ACCLAIM FOR ZAKES MDA

The Madonna of Excelsior

"A lightning flash of a novel from start to finish—inspired, revelatory, and exhilarating."

—*Time Out* New York

"Graceful . . . Sharp and unsparing . . . Mda refuses to undermine his nation's problems with cheap melodrama. Yet his gift, in addition to being an extraordinary writer, is to infuse the past with meaning, to make urgent the challenges of the present, and to reveal the gentle, often stinging, human comedy in both."

—*The Boston Globe*

"Black South Africa has found a strong new voice in Zakes Mda, a marvelous storyteller."

—*The Economist*

"Captivating... In vibrant prose infused with equal parts satire and social criticism, Mda charts new emotional terrain exploring the Madonna-whore complex in a South African setting."

—*Publishers Weekly*

"Resplendent images of emerging African independence . . . There's a *lot* going on here. A gorgeously colored picture of personal and cultural metamorphosis. Exhilarating stuff."

—*Kirkus Reviews* (starred review)

"Zakes Mda . . . has taken our literature to new heights."

—*Sunday Sun* (South Africa)

"A deeply positive vision for the future . . . Mda's work penetrates the mystical, the magical aspects of our lives, sometimes reshaping real events, sometimes inventing new ones. He is compelled by the need to tell a story."

—*Independent* (South Africa)

"Warm, exuberant, and . . . very funny . . . Running through the book like

sunlight is Mda's love of nature and of the country. It is there in all its openness and beauty, vibrancy and color, as a healing, liberating force."
—*Citizen Weekend*

"A brilliantly observed study of the inner workings of small-town South Africa."
—*O, The Oprah Magazine*

"By turns earthy, witty, and tragic, this energetic novel deftly handles issues of racial identity, rape, and revenge.... This is Mda at his best."
—*Pretoria News* (South Africa)

The Heart of Redness
A *New York Times* Notable Book
Best Book, Africa Regional Commonwealth Writers' Prize, 2001
Sunday Times Fiction Award (South Africa), 2002
Hurston/Wright LEGACY Award for Fiction, 2003

"Brilliant . . . A new kind of novel: one that combines Gabriel García Márquez's magic realism and political astuteness with satire, social realism, and a critical reexamination of the South African past."
—*The New York Times Book Review*

"A major step in the new South African novel—now a polyphony of voices, suddenly freed yet still shadowed by deep and immense riddles."
—*The Village Voice*

"Quiet, subtle, and powerful . . . Mda's enormous skills as a storyteller are everywhere in evidence, making the book impossible to put down."
—*The Washington Post*

"This emotionally rich novel dares to seek redemption amid desolation. In these devastated lives, Mda finds grace, tenderness, even the kind of world-weary humor that is born of hardship."
—*The Boston Globe*

"A postcolonial, postapartheid revelation . . . a humorous, mythic, and complicated novel."
—*San Francisco Chronicle*

"Jumping handily between past and present, Mda deftly renders the tensions between maintaining an indigenous culture and altering it in the name of progress."

—*Entertainment Weekly*

Ways of Dying

Winner of the M-Net Award for best novel, 1997
Winner of the Olive Schreiner Prize, novels, 1997
Special mention, the CNA Award for best novel, 1996
Honorable mention, the Noma Award for best book in Africa, 1996

"Tender humor and brutal violence vie with each other in Mda's pages, as do vibrant life and sudden death. The struggle between them creates an energetic and refreshing literature for a country still coming to terms with both the new and the old."

—*The New York Times Book Review*

"A rollicking, at times whimsical tour through the dying days of apartheid as witnessed by the Professional Mourner, Toloki, who wanders from township funeral to township funeral with the hapless wonder of a Chaplinesque loner."

—*The Village Voice*

"Once you have finished *Ways of Dying*, you won't know whether you read the novel or dreamt it. Zakes Mda has gathered up all the human waste and political detritus of South African life and distilled it into a magic realist text of great beauty, humor, and pathos. . . . Mda's novel, with its jewel-like moments of pure imagination, its gentle upward narrative structure, and its repertoire of distinct, intricately carved characters whose lives mean much more than their deaths, bears out this paradox."

—*Sunday Independent* (South Africa)

THE MADONNA OF EXCELSIOR

Zakes Mda

PICADOR

FARRAR, STRAUS AND GIROUX

NEW YORK

THE MADONNA OF EXCELSIOR. Copyright © 2002 by Zakes Mda. All rights reserved. Printed in the United States of America. For information, address Picador, 175 Fifth Avenue, New York, N.Y. 10010.

www.picadorusa.com

Picador® is a U.S. registered trademark and is used by Farrar, Straus and Giroux under license from Pan Books Limited.

For information on Picador Reading Group Guides, as well as ordering, please contact the Trade Marketing department at St. Martin's Press.
Phone: 1-800-221-7945 extension 763
Fax: 212-677-7456
E-mail: trademarketing@stmartins.com

Designed by Cassandra J. Pappas

Library of Congress Cataloging-in-Publication Data

Mda, Zakes.
      The Madonna of Excelsior / Zakes Mda.
            p. cm.
      ISBN 0-312-42382-9
      EAN 978-0312-42382-7
      1. Apartheid—Fiction. 2. Rape victims—Fiction. 3. South Africa—Fiction. 4. Group identity—Fiction. 5. Mother and child—Fiction. 6. Racially mixed children—Fiction. I. Title.

PR9369.3.M4M33 2004
823'.914—dc21   2003054728

First published by Oxford University Press Southern Africa, Cape Town

First published in the United States by Farrar, Straus and Giroux

D 10 9 8

On 10 May 2000, together with a phalanx of my daughters,
I visited Father Frans Claerhout at his studio in Tweespruit, Free
State. I had always wanted to meet him. He had mentored some
artist friends of mine, James Dorothy in particular.
Claerhout presented me with a book on his work written
by Dirk and Dominique Schwager. But first he painted
a golden bird on the black flyleaf and signed his name.
I dedicate this novel to the bird.

THE MADONNA OF
EXCELSIOR

WOMEN, DONKEYS AND
SUNFLOWERS

ALL THESE THINGS flow from the sins of our mothers. The land that lies flat on its back for kilometre after relentless kilometre. The black roads that run across it in different directions, slicing through one-street platteland towns. The cosmos flowers that form a guard of honour for the lone motorist. White, pink and purple petals. The sunflower fields that stretch as far as the eye can see. The land that is awash with yellowness. And the brownness of the qokwa grass.

Colour explodes. Green, yellow, red and blue. Sleepy-eyed women are walking among sunflowers. Naked women are chasing white doves among sunflowers. True atonement of rhythm and line. A boy is riding a donkey backwards among sunflowers. The ground is red. The sky is blue. The boy is red. The faces of the women are blue. Their hats are yellow and their dresses are blue. Women are harvesting wheat. Or they are cutting the qokwa grass that grows near the fields along the road, and is used for thatching houses. Big-breasted figures tower over the reapers, their ghostly faces showing only displeasure.

People without feet and toes—all of them.

These things leap at us in broad strokes. Just as they leapt at Popi twenty-five years ago. Only then the strokes were simple and naïve. Just a black outline of figures with brown or green oil paint rubbed over them. Men in blankets and conical Basotho hats pushing a cart that is drawn by a donkey. Topless women dancing in thethana skirts. Big hands and big breasts.

That is one thing that has not changed, for Father Frans Claerhout is still a great admirer of big hands and big breasts. He is, after all, still the same trinity: man, priest and artist. The threeness that has tamed the open skies, the vastness and the loneliness of the Free State.

Twenty-five years ago Popi peered from her mother's back at the white man as he warmly and masterfully daubed his broad strokes. At five she was precocious enough to wonder why the houses were all so skewed. And crowded together. She thought she could draw better houses. Her people, those she sketched on the sand in the backyard of her township home, were not distorted like the priest's. They were matchstick figures with big heads and spiky hair. But they were not distorted. Yet his very elongated people overwhelmed her with joy. She saw herself jumping down from her mother's back and walking into the canvas, joining the distorted people in their daily chores. They filled her with excitement in their ordinariness.

"Popi, we must go now," her mother said.

"Awu, Niki, I am still watching," appealed Popi. She always called her mother by the name that everyone else in the township used.

"The Father has no use for me," said Niki as she walked out of the gate of the mission station. Popi was sulking on her mother's back. She had wanted to stay with the distorted people in their skewed houses.

"We cannot waste time with your silliness," said Niki.

She had a long way to go. She was going to hitch-hike all the way back to the black township of Mahlatswetsa in Excelsior, thirty kilometres from the Roman Catholic mission in Thaba Nchu. Traffic was sparse on these roads. She knew that she would have to walk for miles before a truck would stop to give her a lift. Truck-drivers were really the only people who felt sorry for hitch-hikers.

But trucks were few and far between on these provincial roads. She would have to walk for miles with only cosmos, the qokwa grass and sunflowers for company. Popi would be fast asleep on her back.

Although her visit to Thaba Nchu had not been a success, she was grateful that the priest had given her a few coins for her trouble. But she was disappointed that he had no use for her. She had heard from the women of his congregation that he painted naked women. In all the neighbouring townships and villages, women walked out of their skewed houses to pose in the nude for him. He paid his models well. Niki had hoped that she would also be able to pose for him.

But the priest had no need of a model. He was not in his nudes-painting mode. He had a few canvases of distorted people and skewed houses and donkeys and sunflowers to complete. Then, in a few weeks' time, he would be painting the madonna subject. If Niki and Popi could come back then, he certainly would use them as models.

The priest was captivated by Popi. He loved all children. Even those who were emaciated and unkempt. Though Popi stayed on Niki's back all the time they were in his studio, he played with her, making all sorts of funny faces. Then he tore out a page from a magazine and shaped her a donkey. He gave it to her and pranced around the room, braying like a donkey. The stocky trinity with his broad face and snow-white mane brayed and brayed, and Popi laughed and laughed.

All this time Niki was nervous. She knew that the priest must have been wondering why Popi was so different from other children. Why she was so light in complexion. Why her eyes were blue, and why she had flowing locks.

We who know the story of Excelsior do not wonder.

As Niki trudged the black road until she became one with it, Popi's mind wandered back to the man who loved women, donkeys and sunflowers. And to his creations.

Woman and girl melted into God's own canvas.

THE GARDEN PARTY

*P*OPI TELLS US that it all began when the trinity was nourished by Flemish expressionists. Theirs were ordinary subjects: sympathetic men and women living ordinary lives and performing ordinary rituals. Popi knows all these things, and shares them with all those who care to listen. We suspect that there are many other things that she knows, but keeps to herself. And there are others that she has decided not to remember.

Twenty-five years ago she saw the thin outlines that defined the concertina player and the dancers. At the time she knew nothing about Flemish expressionists. She had not experienced, through the broad pages of colourful coffee-table books, their mystique that embodied protest.

She was only five. And she was with Niki.

The strokes were not broad like today's strokes. The trinity had not started with broad strokes. They got thicker and rougher as he became more comfortable in his own style. The strokes Popi saw did not stand out. The surface was smoother. The finish was grainy. The colours were fruity. Thick fingers like bunches of bananas pressed the concertina keys. White and brown strokes marked the folds of the instrument as it breathed heavily in and out.

The musician's hat was an overripe tomato. Brown hair peeped under the brim. He was intent. The song had drawn his eyes into his skin, and they had become brown slits. His long nose was sunburnt. He squeezed the concertina. It squealed. Men and women danced. Full-figured women in Starking apple dresses. Skirts of golden pears and Granny Smiths. Pink blouses. Out-of-step men in brown hats and brown suits. Or in light blue shirts and green pants. Sleepy-eyed men with big groping hands.

The musician squeezed the instrument and it wailed a graceful wals. Men and women floated on the clouds. Then he squeezed a lively vastrap. Quicker, quicker than the wals. He was playing Japie Laubscher's *Ou Waenhuis*, the famous composition about an old barn. The zestful party danced in a circle. The men's arms were around the women's waists. The women's arms were around the men's shoulders. Feet close together, turning on the same spot in a fast tiekie-draai.

Rosy-cheeked girls in pink dresses screeched their laughter under the architrave. Then they ran to the lawn to make a nuisance of themselves to the boys who were playing with a rugby ball, practising throws that might see them being picked for Haak Vrystaat, or even the Springboks, in later years. There were no flowers in the garden. Just the lawn. And the small shrubs that would one day grow into a hedge along the short wrought-iron fence. The girls chased one another among the boys. The boys didn't take kindly to this. They chased the girls away until they disappeared behind the whitewashed house.

The house was an imperfect copy of an English bungalow. But it was more exuberant than an English bungalow. As exuberant as the fruity dancers. Two bay windows with ornate stained glass on each side of the brown double doors, which also had painted glass panels. Purple columns supporting the purple architrave. Pillars whose crude capitals were halfway between Ionic and Corinthian. The roof was green. It was made of corrugated-iron sheets instead of tiles. Purple gutters. Green and white chimneys on opposite ends, one with a cowl and another one with a television aerial attached to it. Television was only a few months old in South Africa. This house, therefore, belonged to a man who not only had the money for such novelties, but was also determined to set the trends.

The boeremusiek of the concertina was relentless. The liedjies, or tunes, were getting louder. The volkspele or dances were getting exaggerated, as the concertina filled the dancers with even higher spirits. It had something to do with the cherry liqueur. The circle of buoyant rounded figures danced in and out of the wide doors. Niki passed the time by trying to identify each of the revellers. Popi couldn't be bothered. She was busy sketching houses on the sand just outside the gate. She was concentrating very hard, determined that her houses would not be skewed like those she had seen at the trinity's studio a week before. Her houses would stand straight.

Niki knew almost all the revellers. There was Sergeant Klein-Jan Lombard with his voluminous wife, Liezl, stamping the ground as if they were in a military drill. He of the South African Police, who also acted as a prosecutor at the magistrate's court. She of the yellow cherry jam that had made her famous throughout the entire district. There was Groot-Jan Lombard, Klein-Jan's doddering father. There was the Reverend François Bornman, the dominee of the local Dutch Reformed Church, dancing with a woman Niki could not identify as she had her back turned most of the time. The dominee—one marble eye from a gun accident five years ago—was not in his usual black suit and white tie, but in a brown safari suit. There was Johannes Smit, a very prosperous and very hirsute farmer with a beer belly. He didn't have a partner. And, of course, there was pint-size Adam de Vries, and his strong-boned wife, Lizette. This was their house. This was their garden party.

Adam de Vries ran a small law practice in addition to being the mayor of Excelsior. Like most of the revellers present, he prided

himself on the fact that his grandfather had been one of the
founders of this town, back in 1911. It had been established on an
old farm called Excelsior. People came from surrounding farms to
settle here. And since then various members of his family have
worn the dynastic mayoral chain. Except on a few occasions when
there was no clear candidate from the family. Like when the late
and lamented butcher, Stephanus Cronje, became the mayor.

More families of farmers and businessmen were arriving. All
pillars of the local Afrikaner community. The very cream of Excelsior society. And of other nearby towns such as Tweespruit,
Brandfort and Verkeerdevlei. Niki could see their old bakkies or
trucks and veteran Chevrolets approach on the one-kilometre
stretch of road that was lined with black iron-bark bluegum trees
on both sides. Then the cars would disappear, masked by Reverend Bornman's church that looked like hands in prayer, only to
appear again on Adam de Vries's street behind the church. They
parked in the street and the visitors walked in through the gate
without giving Niki and Popi a second glance. They joined the
sitees—a much slower dance than both the wals and the vastrap.
Even with the fuel of the cherry liqueur, the dances had become
languid and the laughter louder.

The rugby-playing children had increased in number and the
garden was becoming too small for them. A boy threw the ball too
hard. The catcher failed to catch it. It dropped in the street and
bounced until it stopped in front of Popi and Niki. The catcher ran
out of the gate to get the ball. Niki knew him immediately. Tjaart
Cronje. She had not seen him since he was seven. Since the days
when he used to insist on being carried on her back, even though
he was ridiculously big for that mode of transportation. She would
indulge him because he was such a respectful boy. But she stopped
when she realised that whenever he was strapped in a shawl on her
back, he induced an erection and worked himself up with unseemly
rhythmic movements. All that time the boy had been pretending to
play horsey-horsey, he had in fact been in venereal heaven at her
expense. Now here he was, a gangly lad of twelve.

Tjaart took the ball and threw it to Popi.

"Catch!" he said.

Popi missed it. Tjaart laughed. She ran after the ball and got it. Instead of throwing it, she walked to him and handed it back. He looked at her closely and then at Niki. It was obvious that he no longer remembered who Niki was. Five years can be a lifetime in the memory of a boy. Also, her face had changed. The chocolate-smooth complexion was now marred by black, brown and reddish chubaba patches.

"Why are you sitting here?" Tjaart asked.

"I was hoping to get the bones . . . or any leftovers . . . after the party," she said haltingly. "Something for me and my little girl."

"Your little girl? This can't be your child!" said Tjaart. "She looks like a hotnot child. Like a boesman. You must have stolen her."

Then he ran back to his rugby game.

But soon he came back with a slice of cake, broke it into two, and gave a piece to Niki and another one to Popi. The woman who was dancing with the dominee saw him and hurried to the gate. For the first time, Niki got a good look at her. She was face-to-face with Cornelia Cronje, Tjaart's mother. Five years had changed her. She looked old and tired. Cornelia recognised Niki too. And glared at her. Niki glared back. Straight into Cornelia's eyes. Niki did not cringe. She did not cast her eyes down as was expected of her. Cornelia laughed. It sounded hollow and crude. Not rich and full-bodied, like the laughter Niki knew when she worked for Cornelia all those years ago. Then deadly anger flashed in Cornelia's eyes.

"What the hell do you want here?" she asked.

"I can be here, Madam Cornelia," said Niki calmly. "It is not your house. I never go to your house."

"Tjaart!" cried Cornelia. "What are you doing with these people? Come back here at once!"

Tjaart looked at his mother. And at Niki and Popi. He walked back to the rugby game.

ALL THESE MADONNAS

ADONNAS ALL AROUND. Exuding tenderness. Burnt umber mother in a blue shirt, squatting in a field of yellow ochre wheat. Burnt sienna baby wrapped in white lace resting between her thighs. Mother with a gaping mouth. Big oval eyes. Naked breast dangling above the baby's head. Flaky blue suggesting a halo. Unhampered bonding of mother and child and wheat.

Brown madonnas with big breasts. A naked madonna lying on a bed of white flowers. Her eyes are closed and her lips are twisted. Her voluptuous thighs are wide open, ready to receive drops of rain. A black pubic forest hides her nakedness. Her breasts are full and her nipples are hard. Under her arm she carries a baby wrapped in white lace. A naked madonna holds a naked child against a blue moon on a purple sky. The mother is kissing the back of the child's head. Another madonna kneels, her head resting on the ground near the child in white lace, and her buttocks opening up to the sky. Ready to receive drops of rain. The fattest of the madonnas stands among red flowers, looking at yellow fields that cover large patches of the red and brown and green land, and that stretch for kilometres until they meet a blue and white sky.

The madonna of the cosmos and sunflowers and open skies. Like all the others, she is naked. Tightly to her chest, she holds a baby wrapped in white lace.

After twenty-five years, these naked madonnas still live. Popi tells us that they will live forever because such things never die. So will her memory of the excited trinity surrounded by canvases of naked madonnas on easels, with a naked Niki sitting on a stool holding a naked Popi. Popi thought these madonnas looked nothing like Popi-and-Niki of the flesh, even though Popi-and-Niki of the flesh had modelled for them. They were distortions of Popi-and-Niki of the flesh.

It did not matter to Niki that the trinity failed to capture their real images. It was boom time for madonnas. Mother and child had been modelling every day for a month. Mother and child would not need to sit outside another garden party for a long time.

Initially, Niki had been embarrassed to be seen naked by this old white man. But the trinity was gentle. At first he allowed her to pose fully clothed as he painted the madonna in a blue shirt. And the blue mother. The one with an angelic face and flowing locks like Popi's, holding a baby who wore nothing but white socks. Then the trinity eased Niki into taking her clothes off. She cringed in shame. But when she remembered the mortifying garden party, her garments fell on the floor, one by one, until her smooth body glowed before him in all its glorious blackness.

It was not the first time a white man had seen her naked. But this one was different. He did not seem to see her nakedness, even though he painted it.

IN THE VERY BEGINNING,
THERE WERE THREE NAÏVE GIRLS

*H*ERE IN THE Free State the sky is big. A red sun oozes out of the sky. It drips down on the yellow fields. It melts everything it touches, eliciting a feast of colour. Thirty-five years ago, the sky was just as big. The sun dripped on the yellow fields. Colour ran amok. But the trinity's world was of dark and sombre tonal values. Charcoal on white. Figures in tight embraces. Naked women being observed by floating heads. Flowing figures in squiggles that become lace. Three birds of prey perched on the naked buttocks of a woman. Naïve women and children in a naïve black and white world. A world of sinless doodles.

Even then the trinity's was clearly a male gaze. We do not forget that one of his threeness is a man.

Three naïve girls walked out of the trinity's naïve world. Each carried an empty sisal sack. They walked among the cosmos flowers that grew between the fields and on the edge of the road. They had no cares in the world and were singing and humming joyously. They sang about the red railway bus that took fathers, brothers and lovers to the gold mines of Welkom, leaving only the dust in Excelsior. Every time the girls came across dry cow-dung, they picked it up and put it in their sacks. And moved on in a rhythmic step in time to their song.

One of the girls was Niki. She was eighteen years old and looked pretty as a doll in her brown pleated Terylene skirt and white frilly blouse. The only outfit she owned both for happy and sad days. She wore blue rubber sandals that we called "flops" because of the noise they made, especially when one was walking fast. Her body had the fullness of the moon. We thought she was blooming into such a unique flower, and we exclaimed so whenever we saw her. A rare flower in the middle of the desert that was Mahlatswetsa Location. Her skin was chocolate brown and smooth. It was not glossy, for she applied Pandora matt cream generously, which gave her face a ghostly finish. Her hair was rich and sheeny. Only the previous night she had used a red-hot stone to straighten it.

Niki was the only one dressed in her Sunday best. She had just returned from church when her two friends, Mmampe and Maria, came to ask her to join them in a cow-dung collection expedition. She didn't hesitate because she was running out of the essential dung that was used as fuel to cook food and warm the single-room corrugated-iron shack she shared with her father. Also, such expeditions were great fun. Girls got to enjoy the freedom of the big sky and to share the latest titbits on the ups and downs of boy-girl relationships.

Bees were swarming on a bush, and the naïve girls kept their distance, even though next to the bush was a pile of dry dung. Swarming bees could be dangerous if they were disturbed. These were contemplating creating new brood chambers under the rocks next to the bush, so as to be near the nectar and the pollen of the sunflowers and cosmos.

"Eeii!" screeched Mmampe.

"What is it?" asked Niki.

"You want to provoke the bees!" cried Maria at the same time.

"Hairy Buttocks," said Mmampe softly.

It was Johannes Smit. He had materialised before them with a whip in his hand. He cracked it and laughed. Niki was scared. She wanted to run away, but the squat hairy gorilla blocked her way. Mmampe and Maria giggled. They had played this game with Johannes Smit before. Niki only knew of the game from fireside stories. She was not looking forward to it. She had heard of white farmers whose great sport was to waylay black girls in the fields. They chased them around and played harrowing games with them. She had never experienced these games herself. And now it seemed it was her turn. Hairy Buttocks was standing in front of her brandishing a whip.

She knew Johannes Smit vaguely as the farmer her father sometimes worked for. Her father was a handyman who did "piece-jobs" for the farmers and traders in the district.

The hirsute man with a beer belly smiled benevolently, searched the pockets of his khaki shirt, then of his khaki shorts, fished out some bank notes and gave the girls one rand each. Niki hesitated. But when she saw her friends gleefully grabbing the money, she took it too.

Johannes Smit gave Niki another one rand note.

"This is for your mother," he said in Sesotho.

Niki took it, even though she expected Johannes Smit to know that her mother had died many years ago. Surely her father must have told him when working for him.

He gave her yet another one rand note.

"This is for your father."

The two naïve girls gave Niki knowing winks.

"He wants you," whispered Mmampe.

Johannes Smit cracked the whip in Niki's direction.

"Follow me," he commanded.

Niki just froze.

"Don't be foolish, Niki," said Maria. "He will give you more money."

"Then why don't you go with him yourself?" asked Niki.

"He wants you, not me," said Maria.

"He chose you," added Mmampe.

Johannes Smit grabbed Niki by the arm and dragged her into the sunflower field.

"You wait there and whistle if you see people approaching," he barked to the two girls.

Deep in the sunflower field, Johannes Smit pulled off Niki's Terylene skirt. She tried to hold on to it, but he had the strength of ten demons. He threw her on the damp ground. Then he pulled down her panties and took them off. He sniffed them, which seemed to raise more demons in his quivering body. He stuffed the panties into his pocket.

Yellowness ran amok. Yellowness dripped down with her screams. He slapped her and ordered her to shut up. Her screams were now muffled with his hand on her mouth. His pants were at his ankles. He lay on top of her and pleaded, "I am sorry, I didn't mean to hurt you. But if you make noise, people will come and spoil our fun."

Niki wept softly as his hardness touched her thighs. Intense heat sucked out his slimy seed before he could penetrate her. He cursed his pipe as it leaked all over her. He damned its sudden limpness. He just lay there like a plastic bag full of decaying tripe on top of her. She heaved him off her body and jumped up. She grabbed her skirt and ran like a tornado, destroying a swathe of sunflowers in her wake. Johannes Smit's accomplices called after her, "Niki! Niki! Wait for us!"

At home she got under the blankets and cried for a long time, until she fell asleep. She woke when her father arrived in the evening, drunk as usual. He was fuming because she had not cooked any food. She tried to explain that she was not feeling well. And in any case, there was no food to cook because he had not left her any money. But he was not prepared to listen to any lame excuses. He was going to beat the laziness out of her. He was going to lash her buttocks with a belt until they were sour. To placate him, she ran to the tuck shop and used Johannes Smit's money to buy her father a loaf of bread and a big can of pilchards in tomato sauce.

There was a lot of change left over.

M ARIA AND M MAMPE CAME the following day. They were eager to lap up every morsel of gossip.

"How did things go with Hairy Buttocks?" Maria wanted to know.

At first Niki did not want to speak to them. She accused them of being traitors. They must have knowingly led her into a trap. They, of course, denied having been Hairy Buttocks' agents. They bubbled with excitement until they melted her anger.

"Did it enter?" asked Mmampe.

"No . . . it just . . . it just . . ."

The two girls shook the corrugated-iron shack with shrieks of laughter.

"It never enters," said Mmampe.

"His desire is only in the heart," explained Maria, "but his manhood always fails him."

"It happens like that with all the girls he has seduced with money," said Mmampe.

"Perhaps we should call him Limp Stick in addition to Hairy Buttocks," suggested Maria.

"Or Sleeping Horn," said Mmampe.

"Lame Horn."

"Horn of Sorrow."

Niki was not amused. "I am going to report him," she cried. "I am going to tell the police about what he has done to me."

"Don't be foolish, Niki," admonished Mmampe. "Do you think the police will believe you had nothing to do with it? You took his money, didn't you? They will arrest you and charge you with the Immorality Act. Haven't you heard of black women who are in jail for sleeping with white men?"

"But he forced me! You were there! You saw it happen!"

"He will deny everything," said Mmampe. "And we didn't see either. We were not in the sunflower field with you. Don't be stupid, Niki. You can make a lot of money from this foolish white man. Just give him what he wants and eat the money."

"For sure he'll be back," added Maria, laughing. "Just take the money and let the man water your thighs."

HE CAME BACK. That very afternoon. A child came in and said there was a white man in a battered bakkie outside, looking for Niki's father.

"Tell him he is not here," said Niki. "He can go and search for him in all the shebeens of this location."

The child came back again.

"He is calling you."

"Tell him to go to hell."

But Johannes Smit did not go to hell. He walked into the shack instead.

"What do you want?" asked Niki.

"I am returning your broeks," said Johannes Smit, throwing her panties at her. She did not catch them. They fell on the cow-dung floor.

"If you try anything, I'll scream," threatened Niki.

"Is that the way to welcome your lover?" demanded Johannes Smit.

He leapt at her. She jumped away and ran out of the door.

JOHANNES SMIT WAS a persistent man. His offers of cash mounted with her stubbornness, until her good friends prevailed on her. After all, it would not enter, they assured her. A full stomach at bedtime and new leather shoes under the bed would be worth the filth on her thighs. She relented. On every occasion in the yellow fields, she just lay there and became a masturbation gadget. Then she went home and secretly wept while she bathed him off her body. But he was an obstinate stain.

To his utter amazement one day he entered her, rupturing and haemorrhaging her maidenhood. He howled that he was dying such a beautiful death. She tried to vomit him out. Only the last meal and bitter bile came out. For many days she tried. For many days, only half-digested food came out.

She vowed: never again!

His thirst for her could not be quenched, while she imagined the most cruel death for him.

THE WEDDING

*T*HE BRIDE IS in turquoise calf-length taffeta. The scrappy palette-knife-created white lace that hangs from her head right down to her powder-blue shoes makes her look very delicate. She wears a crown of purple and white cosmos blooms. A shoeless full-figured woman is giving the bride a cuddle. She is saved from total nakedness by a pink giant cosmos that covers her jewel like Eve's leaf of shame. Another giant cosmos grows out of the fissure of her buttocks. She also wears a crown of cosmos. Big feet. At last the toes!

The round-eyed groom is in brown overalls and yellow woollen cap. His face is well fed and is round like his eyes. He steps gingerly on the yellow ochre mud in his black rubber boots. A naked bridesmaid embraces him tightly. Her thick thigh is raised to his stomach. Another naked bridesmaid is tickling his ear with a pink cosmos. Full figures. Round stomachs. Each of the women wears a white lace veil that flows to the ground and has pink cosmos attached to it. The frills are tattered. The women's bare feet are attached to elephantiasis legs. They stamp on the yellow ochre mud with stern dignity. They too have toes!

Three blue moons shine out of a violet sky.

Earlier that morning vows were made and papers were signed
before the minister, who had taken the opportunity to complain
about the leaking roof of the church and the tightfistedness of his
congregation. Now opposing sides stamped on the yellow ochre
mud. It had rained all morning. Rain always came with blessings.
The wedding was blessed. Girls and boys from the groom's side
sang of the blessings. But the blessings were wasted, they lamented
tunefully, as the handsome Pule was marrying this Niki, who was
world-famous for her laziness. The beautiful round-faced Pule was
going to die of hunger as soon as he set up house with this clumsy
Niki. They danced around the blessed couple as they heaped scorn
on the bride. Boys and girls from the bride's side responded with
their own musical derision. Pule, they sang, was so ugly that when
he walked out of the house at midday, the sun was bound to set
and the world would be covered in darkness. His was the ugliness
that banished the light of day. How could Pule think that he
deserved a seponono—a woman of soaring beauty and dimpled
smiles—like Niki?

For the whole day, the bride and the groom's parties threw ver-
bal mud at each other. Each side had spent every evening for one
whole month practising new songs that would excel in mocking
the other side. Biting songs under a fluttering white flag that had
announced the wedding for weeks in advance.

After thoroughly disparaging each other, both parties settled
down in an old red and white marquee and shared mutton, samp,
beetroot, ginger beer and cookies. Boys and girls exchanged addresses. Other weddings could result, since weddings gave birth to
more weddings. Just like funerals.

IN THE WHITES-ONLY pub of Excelsior Hotel, Johannes Smit
drank himself silly and cried real tears into his frothy beer.

That evening, Pule took his new bride to her new home: a
brand new shack built of shimmering corrugated-iron sheets a few
streets from the old shack she had shared with her drunken father.

On a moseme grass mat—the only furnishing in the house—he spread layers of blankets. Grey, purple and fawn. She sank into the store-smelling softness. While the song of the bridesmaids gibed and taunted outside, she sucked him in. He danced inside her like a whirlwind, until they both exploded. The hollowness that had existed since the yellowness dripped with her screams was filled. The stubborn stain was bleached away. Once more she was whole. Once more she belonged to herself. And she gave herself permission to share herself with someone else.

The following day, Pule boarded the red railway bus back to Welkom. There to be drained by the gold that he extracted from the dust of the depths of the earth.

JOHANNES SMIT CONTINUED to be a slave to his secret desires. She shooed him away. His unrequited shadow dogged her path. It loomed large even when she got a job at Excelsior Slaghuis, Stephanus Cronje's butchery. She was one of five women who kept the butchery clean, cut the meat, weighed it and generally served the customers. But, of course, none of them were allowed near the till. Cornelia Cronje herself—Madam Cornelia to Niki and the other "girls"—sat behind the till. Sometimes her husband, Stephanus Cronje, manned it. Niki's special assignment involved acting as a nanny to young Tjaart Cronje, in addition to her work at the butchery.

Johannes Smit took to buying meat at odd times. And made a point of being served by Niki. When his deep freeze was full of meat, he took to visiting Stephanus Cronje at work, even though everyone knew that their politics had taken divergent routes. Stephanus Cronje was the secretary of the local branch of the ruling National Party and the mayor of Excelsior. Johannes Smit had recently abandoned the National Party to join the breakaway Herstigte Nasionale Party, an ultra-conservative political grouping of those Afrikaners who felt that their formerly beloved National Party had become too soft and liberal towards blacks, and was beginning to relax some of the more stringent but God-given apartheid laws.

Stephanus Cronje thought Johannes Smit was beginning to regret the errors of his ways and wanted to return to the fold. He did not notice that during these visits Johannes Smit always tried to catch Niki's eye, and would then furtively wave some bank notes at her. Niki would ignore him. She continued to ignore him when he followed her and the other women in his battered bakkie on their way back to Mahlatswetsa after knocking off work. These women, who sometimes included Mmampe and Maria, knew all about Hairy Buttocks and took his misery as something that enriched their lives with laughter.

Niki, on the other hand, found this attention irritating. Inside her another life was ticking. She wanted to think only of its expected kicks in a few months' time, and not of things that reminded her of her humiliation.

BLUE AND RED dominate. Three women are surrounded by white light. White against a blue wall and a blue skewed window. One has a blue face and wears a blue doek on her head and a blue shawl over her shoulders. The second woman has a red face with tinges of grey. She wears red lipstick and a red and blue blanket. A blue woollen cap sits on her head. The third woman has a black face and red eyes from which flow red tears. She wears a red T-shirt and a red beret.

The three women are standing next to the bed on which recline the figures of a blue-faced woman and a newly-born baby. Both she and the baby wear blue woollen caps. Their heads rest peacefully on a fluffy white pillow. The mother is covered in a red and blue blanket and the baby is in white. Next to the bed is a side table on which rests a red clay pot and a white bottle. The mother and child are fast asleep while the three women stand guard over them.

The baby boy was Viliki, a product of whirlwinds and explosions.

6

SHE IS HOLDING THE SUN

*S*HE IS HOLDING the sun entwined in her arms. It is
blazing red. With streaks of yellow. She is all impasto
black and blue and yellow. The sun glows through her
body, giving it patches of fluorescent red. She sits like a Buddha
embracing the sun. She is wide awake, for night has passed. The
whites of her eyes are milky white and the pupils are black like
the night. Everything around her is fiery red. The sky is red.
The ground is red. Rivers of white run on the red ground. Broad
strokes. She is dark and sinister. And beautiful. Under her impasto
sun, plants are wilting.

Johannes Smit was distracted by an infernal drought that was
incinerating parts of the Free State. And the aphids that were having a field day on his spring wheat crop. These destructive partners
were surely going to lessen the yield. An average of only four bags
per hectare instead of the usual eight. Subterranean rivers were
drying up, and the veld was turning into a smouldering desert. A
westerly wind was blowing. A sure sign that the drought was in no
hurry to go. To add to his woes, a freak hailstorm hit the area,
causing further damage to his crop.

Like Johannes Smit, all the farmers in the district were crying.

And when the farmers cried, the people of Mahlatswetsa cried too. Their livelihoods depended on the grace of weather. Perhaps in December the rains would come. A promise of a good maize harvest. In the meantime, farmers shed what they considered to be excess workforce. Johannes Smit focused on how he was going to repay the Land Bank loan and forgot about Niki.

Niki survived the scorching sun because Tjaart had grown addicted to her back. Viliki toddled by her side. Viliki wondered why he was not the one strapped on his mother's back. Why the big white boy—five times his size—was the one riding his mother and shouting, "Horsey! Horsey!"

THE PAN

*T*HERE IS NOTHING muted about these reds and yellows and blues. An impasto world glares at you noisily. But this is not the kind of noise that turns your insides. It is not discordant. It does not grate on the eye. It is a saintly noise.

People walk out of the skewed houses that form a circle. A blue church completes the circle. The houses are pink with cobalt blue doors. People are floating to the church. People with black faces, each holding a giant white flower. Blank faces. A man in a crimson jump suit, brown shoes and brown conical Basotho hat. A woman in a crimson dress and brown beret. She has no feet. A man in a pink jump suit and brown woollen cap. Footless women in blue skirts and red blouses. Their faces are just black blobs. A woman in a long white dress and white veil leads the procession into the church. The procession glides augustly on the raw sienna path. Blazing light surrounds the solemn procession. Absorbing the devout into a halo of yellowness.

Three giant white flowers grow in front of the church. The blue tower is capped by a black spire that pierces the purple sky into heaven. The sky has streaks of pink and yellow clouds. And a dull yellow ochre sun with a broad black outline.

We saw Niki walk past the church. Viliki was trudging behind her. Three-year-old Viliki. All spruced up in his black shorts and khaki shirt and shoeless feet that had acquired a pink colour after being freshly scrubbed to remove thick layers of black dirt.

Niki was well-scrubbed herself. At twenty-two, she drowned the hearts of Mahlatswetsa in a vortex of desire. But she was unreachable. She could not save them from certain death. She was Pule's wife. Pule, whose very name spoke of many rains. Old Pule who had been married before. And was deserted. Or did he desert?

Shame. Niki was loved so much. You could see it even from the way she walked. Like someone who is loved. Shame. She had a husband who dressed her so well. She glowed in a red two-piece costume with blinding silver buttons and a Terylene cream-white blouse. Her face glowed from Super Rose skin lightening lotion. She had long discarded the cheaper Pandora matt. One of the perks of being married to a man who burrowed in the earth for the white man's gold. Her hair gleamed with braids of very thin lines. A style known as essence because it was first seen on models that appeared in an African-American magazine called *Essence.* Shame. Pule spoilt his young beautiful wife. There was no way she could dress herself and braid her hair like that from her earnings at Excelsior Slaghuis. We all knew how tightfisted the Boers of Excelsior were.

This was our church. It was Niki's church. She belonged here. As she passed, she could hear seeping through the porous walls a hymn about God's amazing grace that distinguished itself by its sweetness. If she had been inside she would also be singing about the amazing grace, while Viliki would be snuffing out with his little thumb termites that traced their path across the aisle up the pew in front of him. She would slap his hand and he would stop. But soon the massacre would resume. Viliki was always bored by solemnity.

She knew by heart what would follow the hymn. The minister

would speak of how the meek would inherit the earth and the poor in spirit would see the kingdom of heaven. How those who were oppressed and persecuted would get their reward in heaven. They were the salt of the earth and the light of the world. But in the meantime, he would plead, while they were still on earth preparing for their inheritance in heaven, it was necessary that the leaking roof of the house of the Lord be repaired. Was it because of the congregation's meanness of spirit that even though over the years appeals had been made for funds to repair the roof, very little had been raised? How did the congregation think the Lord felt about being praised in a dilapidated building with a leaking roof and cracked walls with peeling paint? The congregation would respond with amens. But only small brown coins would find their way into the collection plate.

It was like that every Sunday.

Today Niki was going to another church, the one in town. A distance of twenty minutes at an easy pace. Fifteen minutes if she didn't have someone slowing her down. The Reverend François Bornman's beautiful church built of sandstone and roofed with black slate. Everyone said it was shaped like hands in prayer, but Niki did not see any of that. Often she had tried to work out how exactly the strange architecture translated into hands in anything, let alone prayer.

She got there just as the final bell was tolling. She was right on time for the service. Worshippers in colourful floral dresses and grey suits were scurrying into the church. Some betrayed the fact that they were first-time visitors by pausing to read the inscription on a marble panel next to the door: *Tot Eer van God is hierdie steen gelê deur Ds J.G. Strydom, Jehova Shamma, Die Woning van God, Ezech 48–35B.* In honour of God, this stone was laid by J.G. Strydom— the Lion of the North who was the Prime Minister of South Africa from 1954 to 1958, and made certain that he did not make equal what God had not made equal. He who confirmed to his people: *As a Calvinist people we Afrikaners have, in accordance with our faith in the Word of God, developed a policy condemning all equality and mongrelisation between*

White and Black. God's Word teaches us, after all, that He willed into being separate nations, colours and languages. The house of God.

Niki and Viliki stood outside the gate where they would remain for the rest of the service. It was the nagmaal service, so named after the days when Afrikaners trekked from their distant farms into the towns every few months to attend the evening service in which rites of the Last Supper—the breaking of bread and the drinking of wine—were revisited. Niki was able to catch waves of what was going on inside the church, and she became part of it. She joined the Afrikaners in singing about God's amazing grace that was also very sweet. The red amaryllis—belladonna lilies indigenous to this part of the world—attested to this grace. And so did the clean paved surroundings, sanctified by the organ that backed the angelic voices. The amaryllis bowed their heads along the knee-high wrought-iron fence that surrounded the church. Niki and Viliki bowed their heads too. They stood up when it was time for standing up. They sat when it was time for sitting. She listened attentively to the Reverend Bornman's booming sermon. She was uplifted by St Paul's letter to the Corinthians: *And though I bestow all my goods to feed the poor, and though I give my body to be burned, and have not charity, it profiteth me nothing.* Praise the Lord that the door had been mercifully left open so that her ears could feast on His Word!

Thus she became part of the Great Fellowship.

All this solemnity bored Viliki. He broke away from the holy rites. While Niki sang the Afrikaans hymns, he clambered on the sandstone column near the gate, and traced with his forefinger the names engraved on the marble panel. Under the heading: *Eeufees Ossewatrek 22 Oct. 1938* was a list of the names of the distinguished citizens of Excelsior who had participated in the wonderful commemoration of the centenary of the Great Trek. They were among a group of Afrikaners who re-enacted the great event of 1838 by trekking from Cape Town into the interior of South Africa with ox-wagons. Viliki's reading skills were not advanced enough to decipher some of the prominent surnames in the district.

Niki sat, stood and bowed her head—as the ceremony demanded—through the Bible readings and the paeans and the sharing of bread and wine. In spirit she devoured the body of Christ and imbibed His blood. She listened to the announcements and sang the final hymn.

Then the church's hands opened up, and spilled a flood of rejuvenated worshippers onto the fulfilled paving. Niki could see the Reverend François Bornman shaking hands with his flock, who were obviously congratulating him on an inspiring sermon. The Reverend Bornman in his shimmering black suit and snow-white tie. There was Johannes Smit in an ill-fitting brown suit cracking a joke with the doddering farmer, Groot-Jan Lombard. Smit did not seem to be aware that his beer belly had grown bigger and that he therefore needed clothes a few sizes larger. Niki was glad that he no longer bothered her. Maybe he had found someone else to be obsessed with. There was Sergeant Klein-Jan Lombard and his wife, Liezl, shaking hands with the Reverend. There was Adam de Vries and his wife, Lizette, walking out of the gate to their house, which was just behind the church.

Adam de Vries always had a kind word for everyone. As he passed Niki, he smiled and asked, "Did you enjoy the service?"

"It was good, my baas," responded Niki.

There was Stephanus Cronje, his wife, Cornelia, and their son Tjaart. Seven-year-old Tjaart looked like a grown-up in a navy blue suit, white shirt and grey tie. He saw Niki and Viliki at the gate, and ran to join them.

"So, what are we going to do?" he asked.

"I don't know," said Niki. "You'll think of something."

"I know!" said Tjaart excitedly. "You can carry me on your back."

"No, I will not do that."

"Come on, Niki! Horsey-horsey!"

"Never!"

The boy sulked. Viliki wondered why his mother had lost interest in Tjaart's horsey-horsey game and why she never played it with her own son.

After shaking hands with the Reverend, and with a few friends, Stephanus Cronje and Cornelia went to the gate.

"It was a beautiful service, wasn't it?" said Stephanus Cronje.

"It was very beautiful," said Niki.

"We are grateful you agreed to look after Tjaart even though it's a Sunday," said Madam Cornelia.

"We'll make it worth your while," added Stephanus Cronje.

They walked to their Chevrolet across the street and drove away to a volkskongres—a people's congress—which was going to be addressed by a cabinet minister in the neighbouring town of Clocolan.

PULE SAT on the bed motionlessly, staring at the door. Like a wild cat waiting to pounce on its prey. His head almost touched the roof because the bed had been raised with big paint cans filled with soil to make it more imposing than it really was. And to create enough room under it for the two suitcases that were full of clothes and bedlinen. The double bed with a velveteen-covered headboard dominated the room, making a green "kitchen scheme" table with three chairs cower at one corner, and a small pine cupboard with plates, pots and utensils crouch at another.

Even as Niki entered, leaving the boys to play outside, she was apologising for being late. Three o'clock and he had not eaten lunch yet. She had had to go to the church in town because her employers wanted her to look after their son, she explained. She had had to go to Stephanus Cronje's house first to feed Tjaart and to make him change his church clothes. She was supposed to look after the boy at his home. But she just had to come back because she knew that her husband would be hungry too.

He did not respond. He just sat there and expanded like a bullfrog. Niki imagined him exploding into smithereens. And her picking up the pieces. A different kind of an explosion to the one that happened whenever their bodies were bound together. She was getting used to a sulky Pule. They had been married for over four years now, and he came home from the mines of Welkom every long weekend. He had gradually lost his humour. His face had become harder and colder with every visit. After being drained by gold, he brought back to Excelsior a body that had gone dry of smiles.

"I'll fry you eggs quickly," said Niki.

Still he did not speak.

She pumped the Primus stove and fried him two eggs in an old pan that was twisted and wobbly. She served him the eggs with four slices of bread on a china plate. The white Sunday plate with blue pagodas and blue boats and blue pagoda-trees and blue dragons. Weekday plates were enamel plates. With great deliberation and ceremony he stood up from the bed, went to the "kitchen scheme" table, took the plate of food and smashed it on the floor. Eggs and bits of china spattered all over the cow-dung floor.

"It is Sunday today," he shouted. "Every working man in South Africa is eating meat and rice for lunch. And even beetroot. What happened to the meat I brought from Welkom? You are not even ashamed to serve me this rubbish on a Sunday plate! Why am I not eating meat like all decent human beings?"

"I thought you would be too hungry to wait for meat," pleaded Niki.

"For whom were you planning to cook that meat when I am gone back to Welkom tomorrow? For your boyfriends?"

She did not answer. Instead she reached for a broom and tried to sweep up the mess on the floor.

"Ja, so it is true! You are hoarding my meat for your boyfriends!"

Niki was getting irritated. She had always been faithful to Pule. Now he was assigning motives again. That was the major problem in their marriage. Whenever she did something he did not like, however innocently, he assigned a motive for her actions. And however much she denied his accusations, the assigned motive would stick. It would be the gospel truth as far as he was concerned. He never tried to find out from her the reasons for her actions. He knew exactly why she did whatever she did. And the motives he concocted were always sinister. She was always plotting some evil. Anthills became mountains when one was always suspicious of the motivations of the other. Shadows of bushes in the moonlight became assassins.

Only six months ago, he had promised that he would never do it again.

Six months ago she had come home late from work. Stephanus Cronje's unpaid overtime. Pule decided there and then that she was late because she had been sleeping with white men. "Stories are told of black maids who sleep with their white masters," he said. "You must be one of them."

She pleaded her innocence. She tried to hold him in her arms to assure him that she would never do such a thing. But he violently pushed her away and slapped her, shouting, "Get away from me! You smell of white men!"

She was Johannes Smit in Pule's eyes. She saw the uncontrollable yellowness of the sunflower fields. There was the overwhelming smell of Johannes Smit in the shack. Tears swelled in her eyes as she packed her clothes and Viliki's into a plastic bag. She then left with her son to live with relatives in Thaba Nchu.

Pule remained stewing in misery. He really loved Niki and he missed her. He went back to the mines of Welkom. And then returned to an empty shack. He sent his relatives to Thaba Nchu to plead with Niki to come back. He made endless promises and undertakings that he would never hit her again.

Niki finally decided to go back to her husband. Till death do us part. There was no one at home. She had her own key. Deep in the night he came home singing spiritedly. A drunken female voice accompanied his song. A woman he had picked up at some shebeen as his provision for the night. Take-aways. One-night stress-relief. Balm to a hurting soul. He opened the door without wondering why he had left it unlocked. He struck a match and lit the candle. He uttered one sharp curse. Niki was sitting at the "kitchen scheme" table. Viliki was dozing on the bed. He was up in no time.

"I am leaving you, Pule, and this time it is going to be forever," cried Niki.

"Please, Niki, don't go," Pule pleaded. "There is nothing between this woman and me. I don't even know her name."

"But you were going to sleep with her, weren't you? On my bed too!"

"You scoundrel you!" the other woman shouted at Pule. "You didn't tell me you had a letekatse—a whore—waiting for you at home!"

Niki grabbed Viliki's hand and made to go. Pule closed the door with his huge frame and begged her not to go. The other woman, sensing victory, added her own view that she should indeed go.

"I'll stay only if you hit your girlfriend," Niki finally said.

Both Pule and the other woman looked at Niki in astonishment.

"Come on, beat her up," Niki demanded.

"Beat her up? But she has not done anything."

"I had not done anything either when you slapped me," said Niki calmly.

"I can't just beat her up, Niki," protested Pule.

"You just try to beat me up, you'll see the eyes of a worm," threatened the other woman. She was nevertheless reversing towards the door.

Pule slapped her twice. She ran out screaming that people were trying to kill her for nothing. She stood outside, a safe distance from the shack, and hurled insults at the couple, for all the neighbourhood to hear. She was emphatic that it was Pule's loss, because not even in his dreams would he ever taste what she had been going to give him. When it seemed no one was paying her any attention, she finally walked away, still yelling things about their private parts that would render the innocent deaf.

Pule had on that night promised he would stop blaming her for things she knew nothing about. And so she and Viliki had stayed.

But Pule did not keep his promise. Here he was again assigning motives.

"Now you tell me that I have boyfriends. Did you give them to me?" asked Niki in a sarcastic tone.

Viliki led Tjaart into the house, enticed by the prospect of war.

"They are going to fight," said Viliki to Tjaart.

"Who is going to win?" asked Tjaart, looking forward to a good boxing match.

"Papa is going to win. Then we'll leave him and go to Thaba Nchu where we'll stay in a real house and not a shack," said Viliki, looking forward to another long journey.

He felt very important. Very superior. After all, he allowed the big white boy to share his mother. The big white boy could boast about his bicycle, which he promised to let Viliki ride when he grew older. He too had something to boast about: his mother. When he grew older, he would ride Tjaart's bicycle while Tjaart rode his mother. And now here was another thing to feel superior about: he was going to entertain Tjaart to the spectacle of a fight between his parents.

"Why did you bring this boertjie boy here?" exploded Pule.

"Please children, go and play outside," said Niki, pushing the reluctant boys out.

"It is not enough that you spend all your time attending to the whims of these people, now you have to bring their brat here!" cried Pule.

Niki did not respond. She resumed sweeping the floor.

After cleaning up all the mess, and throwing it into the dustbin outside, she poured some sunflower oil into the pan and fried three big chunks of meat. The pan wobbled on the Primus stove as the hot fat splattered on the table. She looked at the pan with undisguised contempt. It had been used by Pule's first wife, until they divorced. Then it was used by a string of girlfriends. Now it was her turn to use it. The pan yoked her to all the previous women in his life.

She said under her breath, "One day, I'll go and leave him with this pan."

THE BIG SKY IS BEREFT OF STARS

*I*T WAS BEFORE Popi's time. So these are things that she heard from those of us who saw them happen, even though today she relates them as if she herself witnessed them. She is no sciolist. She can indeed experience them in the immortal world that the trinity has bequeathed us. She is able to become part of whole lives that are frozen and rendered timeless. A memoir that conveys our yesterdays in the continuing present.

She experiences how the villagers, to their utmost sadness, discovered that there were no stars in the sky. Men and women stood outside their skewed yellow houses one blue night, and raised their eyes to the big sky. They pointed up and lamented that the sky was bereft of stars. A lonely full moon rose behind distant hills. Fumbling in a sky that had no stars. A yellow moon fluttering its cloudy wings above yellow hills.

The villagers stood outside their black-roofed houses, listening to the restlessness of the night. And to the sweeping rhythms of their clustered houses that leaned in directions that were determined by fickle winds. Then a giant with a boyish face appeared. A giant in a red hat and red boots and yellow overalls. He carried over his shoulder a big star attached to a stick. He jumped over the roofs of the houses bringing the star to the village, flooding the skewed houses with titanium white light.

The friendly giant transformed the blues and yellows into a scintillating light-filled land of promise. A world conceived of beautiful madness. Had he lived here, the trinity once surmised, Vincent van Gogh would have gone mad even earlier.

Niki was mad for a different reason. A different kind of madness. Many months had passed without Pule coming home from the mines of Welkom. White man's gold in the earth held him in its bosom, making him desert his family in Excelsior. Although he hadn't really deserted it. He sent Niki money every month. "She will see my money," he told his mates while sweating in the dark tunnels, "but she will not see me until such time that she learns to appreciate me. You are right, my friends, I have spoilt her by going home every long weekend."

Mmampe and Maria applied a soothing balm to her loneliness by making her aware that Pule's conduct was quite normal. Most men came home only once a year. Those with a higher sense of responsibility came twice a year. It was abnormal behaviour to come home every long weekend. It was the behaviour of a man possessed by demons of jealousy. A man who didn't trust that his wife could be left to her own devices for any length of time without getting into mischief. It was not his love, but his tight leash on her that had made him come home so often. Niki should just be happy that, unlike many other men, Pule supported his family.

And he sent not only money. He sent clothes for Niki and Viliki as well. Two-piece costumes with broad figure-belts. Genuine leather shoes and school uniforms. Things for the house too. Floral duvets for the bed and plastic tablecloths for the "kitchen scheme" table. He even sent a china dinner set, with a note that he was re-placing the Sunday plate that he had broken in a fit of temper months before. It was blue and white like the broken plate. But it didn't have pagodas. He couldn't get one with pagodas. It had flowers instead. Now Niki had a whole set of Sunday plates.

Mmampe and Maria became wary of visiting her because every

time they came, she showed them new things that Pule had sent. Or that she had bought with money sent by him. It became a great strain to sit through these crass displays of wealth.

We thought Niki would resign from the butchery, sit down and eat Pule's money. But she continued to work at Excelsior Slaghuis and to look after Tjaart. Even after shameful things were done to her.

CORNELIA CRONJE HAD started a new custom of weighing workers twice a day to make sure they were not stealing any of her meat. The morning clock-in weight had to tally with the afternoon clock-off weight. Any discrepancy meant that there was some chicancry somewhere.

Niki clocked in one morning and stepped on the black iron heavy-duty floor scale. Her weight was recorded at 61 kilograms. A good weight for a mother of one who still kept the body of her maidenhood.

It was at the end of the month. Workers had received their wages and pensioners their old-age pensions. The butchery was a necessary stop-off whenever people had bank notes burning in their purses and pockets. So, it was a busy day for Niki and the other workers. She could only eat her lunch at four o'clock in the afternoon, an hour before knocking off. She was very hungry. She stuffed herself with a lot of pap and meat, generously supplied by the Cronjes to all their workers every lunchtime.

At five it was time to go. As usual she stepped on the scale while Cornelia Cronje recorded her weight. It was 62 kilograms.

"You are hiding something," said Cornelia Cronje.

"It is not true, Madam Cornelia," protested Niki. "I am not hiding anything."

"Your weight was 61 kilograms in the morning. It can't just increase by a kilo for nothing. You must be hiding meat under your dress," insisted Madam Cornelia.

Curious workers crowded around them. They wondered among

themselves: how could Niki be so foolish? Didn't she know that the penalty for theft was instant dismissal? How could she play with her job like this when jobs were so scarce in Excelsior? Was she not aware that the scale would catch her out? The scale never lied.

Madam Cornelia was determined to teach Niki a lesson. And to teach the other workers by example. She ordered her to strip. Right there in front of everyone. When she hesitated, Madam Cornelia threatened to lock her up in the cold room with all the carcasses, as it was obvious that she loved meat so much that she had now become a meat thief. Niki peeled off her pink overall and then her mauve dress. She stood in her white petticoat and protested once more that she was not hiding any meat on her person. Then she peeled off the petticoat and stood in her pink knickers and fawn bra.

"Raise your arms," ordered Madam Cornelia.

She did.

No chunks of meat rained from her unshaved armpits.

"Take them off, Niki," insisted Madam Cornelia. "Everything! You must be hiding it in your knickers."

No meat hiding in her bra. Only stained cotton-wool hiding in her knickers.

She stood there like the day she was born. Except that when she was born, there was no shame in her. No hurt. No embarrassment. She raised her eyes and saw among the oglers Stephanus Cronje in his khaki safari suit and brown sandals. And little Tjaart. Little Tjaart in his neat school uniform of grey shorts, white shirt, green tie and a grey blazer with green stripes. Grey knee-length socks and black shoes. Little Tjaart of the horsey-horsey game. His father had just fetched him from school. And here he was. Here they were. Raping her with their eyes.

"Magtig Niki," said Madam Cornelia, "where did the kilo come from?"

And she burst out laughing as if it was a big joke. Everyone giggled. Including Niki. But there was no laughter in her eyes.

She put on her clothes and went tamely home.

Niki's triangular pubes loomed large in Tjaart Cronje's imagination. Threatening pleasures of the future. A sapling looking to the starless sky for a promise of rain. He knew already that it was the tradition of Afrikaner boys of the Free State platteland to go through devirgination rites by capturing and consuming the forbidden quarry that lurked beneath their nannies' pink overalls.

For Stephanus Cronje, Niki's pubes, with their short entangled hair, became the stuff of fantasies. From that day he saw Niki only as body parts rather than as one whole person. He saw her as breasts, pubes, lips and buttocks.

While the Cronje men were seized by the fiends of lust, anger was slowly simmering in Niki. A storm was brewing. Quietly. Calmly. Behind her serene demeanour she hid dark motives of vengeance. Woman to woman. We wondered why she did not resign from Excelsior Slaghuis after being humiliated like that. But she knew something we did not know. She was biding her time. She had no idea what she would do. Or when. In the starless nights of Mahlatswetsa Location, she was nursing an ungodly grudge.

9

THE CHERRY FESTIVAL

WE HAVE SEEN how the trinity loves donkeys. That is why this long-eared creature foolishly fills the whole space. It wears blinkers and its long tail touches the green grass on which the ass poses like the monarch of the canvas. The fields are uncultivated. They are brown with patches of green. They stretch for miles, until they reach the small brown hill that peeps over the white horizon. There is no room for anything else, except the red cock that the ass carries in a transparent bag strapped on its back and hanging from its side. The donkey and the cock own the world.

A blinkered donkey led the floats on a Saturday morning. It was the king of the world for that day. It wore a crown of flowers and ribbons. Red, yellow and blue ribbons. Pink and purple carnations. It was not burdened with a red cock. Instead, a black boy in a colourful Basotho blanket perched on its back. And absorbed in his little body the summer heat of the eastern Free State town of Ficksburg, near the Lesotho border. Eighty-nine kilometres from Excelsior.

The donkey nonchalantly led the procession from the Hennie

de Wet Park down McCabe Street, into Voortrekker Street, and up Fontein Street.

All the luminaries of Excelsior were there. They would not miss the cherry festival for anything. There was the diminutive Adam de Vries attired in a grey wash 'n' wear suit and grey moccasins. He was the only one of the Excelsior group who was dressed formally. He was also the only one who came with his wife. Lizette was dressed formally as well: a big straw hat shaped like a fruit bowl with plastic bananas, grapes and apples gracing it. A blue short-sleeved polyester dress with yellow flowers. White seamless nylon stockings and blue pencil-heel shoes.

The couple had to be formal because Adam de Vries was a member of the committee that organised the cherry festival—The Jaycee Cherry Festival Committee—even though he hailed from Excelsior, which did not grow any cherries. Some Ficksburg residents complained about this. Those who wanted to hog the festival and keep it to their district. But His Worship, the Mayor of Ficksburg, told them that people like de Vries worked very hard to make the festival—only in its second year—possible. His legal services had been indispensable. In any case, when the Jaycees had decided to organise a festival around a product unique to this part of South Africa, the intention was to bring to the attention of visitors the charms of the entire region, not just of Ficksburg.

The rest of the Excelsior men were in safari suits. And in a party mood. They had left their wives at home to take care of business. Those who had wives, that is.

The wifeless Johannes Smit was there in all his bulk, squeezed into a brown safari suit, fawn stockings and brown veldskoene. In addition to partying, he had come to sell his cherry liqueur. He was proud of this product. It had taken him many months of patience to achieve its fine quality. First he had acquired Black Biggareau cherries from the neighbouring district of Clocolan. He had pricked each one of them with a darning needle. Then he had dissolved sugar in brandy and poured it over the fruit in a wooden barrel. He had stored it in a dark room in his farmhouse. After three months he had strained the concoction, put it into bottles and corked them tightly. He had then stored the bottles for another three months. Six months of tender loving care.

Now he had a stall at the Hennie de Wet Park where he sold his Excelsior Fine Cherry Liqueur. Another cause for snide remarks from the chauvinists of Ficksburg. How could Excelsior have a cherry liqueur when they did not grow any cherries? Shouldn't they be talking of a sunflower liqueur instead—if there could ever be such a thing?

Johannes Smit couldn't be bothered. Envy, that's all it was. They couldn't make as fine a cherry liqueur as his, so they opted for rubbishing him and his district, he concluded.

He sat at a vantage place where he could see all the parades go by. Next to his stall was one that sold biltong. This was Stephanus Cronje's biltong, also made with tender loving care at his Excelsior Slaghuis. Unlike the hands-on Johannes Smit, Stephanus Cronje did not man the stall himself. While he went from stall to stall sampling the pleasures of the festival in the form of cherry crumble, cherry pudding, koeksusters, braaiwors and brandy—with the likes of off-duty Sergeant Klein-Jan Lombard, Groot-Jan Lombard and the Reverend François Bornman—Niki looked after the stall. Niki in her pink overall and grass conical Basotho hat to protect her from the November sun.

She sat at a wooden table on which a variety of biltong and dry wors was displayed. Under a big red garden umbrella. Johannes Smit sat at a wooden table on which cherry liqueur bottles were displayed. Under a big blue and white garden umbrella. Each pretending the other one did not exist. Each fussing over customers who wanted to taste the potent liqueur or to chew the spiced biltong.

Not many people were buying at that moment. Everyone was more interested in the procession of floats led by the colourful team of donkey and boy. It was followed by a tractor pulling a trailer with bales of hay, on which a number of Afrikaner children sat singing Afrikaans songs. The next float was also pulled by a tractor. It comprised a big red polythene cherry in a polythene bowl with all the colours of the rainbow in their proper order. All eyes were fixed on this float. On top of the cherry sat the Cherry Queen and her two princesses. The Cherry Queen was a twenty-one-year-old sashed blonde, chosen the previous night at the Andrew Marquard Hall by the mayors of Ficksburg and the surrounding cherry towns of Clocolan and Fouriesburg. The Cherry Queen was smiling and waving to her subjects. She was followed by a procession of polychromatic floats on tractor-trailers and lorries, like shapeless cakes in a confectionery. These were sponsored by local firms and cultural bodies, and sported the names of the sponsors prominently.

Johannes Smit had been at the Andrew Marquard Hall when the Administrator of the Orange Free State had crowned the Cherry Queen the previous night. He had been one of the boisterous whistlers rooting for her amid stiff competition from the beautiful Afrikaner girls of the region. The mayors had a good eye for beauty, choosing her from a bevy of twenty. He had been one of those who applauded loudly and wolf-whistled when the girl was handed her prize of vouchers for a two-week holiday trip to Durban and fifty rands pocket-money. Occasionally he had taken a swig from his flask of Klipdrift brandy. By the time Esme Euvrard and her Spanish Troupe were entertaining the guests, he was already sloshed. He saw dimly that on the stage, radio personality Frans Jooste was compèring. His head was spinning as people all around him laughed at Jooste's jokes.

Of course, Niki was seeing the Cherry Queen for the first time. She would not have been allowed into the Andrew Marquard Hall even if she had wanted to attend the pageant. The hall—named after the first principal of the volkskool—belonged only to the volk. And to those visitors whose bodies were blessed enough to have melanin levels that were as low as those of the volk.

Niki had no desire to attend the events at the Andrew Marquard Hall. She was happy with the street parades. With the local high school band and smartly-uniformed drum majorettes that passed a few steps ahead of the donkey. With the Afrikaner school children in fancy dress and comic outfits. With the whole festive atmosphere. With the Cape Coon Carnival on the very first day of the festival on Thursday. That had been funny!

She heard that it was the first time these banjo-strumming minstrels from Cape Town had performed in the Orange Free State. The satin-clad minstrels carried with pride the derogatory name they had inherited from American performers—Negroes, as they called them then—who had visited the Cape in the 1800s. The Cape Coons revelled in the coon image and cherished it. Their faces were painted black with exaggerated white lips. Or white with exaggerated black lips. They wore white panama hats and suits of shimmering red and white. Yellow and white. Purple and white. Matching umbrellas. They were strumming *Daar Kom die Alibama*—singing about the ship that their slave ancestors thought was coming to save them, only to witness it sink in the stormy seas.

The antics of the Cape Coons had made her laugh so much that she had forgotten her concern for Viliki. She had left him with her friend, Mmampe, for the duration of the festival. She knew he would be safe, even though she had never before left him with neighbours for so many days. The entertainment had even enabled her to shelve her constant thoughts about Pule. Her deep longing for him. The emptiness that his long absence caused. The fact that even on those rare occasions when he came home, he was drifting more and more into the murky moods of her dead father. The control. The drinking. The jealousy. Niki should not be seen walking on the same side of the street as a man. But Pule had his beauty as well. He never stopped supporting his family.

After the procession of floats had left the park for the streets, Johannes Smit—his head pounding from last night's drums—turned to Niki. For the first time in the three days of the festival. "Give me a stick of biltong," he said without looking at her. "How much is it?"

Niki told him. He bought a stick.

Silence again.

Then out of the blue he asked, "Where are you going to sleep tonight?"

"Where I always sleep."

"And where is that?"

"What is it to you?"

"I want to visit you."

"Don't you ever give up? I don't want you! I don't want to have anything to do with you!" said Niki vehemently.

"You seem to forget that you are my sleeping partner," said Johannes Smit with a dirty smirk on his face. "Me and you, we go a long way back. To our days in the sunflower fields. Surely you cannot forget that you ate my money. I gave you enough chance to get rid of your wildness. Tonight is the night."

Niki did not respond. She feared that Hairy Buttocks would find out that she was sleeping in a primary school classroom in the black township of Marallaneng where all the out-of-town servants slept, and he would go there and carry out his threat.

When Stephanus Cronje finally showed up late that afternoon, Niki told him that she wanted to get on a bus and go back to Excelsior. After all, tomorrow was the last day of the festival. Everybody would be packing up.

"And who will pack up when you are gone?" asked Stephanus Cronje.

"Ask her what she is running away from," said Johannes Smit.

"He has threatened to come and get me at night," cried Niki. Stephanus Cronje turned red.

"What for?" he asked. "Why?"

"She is my padkos—my provision for the road," said Johannes Smit boastfully.

"Is that true, Niki? Is it true?" asked Stephanus Cronje. He was highly agitated.

Once more, Niki took refuge in silence. She busied herself by packing the biltong into a box. Then she took it to her boss's bakkie, which was parked a few metres away. Stephanus Cronje folded up the umbrella and the table and loaded them into the bakkie. Then he barked at Niki to get into the bakkie.

"I am going to get her when we return to Excelsior," said Johannes Smit as Stephanus Cronje drove away with his prize. Then he packed his cherry liqueur into boxes and loaded them into his bakkie. He walked to the far end of the Hennie de Wet Park to while away time watching the dogs from the Kroonstad prison warders' training school as their brown-uniformed handlers put them through their paces. They were demonstrating how they tracked down and attacked criminals. He found no pleasure in their sniffing around, following the trails of hidden objects. Even the music of the tartans of the Bloemfontein Caledonian Pipe Band, which accompanied the Highland and country dances, did not soothe his troubled soul.

Meanwhile Stephanus Cronje was driving around the streets of Ficksburg aimlessly, with Niki by his side. His brow and nose were glistening with tiny drops of sweat. He was hyperventilating. All the while he was asking, "Is it true, Niki? Did you do things with that Johannes Smit?"

Niki had no intention of answering this question.

"Dammit, Niki," he said frantically, "it is me you should be doing things with, not that Johannes Smit."

Niki just smiled. Stephanus Cronje knew that she was ready and willing. He became brave.

Night had fallen when he drove to a fallow field on the outskirts of town. And on the grass that grew at its borders, she peeled off her pink overall. The same overall she had peeled off on that afternoon of shame. While Johannes Smit was seething at the Cherry Ball, sickened by the aura of excitement and romance that permeated the Town Hall, all dressed-up in a tuxedo without a dance partner, Stephanus Cronje was relieving Niki of her undergarments. While Johannes Smit watched enviously as Adam de Vries and Lizette executed a clinical waltz, followed by the two Lombards, each partnered by the young blood of Ficksburg, Stephanus Cronje and Niki were rolling on the grass.

He was deep inside her. Under the stars. She looked into his eyes in the light of the moon. She did not see Stephanus Cronje, owner of Excelsior Slaghuis. She did not see a boss or a lover. She saw Madam Cornelia's husband. And he was inside her. She was gobbling up Madam Cornelia's husband, with the emphasis on *Madam*. And she had him entirely in her power. Chewing him to pieces. She felt him inside her, pumping in and out. Raising a sweat. Squealing like a pig being slaughtered. Heaving like a dying pig.

Ag, shame. Madam Cornelia's husband. She who had the power of life and death over her. He became a whimpering fool on top of her, babbling insanities that she could not make out. Then there was the final long scream, "Eina-naaa!" A dog's howl at the moon. And two sharp jerks. It was all over. His body had vomited inside hers.

He was in control again. He had the power of life and death.

A BARN FULL OF MOANS

*T*HE ONE in front has big feet. Big brown feet with grey toenails. Five toes on each foot. An occasional departure from the trinity's norm. Feet and toes! She wears a grey knee-length dress and a grey beret. Her sad face is black and her eyes are cast down to the red ground. Her gaunt posture hides the fact that she is a leader. She leads four women in their prime. A woman in a red blanket and red slippers. A grey crocheted hat on a brown head. She has bedroom eyes, and she walks sideways. Her feet point in the direction from which she comes.

She is followed by the one who has thin legs. Grey legs without feet. The only one carrying a baby. There is a softness about her. Soft yellow blanket. Soft grey baby wrapped in a soft yellow blanket. The baby wears a soft grey woollen cap and the mother a soft grey beret. The mother is not really carrying the baby. The baby stands on the palm of her hand. The brown woman behind her holds out her open hand so that it can support the weight of the baby. The brown woman's bare feet point to where she is going. Forwards. She has only three toes. The last woman faces sideways, giving us her back. Giving us her bare heels. Her grey dress has

a matching broad figure-belt. She wears a grey doek. Her black
face is turned to the other women. She is looking in the direction
they are all going. Her hands are raised to the heavens as if in supplication.

Five women sneaked into the barn. Five supplicants walking
into a wanton temple. When they left their homes, they were going
to collect cow-dung in the veld. And everyone knew that. Cow-
dung in the fields and not in a big barn built of corrugated-iron
sheets. There was no cow-dung in the barn. But here they were,
walking gingerly on the hay that carpeted the floor. Bales of hay
were stacked in one corner. Some were scattered around on the
floor. Creating little havens of joy. Five men sat on some of the
bales. Five men in khaki shorts or grey wash 'n' wear pants. Five
men drinking Johannes Smit's cherry liqueur. Two bottles from
the ten that were not sold at the festival. Johannes Smit, threatening to burst out of his grey safari suit. Johannes Smit, proudly serving the dark liquid in beer and coffee mugs. He was the host. This
was his barn on his farm. His territory. The four men and five
women were his guests.

He had made elaborate arrangements for this gathering of the
partakers of stolen delicacies—to the extent that he had neglected
some of his crucial duties. He had, for instance, left his cows at
the mercy of summer pastures. Even though he knew that cows
needed to be fed green-coloured legume hay in order to maintain
high milk yields. Even though he was aware that cows start preparing for their next lactation as soon as they are dried off. The
gathering in the barn was more important than dry cows. More
important than his docile Brahmin cattle, three of which were
loitering outside the barn, collecting strands of hay with their
tongues and dispatching them to their stomachs.

The five men welcomed the five women with drinks. One of the
women, Niki, said no thank you. Johannes Smit, the man who was
offering her a mug, urged, "Come on, Niki, you will see it is much
more fun when you are a bit tipsy."

But another man, Stephanus Cronje, stepped between them and said, "She does not want any of your cherry liqueur, Johannes."

"Today we must swop, Stephanus," said Johannes Smit. "Last time you refused to swop. Everyone swops. You can't keep to one partner all the time."

He was already breathing like someone who had just run a marathon. Niki looked at him as if he was something someone had forgotten to throw into a rubbish bin. She seemed to be the only one of the women who had full awareness of the power packed in her body. And she was using it consciously to get what she wanted. Since the cherry festival, Johannes Smit died of desire every time he thought of her. Especially when he imagined all the things she must have done with Stephanus Cronje. He had hoped that during these partner-swopping orgies, he would have his opportunity. But Stephanus Cronje was obviously becoming unsportsmanly. As if he had the sole ownership of Niki. And this was the same Stephanus Cronje who had a taste of other men's partners when Niki was not there!

"He will not be allowed here if he does not want to share," said the Reverend François Bornman, fondling Mmampe's breasts. She had planted herself on his lap.

"If they banish us from here, Niki, we'll just do our thing in the sunflower fields," said Stephanus Cronje with a tinge of boastfulness in his voice.

They had "done their thing" in the sunflower fields before. In between the barn romps, which happened only once a fortnight. They had even "done their thing" in Madam Cornelia's bedroom, when she went visiting her parents in Zastron. They had used Madam Cornelia's own metal antique bed that looked like a hospital bed to Niki. On Madam Cornelia's own downy duvet. Niki's head resting comfortably on Madam Cornelia's own fluffy continental pillow. Niki's greatest triumph!

"So what do you want here if you won't play by the rules?" asked Johannes Smit, taking his cue from the man of the cloth and fondling Maria's breasts.

"Rules?" cried Stephanus Cronje. "Whose rules? When did we lay hard and fast rules that we'll swop no matter what?"

"He's always been a selfish boy," muttered Groot-Jan Lombard. "Even when he was a baby I knew he was going to be a selfish boy."

"You should say that about your own son, Oom Groot-Jan," said Stephanus Cronje. "He is the selfish one. Klein-Jan eats his black honey on the sly."

The woman with the baby placed the child on the floor at the far end of the barn. She sat on Groot-Jan Lombard's lap and ceremoniously took off his shirt. Then she yanked at the hair in his armpits. With each jerk he bleated like a goat. The pleasurable pain was all he would ever get from these sprees. It was before the wonder of Viagra was invented.

Soon naked hairy white bodies were frolicking on the hay with naked smooth black bodies.

The baby played with an empty cherry liqueur bottle. *Da . . . da . . . daaaa.* The baby who was almost white rolled the bottle on the floor and crawled after it. *Da . . . da . . . daaaa.* Brownish hair like young maize-cob filaments. A product of these barn romps. *Daaa . . . da . . . daaaaaa!* Mummy administering such creative pain to a poor old man. Everybody lost in a dizzying whirl of partner-swopping. Everybody but Niki and Stephanus Cronje. They were lost deep within each other.

The single-titled man became a whimpering baby as before. As always.

Once he carried two titles: boss and Madam Cornelia's husband. Now he was just Madam Cornelia's husband, as he had insisted that she resign from the butchery. She was unemployed. But she didn't have a single regret. She earned more money than she did when she worked full-time at the butchery. Once a week she would send Viliki to Stephanus Cronje's house in town. During the day, when Madam Cornelia was busy ringing up the till at the butchery, counting rands and cents—some of which would end up as Niki's share of the spoils—and weighing workers on the black iron floor scale twice a day. Viliki would knock timidly. Stephanus Cronje would appear at the window. Viliki would give him a note from his mother. He would read it and then put some bank notes in an envelope.

"Give this to your mother," he would say in Sesotho. "And be careful, boy, don't lose that envelope."

Viliki would run like the wind all the way to Mahlatswetsa Location and proudly give the envelope to his mother.

Viliki and Niki were living a wonderfully comfortable life, what with Pule's relentless remittances! And the few coins Niki earned once in a while when Madam Cornelia sent for her to look after Tjaart when the regular nanny had not turned up—attending her grandmother's funeral for the tenth time. Occasions that Tjaart relished because for him there was never going to be anyone who could take Niki's place. Occasions that Niki relished because they kept her in touch with Madam Cornelia. If only to give Madam a self-satisfied smirk. And to rejoice in Madam's blissful ignorance.

The romps on the hay deteriorated into moans. Moans relayed from one pair to another. Simultaneous moans. A barnful of moans. And howls of enjoyable pain. The baby cried. But no one paid attention. The baby bawled and bawled. The Brahmins outside went berserk. With their big ears, they had very keen hearing and were sensitive to strange noises. The Brahmin bulls bellowed and raised dust. No one paid any attention to them. A cacophony of moans, howls, baby cries and the deep bellowing of the bulls.

In the middle of it all, Niki suddenly felt the weight of a chilling ball of iron somewhere between her stomach and her lungs. It was not Stephanus Cronje's heavy body on hers. It was the weight of a memory that was determined to come between her and ecstasy. She had filed the fact that she had missed her times in some dark compartment of her mind. Now it was forcing itself back in the cacophony. More than a month had passed without her visiting the moon. To add to her woes, most mornings she was nauseous. And had a strong desire to eat damp soil.

She wondered what Stephanus Cronje would say when she told

him. And what murder Pule would commit when he got to know of it.

She pushed Stephanus Cronje with both her hands, and shoved him away from her body. Just when his was getting hard and rigid.

He watered the hay.

BIG EYES IN THE SKY

A	MAN IN blue pants, blue shirt and red beret stands on
the black roof of a skewed house one blue night. He
lifts his arms to the heavens in a supplication that is
reminiscent of the five women in their prime. The roof almost
caves in from his weight. Wide-eyed heads appear in the blue and
white and yellow sky. Milky-white eyes with pitch-black pupils staring at the man. Penetrating the house with their amazed gaze.
Disembodied heads like twinkling stars in the blue night. White
cosmos grows wild around the house.

Bright eyes in the sky see everything. They see a newly-born
baby wrapped in white linen. An intrusive star of Bethlehem has
sneaked in through one of the two skewed windows and shines on
the baby's body. It fills the room with light and yellowness. Two
humans kneel on either side of the sleeping baby, hands clasped in
prayer. One is a man in a blue suit and blue beret. The other is a
woman in a blue nun's habit. The big star of Bethlehem suspends
itself above her buttocks.

It had not been easy for Niki, although this was a second child-
bearing. The water had broken. The contractions had flooded
her body. Fewer and fewer minutes apart. It should have been

smoother. But the baby had other ideas. It gave the village mid-wives its back, and remained stuck in the passage of life. The Vase-lined hand of a midwife forced its way into the channel, trying to turn the baby, so that its head should come to the fore instead. A hundred razor-blades were cutting the very depth of Niki's being. Making incisions that bled profusely and throbbed with a pain that she believed would be etched in her memory forever. She moaned and wailed. The midwives softly admonished her: a true woman accepted her lot with bravado. A true woman hid her pain inside her chest and presented an unflinching face to the world. It was a disgrace for any woman to yell like that at the agony of bring-ing a new life to the world. Even more shameful in a second con-finement.

She was tired of pushing. Yet they egged her on. They cajoled and threatened. They mocked and ridiculed. They burnt herbs near the bed, and filled the room with incense. Until the baby turned around. After many hours. After one whole day and one whole night. Just when she thought she was giving up on her life and the baby's, the baby's head mercifully erupted like red molten lava onto the midwives' exhausted hands.

Big eyes in the sky saw Niki's relief. The midwives heard her sigh and joined with their own unison of sighs. The struggle was over. The baby uttered one good yelp. They cut the umbilical cord and clamped the piece that hung from the baby's stomach with a clothes peg. Niki fell into a deep sleep, while the midwives buried the placenta in the ash heap at the back of the shack.

She owed her body a dream-free slumber.

When she woke up, they showed her a beautiful baby girl. A flood of love overwhelmed her. She wanted to hold her tightly against her breasts. And to protect her fiercely against anyone who would dare question her reason for existing. The midwives said the baby looked like a porcelain doll. They jokingly called her Popi, another word for "doll". And that became her name.

When we finally got to see Popi, we were not in the least taken aback that she looked almost like a white woman's baby. The midwives who attended to Niki were not astonished either. Of late they had been helping quite a few black women from Mahlatswetsa Location and the neighbouring farms, who had been giving birth to almost white babies. Or to "coloured" babies, as they were called. As if they were polychromatic. Or as if everyone else in Mahlatswetsa was transparent. Some barn women were already cuddling their own coloured offspring, while others' stomachs were expanding by the day. It was a bursting of forbidden sluices that we were all talking about in Excelsior.

After the baby had been cleaned and wrapped in a soft white blanket, she slept peacefully in her mother's arms. The baby was obviously exhausted after the long struggle. The midwives snickered and whispered among themselves that she shared features with Tjaart Cronje. She had Tjaart's eyes. She had Tjaart's fingers. She had Tjaart's ears. She had Tjaart's nose. She had Tjaart's rosy cheeks.

Niki heard every word, for she was not asleep after all. She had just closed her eyes, enjoying the softness of the baby's body against hers, careful not to hold her too tightly against her breast, lest she squeezed all life out of her tiny body. She wondered how the midwives had suddenly gained such great expertise on the shape of Tjaart's body parts. Her child had nothing of Tjaart's, she convinced herself. The midwives were seeing what they wanted to see. Their ill-gotten knowledge of barn escapades made them reinvent her beautiful baby in the image of Tjaart Cronje.

The image of Tjaart Cronje began to haunt her restful state. It transformed itself into a daymare. Tjaart Cronje. All of seven years old, yet his crush on Niki had persisted. Exacerbated by her naked body that continued to loom large upon the floor scale of his imagination. Exacerbated even more by her big round belly.

Madam Cornelia had continued to use her services as Tjaart's part-time nanny until the very last month of her pregnancy. Part-time in name only, for her services were demanded almost daily, as the boy wanted only Niki, and none of the regular nannies employed to look after him.

It was an unspoken covenant of mutual enjoyment. Tjaart enjoyed caressing her protruding stomach that stretched her maternity dress to its very limits. And laughing at the violent kicks of the baby. Niki secretly enjoyed the calming effect of the little hand. Madam Cornelia meanwhile enjoyed teasing her about "her people" who were always having children in spite of the overpopulation of the world.

"You people never know when to stop," she would observe. "You must ask your husband to take you to the hospital to close you up."

She obviously had forgotten that this was only going to be Niki's second child.

Madam Cornelia's greatest concern was for Tjaart. Who was going to look after Tjaart when the time came for Niki to give birth? And after that, how was she going to look after a new baby and Tjaart at the same time?

PULE HAD NOT returned to Excelsior for almost a year. When he came back, he found a coloured baby in his house. In Welkom, he had heard rumours of his wife's pregnancy. He had written to Niki, trying to find out the truth of the persistent stories. But she had not responded. He had then stopped sending her money, after warning her that if she did not come up with a reasonable explanation concerning her alleged condition, he would stop wasting his hard-earned cash on her. The money that was enabling her to gallivant around was dripping with his sweat, he added. He was indeed true to his word. Hence Niki's willingness to act as Tjaart's nanny, even when she was very heavy with child. She needed the cash.

The fact that there were other families in the location who had coloured children did not lessen the grief that Pule felt to the marrow of his bones.

"Who is the father of this child?" he wanted to know.

Niki dared not reveal Stephanus Cronje's name, in case Pule did something silly. Like going to confront him at his Excelsior Slaghuis, where the man would be sure to gun Pule down. Stephanus Cronje was well known for drawing his gun at the slightest provocation. Like when a customer from Mahlatswetsa Location was foolish enough to complain that a piece of meat just purchased had a distinct stink of putrefaction. Madam Cornelia would say she had already rung the money in the till. There was no way of getting the money out once it was already in the till. If the customer insisted that he wanted a refund, Stephanus Cronje would whip out his gun and ask the customer to disappear from his sight. Sane customers never argued with guns.

Niki wondered how Stephanus Cronje was going to receive the news of Popi's birth. She had not seen him since the day she told him of her missed periods, her morning sickness and her cravings for damp soil and sunflower seeds. It was very clear to Niki that he was avoiding her.

"I have asked you a question," said Pule calmly.

"I have already sinned, Father of Viliki," wept Niki. "I will understand if you never want to have anything to do with me again."

WE SAW Pule exiling himself into a world of silence. Those who worked with him in the mines of Welkom said the silence continued even there. So did the heavy drinking. We pointed fingers at Niki. How could she do this to a man who had shown so much responsibility towards his family? Other women could make excuses that their husbands had deserted their families after falling for the wily women of the big cities of gold—Welkom and Johannesburg. But Pule was well known throughout Mahlatswetsa for his devotion to his wife and son. We knew that even when he spent long periods without coming home, he never forgot to send Niki and Viliki money and beautiful clothes.

Mmampe, who was carrying a load in her womb herself as a result of the barn escapades, had an answer.

"What can we do?" she asked resignedly, "White men have always loved us. They say we are more beautiful than their own wives. We are more devastating in the blankets."

Oh, the burden of being loved! Of being devastating!

The news of Popi's arrival reached Johannes Smit, who bitterly boasted to Stephanus Cronje, "Even if you scored a bull's-eye, I had Niki first. Before any other man."

But Stephanus Cronje was in no mood to rejoice over any bull's-eye. Or to engage in puerile contests. He was busy plotting ways to stop the news from reaching Cornelia's ears.

A TRULY COLOURED BABY

*H*IS PURPLE SHOES look like a ballerina's dance slippers. The broad brim of his purple hat covers his eyes. His face is downcast, as if he is contemplating the burnt sienna ground. His khaki pants are bulging at the pockets. One hand is in his pocket and another is holding a white umbrella. He is using the closed umbrella as a walking stick. His shoulders are raised high. His elbow-length purple sleeves hang loosely from his khaki waistcoat. The ground has streaks of green. White cosmos surround him.

The Man with the Umbrella walked hesitantly towards Niki's shack. Black piglets grunting around the corrugated-iron shack and speckled hens pecking at unseen morsels scattered in different directions at his approach. He used his umbrella to knock at the open corrugated-iron door.

Niki in a white doek, yellow blouse and black skirt sat on the bed, Popi nestling in her arms, a pacifier in her mouth. Although it was very hot under the low corrugated-iron roof, the baby's head was in a woollen cap. Only her round face could be seen.

"I thought I should warn you," said the Man with the Umbrella, "they are searching all over the district. From house to house. They follow every rumour."

He was talking of the police. They had uncovered twelve light-skinned children who they claimed had mixed blood. They were already in jail with their black-skinned mothers. There was a doctor too. All the way from Bloemfontein. His work was to take blood tests and to confirm that the blood was indeed mixed.

Niki wondered how it was possible for the doctor to tell if the blood was mixed or not. Mixed with what? Was it not all red?

"They will come for you too," said the Man with the Umbrella. "Take your baby away. Go hide in Thaba Nchu. Or better still, in Lesotho. I have heard that in Lesotho they don't mind when the child's blood is mixed. They are ruled by a black prime minister there. You must have relatives in Lesotho."

It was difficult for Niki to take this whole matter seriously. Especially as the news came from a stranger with a white umbrella and funny shoes.

Thaba Nchu would give her no succour. The arm of the law was long enough to reach there. She would not exile herself to Lesotho either. She had never been there in her life. She knew that, like most Mahlatswetsa Location people, she had distant relatives in that country. But surely she could not just pack up and go. In any case, the one who had been wronged by her actions had forgiven her. Pule had said so in his letter: he had forgiven her because it was not for him to judge. Yes, he had not come back to Excelsior for eight months—not since he left the day after Niki's refusal to name the father of her coloured child. But after a few months' silence, which he spent digesting what had befallen him, he had explicitly written that he forgave her. He had become a mzalwane—a born-again Christian. We observed with mirth that Niki's infidelity had had a commendable by-product. It had driven him into the comforting arms of salvation.

If the one who had been wronged had forgiven her, what business was it of the police? Why would the government not forgive her as well?

She was still not totally convinced of any imminent danger when the Man with the Umbrella pointed his funny shoes towards the door and left to warn others.

Niki carried Popi on her back, wrapped in a red and blue tartan shawl, and briskly walked to Mmampe's shack three streets away. Mmampe's ageing mother sat forlornly on the mud stoep in front of the door. She expressed her surprise at seeing Niki walking the free earth of Mahlatswetsa. Her own daughter and her light-skinned granddaughter were in jail. The police had come for them in the middle of the night. Three police vans in all. Each with five heavily-armed Afrikaner policemen. They kicked the door down and shone torches in the eyes of a startled Mmampe and her mother. Mercifully, they gave Mmampe the opportunity to put a dress on over her nightie, before they frogmarched her into the street with the bawling baby in her arms. They bundled Mmampe and the baby into the back of a van, ignoring the old lady's pleas that they leave the baby with her. There were already other women and babies in the van. They drove away in a triumphal convoy.

"Maria!" cried Niki. "I must warn Maria."

"Maria and her baby boy were picked up the night before," said Mmampe's mother.

"Why didn't anybody tell me?"

She did not wait for an answer. She scurried back to her shack. Like a field-mouse sensing a rainstorm.

She retrieved the brazier from the back of the shack where it had been gathering summer rust, waiting for its winter tasks of warming the house and cooking the food. She carefully placed dry grass and twigs at its base. She piled dry cow-dung on the twigs and ignited the dry grass.

While the fire was burning outside, she pumped the Primus stove and boiled a little water in a kettle. She poured the water into a blue enamel washing basin, placed it on a grass mat and knelt next it, holding Popi's head over the steamy water. The baby cried as her mother worked up a rich lather of Lifebuoy Soap on her head. Her hair slid between Niki's fingers like green algae filaments. The top of the head was pulsating like a wild heartbeat. With a Minora razor blade, she shaved her daughter's little head clean. No stranger would know that the hair that belonged on that bald head was not black and matted. Not nappy. Not frizzy.

But Popi was still pink. They would see that she was of mixed blood.

Niki took the smoking brazier into the shack and placed it on the floor. She held a naked Popi above the fire, smoking the pinkness out of her. Both heat and smoke would surely brown her and no one would say she was a light-skinned child again. The baby whooped, then yelled, as the heat of the brazier roasted her little body and the smoke stung her eyes and nostrils. Cow-dung smoke is gentle in reasonable doses. But this was an overdose. There was so much that it made even Niki's eyes stream. She assured the baby that it was for her own good. She sang a lullaby as she swung her over the fire. Rocking her from side to side. Turning her round and round so that she would be browned on all sides. Evenly.

FOR FIVE DAYS, they did not come for Niki. The nights became too long to bear, for they were unaccompanied by sleep. Days were tiresome and teary, for she spent them hovering over a smoky brazier, browning her little girl. Singing lullabies and hoping the baby would get used to the heat and would stop crying so. Singing lullabies until the baby became red instead of brown. Until the baby's skin began to peel from her chest right up to her neck. Until the baby became truly coloured, with red and blue blotches all over.

Just when Niki was beginning to relax, and to brown Popi for shorter and shorter periods, the police pounced on her. Not in the night, but in the glare of the day when the whole world could see.

Two police vans stopped outside her shack. Four burly policemen walked into the house and dragged her out. Her resistance had no effect. Popi dangled from her hand like a raggedy doll.

When Viliki came back from playing in the street the door was ajar, but there was no one at home. There was nothing to eat either. He sat outside, hoping that Niki would return soon. When darkness fell, he began to cry. Then he walked to Mmampe's home, three streets away. Mmampe's mother knew immediately what had happened. She gave him sugared water and a chunk of steamed wheat bread.

SHADOWS SHIFTED around, creating space for her to sit on a mat of grey blankets spread on the concrete floor. She could see their dark outlines vaguely. Shadows holding babies. Gurgling babies sitting on their laps. She could hear Popi crying as a warder walked away from the cell with her.

"Bring back my baby!" Niki screamed. "What are they going to do with my baby?"

"Don't worry, Niki," one of the shadows said. "They will bring her back. They are taking her to be examined by the Bloemfontein doctor for traces of whiteness."

It was Maria's voice. Niki's eyes were getting accustomed to the dimness. She could see Maria sitting near the toilet bucket, rocking her baby to sleep. The cell was too small for the ten women packed in it. They barely had enough room to sit with their legs outstretched. Niki knew most of them. Those she could not identify she suspected came from other towns. The sex ring had expanded to include women from farms in neighbouring districts such as Brandfort and Clocolan. Even Marquard, a hundred kilometres away.

"Where is Mmampe?" asked Niki.

"They took her to another cell," said Maria.

Niki learnt that the warders had had to move Mmampe to another cell because the other women were threatening her with grievous bodily harm. They accused her of exposing their activities to the police.

"How do you people know that Mmampe did that?" asked Niki indignantly. "Mmampe would never do anything like that."

"She did! She did!" shouted the women in unison.

"Read her the newspaper, Susanna," said Maria to one of the women.

The woman—Niki learnt later that she was a teacher at a farm school—took out a piece of paper from her deep cleavage. It was a cutting from *The Friend* newspaper. She shifted closer to the toilet bucket where there was better light. She read with histrionic panache:

AFRICAN WOMAN TOLD POLICE ABOUT AFFAIR

The Minister of Justice, Mr P.C. Pelser, said that all kinds of rumours had been doing the rounds in Excelsior for some time before the police took action. As a result of this a police officer from Ladybrand had given instructions to a warrant officer at Excelsior to investigate the matter. On 21 October he had called a Bantu woman, Mmampe Ledimo, to the charge office and had questioned her. She had admitted that she had had relations with a certain White man. She had, however, added that she had not been the only non-White woman who had done this, and had mentioned a number of others. As a result of this information seven Whites and fourteen non-Whites had been arrested.

"I refuse to believe this nonsense!" said Niki, clearly unable to convince herself that she unreservedly disbelieved the report.

"It's right here in the newspaper in black and white," said the farm schoolmistress.

"A newspaper cannot lie," added Maria.

"The bitch!" cried Niki.

GLORY

*T*HESE WERE DAYS when sunflower fields lost their yellowness and assumed a deep brownness. Days when the trinity's palette became warm and sombre. Dominated by siennas and umbers.

Niki and Popi frolicked in the wide-open spaces that the trinity created for all those who loved wide-open spaces. Those who relished big skies that merged with the earth. Eliminating horizons. Making it impossible to determine at which point the earth ended and the sky began. It was a rapturous sight. Popi, truly coloured in red and blue patches, running among the brown sunflowers. Petals wilted and lost their yellowness. Popi naked and unevenly coloured. Not old enough to crawl. Not old enough to toddle. Yet frolicking and running in the brown field. Niki, naked and free, running after her. Popi and Niki gambolling in the field whose wilting colours formed a fading image. Like one big veronica. Until woman and infant merged with Payne's grey. And became one with it. Disappearing into the trinity's splashes and becoming part of the compassion they evoked.

No one would ever find them.

The clanking noise of the keys, and the grating sound of the metal bowls of sugarless maize porridge being pushed across the rough concrete floor, did find them. And dragged them protesting out of the splashes. They had not merged strongly enough. Deeply enough. Their guilt-ridden contours had stood out among the innocent strokes. They were found and brought back into the world of fluster and bewilderment. Of catty women and screaming babies.

Niki was living among them in the stuffy cell. Yet she felt isolated and lonely. She faced each one of the seven days in a daze. She saw things happening to her as if she had another life outside of her body. As if they were happening to someone else. As if she was living in someone else's dream. Someone else's nightmare. Daymare. Eveningmare. Morningmare. Every-hour-mare.

Whispers buzzed around her like annoying green flies. Whispers of what Stephanus Cronje had done to himself. The coward. He had taken the easy way out, she mused. Leaving her to face the wrath of the law alone. He had shirked his responsibility right from the beginning. What would happen to Tjaart? She chastised herself for thinking of Tjaart when she and Popi had their own troubles to deal with. When she had been separated from her son, Viliki.

The stench of sour milk from lactating breasts also sought and found her. Milk that had soaked into the babies' unwashed flannel vests. Yellowing garments made of curdled milk. And the vapours that released themselves from the open toilet bucket. And from the bodies of the interned. Lacteal odours took second place to stronger fetidities when the babies decided to release their bowels. Those who had already been potty-trained before their incarceration sat on the bucket, mothers holding them tightly around their little chests so that they would not fall into it. And sink. A baby could drown in the bucket. It got full very quickly, since the women took turns to empty it only once a day—in the morning before breakfast.

Popi was still too small to be toilet-trained. She did everything on the single nappy she had been wearing when she and Niki were

arrested. Niki washed it once, in the morning, with the same water
she had used for washing herself in a metal basin. While it dried
on the high barred window, she wrapped Popi in her petticoat.
And held her close to her bosom. Rubbing her chin gently on
Popi's head. Hair was beginning to grow. Not kinky. Not frizzy.
Straight hair lying flat on her scalp. Brain throbbing under the skin
of the head where the bones of the skull had not yet closed ranks.
Bubbling in a slow rhythm like porridge under a low flame.

WHEN THE MAIN ACTORS of the unfolding drama began to arrive, we were already crowding outside the Excelsior Magistrate's
Court. There were more strangers than us, the people of Excelsior. Strangers from Johannesburg and from as far afield as
London and New York. Strangers with cameras and notebooks.
Talking to us and asking us questions. Big television cameras that
none of us had ever seen before. Taking pictures of Excelsior and
sending them directly to the living rooms of England and America. Transmitting our lives through the big masts that had been
erected outside our post office. Twenty television masts outside one
little post office in a one-street town. Unfortunately, none of these
pictures would be seen in South Africa. There was no television
service in the country yet.

Busybodies spreading the shame of Excelsior to the world. Even
invading decent volk working in their gardens. Bombarding them
with inane questions.

"Leave us alone in our trouble," we heard Oom Gys Uys
screaming from his garden at one of these scandalmongers who
had asked him what the community thought of its disgraced elite.
"Don't interfere with us!" warned Oom Gys as he turned his back
and walked away.

We saw Adam de Vries walking from his black Chevrolet sedan
towards the courtroom. He was holding a big black briefcase in
one hand and a wedge of files in the other. He looked like a member of the Cape Town Parliament in his pinstriped suit and black

Battersby hat. As soon as the vultures with cameras and notebooks saw him, they pounced on him, asking him questions all at once, shoving microphones into his face. Unlike Oom Gys Uys, he didn't seem to be perturbed by all this attention. He seemed to be enjoying it. He could not spend too much time answering their questions, however, for two men from the British Broadcasting Corporation—one with a microphone in his hand and another with a camera on his shoulder—were waiting for him on the steps of the courthouse.

"Excelsior has become the best-known town in the world this week," said the BBC man talking into the microphone and facing the camera. "The small farming community—population seven hundred—was rocked a few weeks ago when some of its prominent citizens were arrested with their black maids for contravening the Immorality Act. The white accused include the secretary of the local branch of the National Party and some of the wealthiest farmers in the district. Mr Adam de Vries is the lawyer representing the white men."

By this time, Adam de Vries had reached the steps and was facing the camera with studied graveness.

"Mr de Vries," said the BBC man, "what are your clients' chances?"

"They are innocent," said Adam de Vries. "We'll show the court that they have been framed."

"What about the babies? Surely those babies come from somewhere," said the BBC man.

"Certainly not from my clients," said Adam de Vries confidently. "The state has no case against my clients."

Then he hurried into the courtroom, his face hardly betraying his inner joy at the prospect of being seen on the screens of faraway London.

These were days of glory for Adam de Vries.

They were days of shame and humiliation for Cornelia Cronje. We saw her walk unsteadily into the courtroom. A sad figure in the comforting company of Lizette, Adam de Vries's wife. We had not expected to see her here so soon after the calamity that had befallen her family. Stephanus Cronje had shot himself dead only a few days ago. He had been released on bail of two hundred rands. The following morning, after leaving his wife at work, he had locked himself in the guest bedroom, to which Cornelia Cronje had exiled him while she slept alone in the master bedroom they used to share in happier times. They no longer shared a conjugal life since the exposure of his activities with Niki. When she returned from work that day, something made her suspect that all was not well with her husband. She had asked the gardener to break down the bedroom door. And there he was. Stephanus Cronje. Bloody-faced. A rivulet of blood tracing its way from his temple to the foot of the bed. The shotgun with which he used to threaten us lying between his legs.

If Cornelia Cronje had been one of our people, she would be sitting on a mattress in an unfurnished bedroom, weeping softly, and being comforted by female relatives. Even if betrayal had killed all her feelings for the deceased, she would still have been required to go through the regulatory mourning rituals. But the customs of her people did not include brooding in ceremony over death. Here she was, attending a court case, eyes full of undisguised anger. And loneliness. Scurrying away from photographers into the courtroom.

We saw the white men arriving. Dodging photographers. Five white men charged with indulging in stolen pleasures. They were all out on bail of two hundred rands each, while their partners in crime remained incarcerated in the fester that was Winburg police cells. Adam de Vries had had to battle to get the magistrate to grant one of the accused, Groot-Jan Lombard, bail. The prosecutor—imported all the way from Ladybrand—had opposed the bail application. He had submitted that Groot-Jan Lombard had been involved in a case of violence in which an African woman had been killed.

"He used violence on a previous occasion," Christiaan Calitz, the prosecutor, had said, "and as a result he was convicted and given a suspended sentence."

Adam de Vries had stood up in defence of his client.

"Mr Lombard has undergone a total personality change," he had said. "Previously he had a violent temper. But now he is a different man. He suffers from heart trouble and cannot survive in a prison cell. Also, his farm cannot do without him."

These had indeed been compelling reasons. The magistrate had released him on bail of one hundred and fifty rands.

"You cannot take photographs of these men," said an exhausted policeman. "The law does not allow you to publish photographs of accused persons."

"We aren't publishing them in South Africa," responded a Cockney accent.

First to arrive was Johannes Smit, punishing his grey suit by stretching it almost to bursting point. We really were not surprised that he was one of the accused. Among all the Afrikaners of Excelsior, we knew him as an openly lecherous man. Why, he even drove to Mahlatswetsa Location on occasion to hunt for his quarry. He was known to bribe little boys with bottles of milk from his Jersey cows to "organise" him their sisters. He was the only white man we had seen actually doing this.

Then followed Groot-Jan Lombard. Tottering with a walking stick. Supported by Liezl, Klein-Jan Lombard's sizeable wife. Groot-Jan Lombard did not hesitate to use his cantankerous stick to clear his way through the vermin that were pointing cameras at him.

"Sies!" exclaimed a white female spectator, attired in a Voortrekker costume with kappie and all. "This man was revered by all of us because he took part in the Great Trek commemoration of 1938. His name is there for all to see on the plaque at the church. But here he is, involved in this evil! The world is coming to an end!"

"How dare you judge?" responded a white male spectator.

"These men are innocent. They have been framed by the blacks. Oom Groot-Jan Lombard occupies a place of honour in this community. He will continue to occupy it after this trial because he is innocent."

While the spectators were debating the black conspiracy, two other accused arrived. We did not know them. They must have come from outlying farms. Later we heard that one of them was a policeman.

The Reverend François Bornman was the last to arrive, accompanied by his sickly wife. They were both in funereal black. If ever there was a person who had been framed, then it had to be the dominee, we all agreed. We knew of him as a man of God who preached obedience to His laws. Laws against adultery and miscegenation. Why, he had even been responsible for running Konstantin Dukakis and his sinful family out of town.

Dukakis was a silver-haired Greek who had come to Excelsior ten years earlier to establish a corner café. We remembered him very well because he had punched a few of us when we had complained that the fish he had sold us was stale. Or that the chips were charred. He would hurl our change at us. We would chase the coins as they rolled on the concrete floor. He and his son, Ari, found this most entertaining. Their guffaws would follow us as we fled the café, only to come again the next day for more doses of rudeness. What could we do? His was the only café that sold fish and chips, which we ate when we were giving ourselves a treat.

We also remember him for the glossy magazines that he sold at his café. He introduced to our town *Kyk*, a picture-story magazine whose pages took the citizens of Excelsior to great flights of fanciful romance. And *See*, which was the English version of *Kyk*. He also introduced *Mark Condor*, a picture-story magazine of adventure, spies and crime-busters. Issues of this used to circulate among our boys, who would hide them in their exercise books and read them in class. Then there was *Scope*, a magazine whose pages were full of white women with stars on their tits. If the Afrikaner men of Excelsior caught a black man reading *Scope*, they would beat him to pieces. Black men had no business ogling topless white women. But the brave men of Mahlatswetsa Location had no qualms about risking broken limbs by smuggling the magazine under their shirts. To this day, many of us believe that white women have black stars on their breasts instead of nipples.

Besides the young soldiers and their fathers who came to the café to buy *Scope* magazine discreetly, and the schoolboys who came to peek through its pages stealthily, the Afrikaner community kept Dukakis at a polite distance. They left him alone to bully the folk of Mahlatswetsa Location in peace. Until one night when his son, Ari, was caught necking in Dukakis' old Studebaker with Jacomina, the Reverend Bornman's daughter. The Afrikaners of Excelsior, led by the dominee himself, could not hide their outrage. They said Greek boys had no right to smooch with Afrikaner meisies. Greeks were not white enough. They were no different from the Portuguese. Greeks were wit kaffirs. They put it to him frankly that the likes of him were no longer welcome in Excelsior.

The Dukakis family had had to pack up and leave.

ADAM DE VRIES. Mayor of Excelsior. Elected by the town council only a month before the erstwhile mayor, Stephanus Cronje, took his life. District Chairman of the ruling National Party. With the emphasis on *ruling*. His gait befitted that of the attorney of record of the five white men accused of sleeping with black women. He walked to the dock to confer with his clients in a manner that would have been august if only he had been of bigger stature. His stride was that of a man savouring moments of glory. Here at last was a case that would afford him the opportunity to display his greatness as an attorney-at-law. Not the petty stock theft cases that occupied most of his time. Not the tedious drawing of wills and deeds of transfer and the administering of estates of deceased farmers.

He whispered something to Johannes Smit, but went quickly back to his table when the accused women were led into the courtroom. Fourteen black women, twelve with babies in their arms or strapped to their backs. Gasps from the volk, packed into the gallery, at the sight of so many coloured babies. The gallery had been full one hour before the trial. Spectators came from as far as Reddersburg, one hundred and forty-five kilometres away. Hairy farmers in safari suits with combs in their socks. Wives in floral dresses and wide-brimmed straw hats. Tannies carrying picnic baskets and Thermos flasks of strong coffee.

None of us were allowed to sit on the seats. Those few of us who could get into the courtroom stood against the wall at the back.

We saw the court orderly policeman arrange the women so that each of them stood next to the man she was being charged with. He read the names of the women from a sheet of paper. When a woman acknowledged her name, she was pulled by the arm to the spot where the law had determined she belonged.

Johannes Smit was charged with five women, one of whom was Mmampe. Groot-Jan Lombard with two. The Reverend François Bornman with two, one of whom was Maria. The farmer we did not know was charged with three women, and his policeman friend with one. Niki was charged alone, since Stephanus Cronje no longer walked this earth.

General nervousness and fidgeting among the men and women of Excelsior and its environs, as they stood side-by-side in the dock.

Klein-Jan Lombard, in his neat police officer's uniform, entered and sat at the prosecutor's table, next to the prosecutor, Christiaan Calitz. We wondered how he had escaped arrest, as the women of Mahlatswetsa Location had revealed at stokvels and at the fundraising gatherings of the Mothers' Union that he had also occasionally indulged in the wicked pleasures. Now here he was, ready to prosecute his own father.

When the burly magistrate, Karel Bezuidenhout, entered, all those who were sitting down stood up. Including Adam de Vries, Christiaan Calitz and Klein-Jan Lombard. Those of us who had

been leaning against the wall stood up straight. Karel Bezuidenhout surveyed his court, then sat down. The rest of the people sat
down too. We leaned against the wall.

"One of the accused is your close relative," said the magistrate,
looking at Klein-Jan Lombard kindly. "You cannot prosecute this
case."

"I thought I could perhaps assist Mr Calitz, Your Worship,"
said Klein-Jan Lombard humbly.

"I have no doubt that you are a man of integrity," said the magistrate patiently. "But you'll still have to recuse yourself. Mr Calitz
can manage fine without you."

Klein-Jan Lombard made a deep bow in front of the bench,
and walked out of the side door that led to the prosecutors' and
magistrates' offices.

The prosecutor said that the women had all agreed to plead
guilty and thereafter to give evidence against the white men. This
obviously came as a shock to Adam de Vries. He stood up in a huff.

"They are accomplices!" he cried. "Their evidence alone will
not be enough to convict my clients."

"My learned friend should not worry about that," said Christiaan Calitz with a wicked smile. "There are other eyewitnesses.
And of course there are the children. Blood tests have been carried out on the accused and the children."

He looked at the babies benevolently.

Popi made friendly noises in Niki's arms. Niki fondled her face.

The magistrate said the court was not dealing with the merits of
the case at that moment. The proceedings would be adjourned
until the following week. Bail for the women would be set at fifty
rands each.

Popi began to cry as the women were led away by the prison
warders and policewomen.

We waved at the women and their babies as they were loaded
into the back of a big police truck with meshed windows. None of
them were able to post bail. They would all remain in custody at
the Winburg police cells.

A SUNBURNT CHRIST

A BROWN CHRIST crucified in a field of pink and white cosmos. His face has streaks of red from the red sun that burns from the safety of a green ball suspended against a blue and white sky. He wears a black loincloth and hangs on the grey cross like a bird in flight. One big sunflower grows next to the cross, its yellow petals touching the bent knees of the Christ. Another big sunflower stands behind the cross. Sunflowers always face the sun and thrive on basking in its rays. But these two giant sunflowers have turned their backs on the sun in silent defiance.

A black-roofed house camouflages itself among the cosmos and blue and green grass. Yellow light shines from a single window. Red blood seeps from the green door. A procession of women in blue dresses and shawls passes between the house and the big sunflower behind the cross. The sun has painted streaks of red on their Basotho hats. Their bodies are bent forward from invisible burdens. Four stooped women led by an upright nun in a blue head-veil march to pay homage to the hanging Christ. Round-eyed nun with bare breasts and black nipples. A black navel planted on a brown round stomach. A stomach full of life hangs above a blue skirt with a frayed knee-length hem.

A sunburnt Christ. Like Niki's face. Although hers was not burnt by the sun. It had been devoured by the chemicals that the Krok brothers put into their Super Rose skin-lightening lotion. The Krok brothers were diminutive identical twins from Johannesburg who used huge doses of hydroquinone to turn black South Africans into white South Africans. They were reaping great rewards in the process, since millions of black people had taken to their skin-lightening products like bees to nectar and pollen.

Niki was no exception. For even quicker results, she had changed from the regular Super Rose skin-lightener to Super Rose He-Man, specially brewed by the twins to lighten the tough skins of black men. It was even stronger than American products such as Ambi Extra and Artra. Hydroquinone did lighten the skin. But only for a while. Then it fried it until it became discoloured and hard like the skin of an alligator.

Niki's world was falling apart with her skin. It had caked and was beginning to crack. Fire was burning in her cheeks. She blamed it on her incarceration. Had she been at home, she would have applied more Super Rose He-Man to her face. Her skin was crying out for Super Rose He-Man. They had not given her the opportunity to take any toiletries when they arrested her.

But Susanna, the farm-school teacher, told her that her skin would have broken into cracks and patches even if she had been as free as a bird. Super Rose He-Man did that to the skin in the long run. She was speaking from experience. Her own face had chubaba patches. But fortunately she had stopped using skin-lighteners as soon as she realised that they did not agree with her skin. Then one day she had read in some magazine about the ravages of hydroquinone and about the Krok twins, Abe and Solly, who were amassing untold fortunes as a result of black women's quest for whiteness.

"The only way you can save your skin from further corrosion is to stop using skin-lightening creams," said Susanna. "Go back to the harmless creams that treat our skins gently: to Beauty and Pandora."

Her listeners laughed at the memory of those cheap pink creams that they had outgrown since adopting Super Rose, Ambi and Artra, in line with the trends set by the city women that they saw in magazines. How could Susanna suggest that they go back to an age of darkness?

Niki did not understand any of this. It seemed that Susanna was talking politics. Her face had nothing to do with politics. Susanna had this annoying habit of seeing politics in everything. Niki therefore did not join the others in their laughter.

"At least we can still laugh in spite of our troubles," said Mmampe.

"And by the way, who is the cause of these troubles?" asked Maria cruelly.

"When will you people understand that I did not cause our arrest?" asked Mmampe. "How many times must I tell you that they knew everything already when they came to arrest me? They merely asked me to confirm it!"

Thirteen women looked at her in disgust. Well, twelve women, because Niki did not look at her at all. Niki fixed her eyes on her baby as she rocked her in her arms. Mmampe saw the hate in twenty-four eyes. It still was not safe for her to be in the same cell as these vicious women.

The women were silent for a while, and focused on fussing over their babies.

Fourteen women sitting against the wall of the Excelsior Magistrate's Court. Twelve of them with light-skinned babies nestling in their arms. One of them almost recovered from being a truly coloured baby. Three weeks had healed the blotches of red and blue. But her neck and chest were still peeling.

Twelve madonnas, sitting in a row outside the courtroom, breastfeeding their babies. Coo-cooing and talking baby talk. Promising the little ones that they would be home soon. Or pretending they were already home and making references to beautiful things in the home surroundings with which the babies would be familiar. Making futile assurances: "Grandma will come and fetch you."

They had been transported in a truck at dawn from the Winburg holding cells, fifty-five kilometres away. They had been waiting the whole morning. They did not complain. It was better than being locked up in tiny cells for days on end. Here there was ample fresh air. Also, they were able to update themselves on the latest news from the township and farm villages. Friends and relatives, crowding a short distance away, let snippets of gossip drift across to them. They talked to the prisoners obliquely in their loud conversations among themselves.

By midday, no one had called them into the courtroom. The female warders hovering over them told them that the magistrate had not yet arrived. Something must have happened, for Karel Bezuidenhout was usually a stickler for time. The women were not bothered. They were not hungry either. Their friends and relatives had brought them fish, Russian sausages and chips. The warders were kind enough to allow them to receive food from the outside world. No one had brought anything for Niki. Mmampe and Maria shared their food with her.

The babies were getting restless, though. Popi was crying. Niki pushed her breast into her daughter's mouth. She made an attempt to suckle. But she soon spat the milk out because it had a painful taste.

Thirty minutes after midday. The women were led into the courtroom. And into the dock. The accused white men were already in the dock. But there were only four of them. The Reverend François Bornman was not among them. The attorney for the defence, Adam de Vries, was not there either. Prosecutor Christiaan Calitz looked bored. He was busying himself paging through a law report, without really reading anything. The usual spectators, including press people, filled the gallery.

"All rise!" announced the policeman who also acted as a court orderly, as Karel Bezuidenhout entered. Everybody stood up, and only sat down once the magistrate had taken his seat at the bench.

It was at this point that Adam de Vries rushed into the courtroom. He apologised as he bowed before the magistrate. He placed his black briefcase and files on his table.

"I spent this whole morning at the hospital in Bloemfontein," said Adam de Vries breathlessly.

"How is he?" asked the magistrate.

"He will live," said Adam de Vries, much to the relief of the magistrate, the prosecutor and the men in the dock. "But he will lose his eye."

"You might have heard that one of the accused, the Reverend François Bornman, allegedly made an attempt on his life with a gun this morning," announced the magistrate to the rest of the court. "He allegedly shot himself in the right eye. That is why the court had to start so late today."

The women looked at one another with eyes full of question marks. Maria's eyes had exclamation marks in addition to question marks. Her lover had failed in his bid to join Stephanus Cronje. The scoundrel was trying to escape responsibility. He had proved to be just as cowardly as Niki's lover.

"Today we shall only deal with bail matters and then adjourn," announced the magistrate.

"Your Worship," said Adam de Vries, "on the instructions of my clients, I have arranged that the bail of fifty rands set by this court be paid for each one of the women charged with my clients."

Christiaan Calitz shook his head in wonder. Karel Bezuidenhout squinted his eyes and looked at Adam de Vries closely. Also in wonder.

Outside the courthouse, we saw journalists crowding around Adam de Vries. They were firing questions at him, all at once. Why did his clients pay bail for the women? Was it an admission on their part that they knew these women and had had intimate relations with them? Why would they post bail for women who were allegedly framing them?

But Adam de Vries had a ready answer: "I arranged for their bail because I did not think it was fair that they should have to remain in custody because they did not have the money, while my clients were free because they could afford bail."

"Is it not a coincidence that your clients are paying bail for the women only now that the women have indicated that they are withdrawing their admission of guilt and will not give evidence against the men?" asked one impertinent reporter.

"I do not know what you are talking about," said Adam de Vries calmly.

"Dr Percy Yutar, the Attorney-General, reported that his office in Bloemfontein received a telephone call from Excelsior conveying the information that the women were no longer prepared to plead guilty, that they had briefed counsel and that they were to dispute the admissions," said the reporter, with a flourish more typical of defence counsel.

"What are you insinuating?" asked Adam de Vries, finding the experience of being put on a witness stand by an upstart repugnant.

"It is not an insinuation, Mr de Vries," said the persistent pest. "It is a question. Isn't it rather strange that the men post bail for the women soon after the women have declared that they are no longer prepared to give evidence against them? How are the women able to afford to brief counsel?"

"I am not going to tolerate this line of insolent cross-examination," said Adam de Vries, pushing his way out of the circle of vermin.

We saw the women walking away from the courthouse, back to the freedom of Mahlatswetsa Location and the neighbouring farms. Babies strapped on their backs. Excited friends and relatives jumping about. Fawning. Like dogs at the return of the master after a journey of many days. But Niki was not among them. We saw her being escorted to the police truck by a warder, Popi held close to her bosom. Nobody had paid any bail for her, as her lover had taken the easy way out. We saw Johannes Smit looking at her with a smirk on his face. And then giving her a silly wave. Rubbing it in that had she accepted his advances, she would have been walking home to Mahlatswetsa Location with the rest of the women. We saw Mmampe running to the truck as it drove away with Niki and Popi, shouting: "Don't worry Niki, I will look after Viliki!" We heard Niki shout back through the meshed window: "Please do! I cannot thank you enough, Mmampe."

THAT NIGHT, many families in Mahlatswetsa Location were celebrating the return of their daughters, wives and mothers. And of the light-skinned babies. But Niki's shack was deserted. It was not the only home that was deserted, however. Stephanus Cronje's home was deserted as well. A neighbour said that Mrs Cornelia Cronje and her son, Tjaart, were away. She did not know where they had gone. Maybe to her family in Zastron. A woman leaving the premises of Excelsior Slaghuis denied to the journalists that she was Mrs Cronje, and that she even knew her.

Cornelia Cronje disappeared immediately after the inquest. Soon after she gave evidence of how she had found the body of her husband upon returning home from work. She had testified that her husband had been released on bail after being charged with contravening the Immorality Act. He had driven her to the butchery the next morning and said goodbye normally before returning home. When she came back home that evening, she had found her husband's wallet on a table beside her bed. As this was unusual, she had gone to his bedroom and knocked. No one had answered. She had tried to open the door, but it had been locked. She had called the gardener, who had used a lever to dislodge the door from its hinges. She had stood aghast at the discovery of the body. Her husband's face was covered in blood and a shotgun was clenched between his legs. She had run to the house of a friend nearby and the friend had telephoned the police.

After the inquest, Cornelia Cronje had gone underground. Obviously she needed to get some breathing space away from the newspaper and television hounds that had practically camped outside her house and also outside her butchery.

There was another home that was deserted that night. That of the Reverend François Bornman. He was at the Universitas Hospital in Bloemfontein. His right eye was wrapped in thick bandages. His loyal wife was at his bedside. They were joined by the elders of the church in their dark suits.

He was not in any physical pain, he told his visitors. His pain was the pain of the heart. The pain of knowing that he had betrayed those he loved and those who loved him. It was the work of the devil, he said. The devil had sent black women to tempt him and to move him away from the path of righteousness. The devil had always used the black female to tempt the Afrikaner. It was a battle that was raging within individual Afrikaner men. A battle between lust and loathing. A battle that the Afrikaner must win. The devil made the Afrikaner to covertly covet the black woman while publicly detesting her. It was his fault that he had not been strong enough to resist the temptation. The devil made him do it. The devil had weakened his heart, making it open to temptation. And he had made things worse for himself in the eyes of the Almighty by attempting to take his own life. He was therefore praying every hour that God should forgive him.

The loyal wife grasped his hand tightly. The warmth of her grip transmitted her complete understanding and unreserved forgiveness. The elders assured him that God had forgiven him. Clearly God did not want him to die yet, for He had a bigger plan for him. He still needed him to be His messenger on earth. God had a greater purpose. That was why He was testing His flock with this scandal that had rocked the Afrikaner nation to its foundations. Men of little faith could not easily understand God's grand plan. It was an arduous road that God had set for His volk. And on the journey, many good men would be lost. Already one good man had been lost. Stephanus Cronje. A stalwart of the National Party, whose father had trekked from Cape Town to the northern Transvaal in an ox-wagon in the wonderful 1938 commemoration of the Great Trek. Together with François Bornman's own father. And Groot-Jan Lombard. And Johannes Smit's father. Although Johannes Smit had rebelled against the political home that had nourished him, and was now counted among the provincial leaders of the ultra-right-wing Herstigte Nasionale Party. Be that as it may, he too remained a good person who had been led astray by the devil in the guise of black women.

The elders of the church bowed their heads and praised the Lord for His magnanimity.

AN OUTBREAK OF
MISCEGENATION

*T*HE ELDERS of the church were right. The devil was on
the loose in the Free State platteland. Grabbing up-
standing volk by their genitalia and dragging them
along a path strewn with the body parts of black women. Parts
that had an existence independent of the women attached to
them. Parts that were capable of sending even the most devout citizen into bouts of frenzied lust.

But wily as Lucifer might be, he was not going to succeed in his
designs to consign the volk to eternal damnation. God always
looked after His own.

These sins of our mothers happened in front of our eyes. Hence
some of us became blind. And have remained so to this day. Those
sins that we did not see with our own eyes, or that we did not hear
about in places where we gathered to celebrate our lives, we read
about in *The Friend* newspaper. Reports of wholesale miscegenation in the Free State platteland abounded. Tlotlo le wele makg-
wabane, the people said. A free-for-all. Open season. A feast of
miscegenation.

The Friend, 7 January 1971:

The first three of a number of persons who will be charged in the Regional Court, Bloemfontein, for offences under the Immorality Act appeared in court yesterday.

Anna Tsomela, a 36-year-old African woman with a light-skinned, fair-haired baby of three months in her arms who, she said, was the child of the White man arrested with her, was found guilty under the Act and sentenced to nine months' imprisonment, suspended for three years.

Constable Johannes David Grisel, of S.A. Police, Reddersburg, gave evidence of how the light delivery van in which she was travelling with a White man of Bloemfontein, Petrus François Smit, was trailed by him and how they were arrested on a lonely farm road near Reddersburg.

He said that as a result of information received, he followed the van when it left Reddersburg at about 7 p.m. on 1 October last year. About 16 km from Reddersburg on the road to Bloemfontein the vehicle turned off into a farm road leading to the farm Mierfontein. Constable Grisel was joined by another policeman working with him and they pursued the light delivery van with their police vehicle.

When the light delivery van left Reddersburg, Tsomela was sitting in the back of the vehicle and the White man was driving. When they stopped the van both were sitting in the front and the baby, obviously of mixed blood, was with them. Tsomela's breasts were bared and her dress was pulled up high. He arrested the couple.

Dr B.J.B. Faul, district surgeon at Reddersburg, said that he examined the child in court in October last year at the request of the police. It was obviously of mixed blood and if Tsomela, who was an African woman, was the mother, the father must have been a White man.

In her statement to the magistrate Tsomela said she started to work for the White man and his family on a farm near Virginia some years ago. After some time the man's wife moved to

Bloemfontein and she had to look after him on the farm. After they had been staying there alone for about two years, he started giving her some of the gin he drank and later they became intimate.

About a year ago she became pregnant. The White man then moved to Bloemfontein and, because there was no accommodation for her in the city, he took her to her sister in Wepener. From there she went to Lesotho where the baby was born and then she returned to her father who was in Reddersburg.

The White man obtained her address by writing to her sister and then also wrote to her. On 1 October he arrived there and told her that he had brought her something. He took her in his light delivery van to a spot on the farm road to Mierfontein where he stopped to show her what he had brought her. There were groceries, bread and meat which he showed her, but before he could show her everything the police arrived.

In her statement Tsomela also said that she had no complaints against the White man. He at least provided for his child. Her other four children she had to bring up on her own.

The magistrate said that Tsomela should realise the seriousness of her offence. She had been committing immorality with a White man over a long period and there had been miscegenation, which it was the purpose of the Act to prevent. The serious light in which the offence was seen by the legislature was indicated by the fact that the maximum sentence provided was seven years' imprisonment.

In view of the fact that she had made a clean breast of everything, that she had no previous convictions and that she was now saddled with the burden of another child to provide for, the magistrate said her sentence of nine months would be suspended for three years, however, on condition that she was not during that period found guilty of a similar offence and that she did not leave the Republic of South Africa before 15 February when she would be required to appear in court to give evidence against Petrus François Smit.

The Friend, 7 January 1971:

In another court a young White man, Johannes J. Oosthuizen (26), of 9 Goddard Street, Bloemfontein, appeared together with a 16-year-old African woman before Mr P. Geldenbuys. No evidence was led and they were remanded until 16 February. Oosthuizen is on bail of R50. Bail of R50 was also allowed for the African girl, but has not yet been provided.

The Friend, 23 January 1971:

A mother of three sat quietly with an arm around her young son outside the Bloemfontein Regional Court while a magistrate, Mr A.W. van Zyl, was told how her husband had put his hand under the dress of a 19-year-old African school teacher and then offered her R5 if she consented to have relations with him.

A 33-year-old former traffic inspector, Barend Jacobus Nolan, formerly of Rouxville, was sentenced to six months' imprisonment suspended for three years after he was found guilty of attempting to contravene the Immorality Act.

According to the evidence led by the key witness, Cecilia Mapeta, of the farm Valbankspoort in the Rouxville district, on the evening of 4 November she heard a car approaching the hut in which she stayed.

She went out to meet the car, which was driven by Nolan. He called to her and told her to tell the pupils she taught not to play in the road. He then told her to get into his car and he would take her to a gate which he wanted closed.

She climbed into the front of the car with him but when they arrived at the gate, he did not stop. Nolan suggested to her that they should have a love affair. She refused him.

They carried on driving until they came to a grove of bluegum trees some 13 km out of Rouxville on the Aliwal North road. Nolan parked the car under the trees, switched off the lights and again suggested to her that they have an affair.

For the second time she refused him. He grabbed her arm and twisted it. She started crying and he hit her. Nolan undid the shorts he was wearing and made an indecent suggestion to her. He also put his hand up her dress. After she pushed him away and told him to stop it, he offered her R5 to have intercourse with him.

While they were arguing, a car's lights appeared and Nolan pushed her off the seat to the floor of the motor car. The car drew up about 12 yards behind Nolan's parked car and a European man climbed out.

She said that while lying on the floor of the car she heard a man ask Nolan what he was doing there. Nolan replied, "Ou Piet . . .", she did not hear the rest. Suddenly the car was started and reversed for about six yards. Miss Mapeta jumped out of the car and ran away.

Const. P.W.A. Nel, of the South African Police, said in evidence that on 4 November, acting on information he had received, he drove in his private car to the spot where Nolan was parked.

He approached the car which, so far as he could see, contained only one person. He recognised Nolan as the person in the car. When he asked Nolan what he was doing there, Nolan replied: "Leave me alone, I have a strange girlfriend with me."

Nolan reversed the car and he (Nel) saw an African woman jump out and run away. He arrested Nolan and took him back to the police station.

In a statement to a local magistrate in Rouxville, Nolan submitted that on the night concerned, he and his wife had argued. He left his home and went to a local hotel where he had been drinking the same afternoon.

The next thing he could remember was that he was being arrested by the police.

It was the Golden Age of Immorality in the Free State. Immorality was a pastime. It had always been popular even before laws were enacted in Parliament to curb it. It became a pastime the very first day explorers' ships weighed anchor at the Cape Peninsula centuries ago, and saw the yellow body parts of Khoikhoi women. But what we were seeing during this Golden Age was like a plague. In various platteland towns Afrikaner magistrates were sitting at their benches, listening to salacious details, and concealing painful erections under their black magisterial gowns. Afrikaners prosecuting fellow Afrikaners with cannibalistic zeal. Afrikaners sending fellow Afrikaners to serve terms of imprisonment. All because of black body parts.

Young Afrikaner boys were eager to taste what their fathers were eating on the sly. They went out on hunting expeditions for what they called swart poes. In the fields. In the veld. In the byways of one-street towns. In the farm villages. And in the kitchens of their very homes, where maids and nannies cooked them their dinners.

The Friend, 17 November 1970:
The son of an Excelsior farmer has been arrested on charges under the Immorality Act. He is to appear with an African woman in the Excelsior Magistrate's Court shortly. He has been released in the custody of his parents.

Within the current month 14 White men in the Free State have appeared before the courts on charges of contravening the Immorality Act.

While miscegenation and immorality were doing the rounds, and the law was saving the Afrikaner man from himself, the trinity was creating nuns in flowing blue habits. Nuns in a procession. Their child-like brown faces peeping through head-veils that flow almost to the ground. Hiding their feet. Five nuns that only live in the continuing present. Their world has nothing to do with the outside world of miscegenation. Yet each one of them is carrying a baby. Babies with slanting eyes. Babies that look grey at first glance, but have the colours of the rainbow if you look hard enough. (God promises us through the rainbow that He will never destroy the world again.) Babies wrapped in blue shawls. Only their round heads are showing. The first three nuns are looking ahead. The fourth nun is looking back at the fifth nun. Looking down at her.

The fifth nun is the shortest of them all. She looks like a child. Her face has the innocence of a child. She is the only one who does not understand why they are carrying the babies and where they are taking them. She is with child. Yet she does not understand how it happens that her stomach reaches any destination before she does.

The nuns' bodies reflect white light on the wall. These second selves follow the nuns like ghosts in a blue night.

THE KAMIKAZE OF THE GEESE

*G*EESE DIVE DOWN from the sky in a sacrificial kamikaze. The sky is overcast with dark purple clouds. A promise of rain. The ground is green. A man in a yellow ochre miner's helmet, yellow face, brown suit and black boots carries a dead goose on his shoulder. A gift from the heavens.

Another gift from the heavens: Dr Percy Yutar, Attorney-General of the Free State, made the astounding decision that all charges against the Excelsior 19 were to be withdrawn. Word got to Excelsior just minutes before the trial could resume. All the accused were in the dock. Except for the Reverend François Bornman, who was recovering nicely at the Universitas Hospital. Adam de Vries had just addressed the court to the effect that the female accused would have legal representation. The surprised Karel Bezuidenhout, presiding magistrate, had just responded that in that case, the accused would have to be tried separately. There would be delays in the trial. Judgement would have to be passed individually on each of the accused according to the merits of the individual cases.

Mr Christiaan Calitz, the prosecutor, was jolted by the Attorney-General's sudden decision. Even as he stood up to announce that he had received an urgent communication from Dr Percy Yutar, his hands were shaking.

"The charges have been withdrawn because in the view of the Attorney-General it is clear that state witnesses are no longer willing to give evidence in the trial," said Christiaan Calitz.

His face did not hide the fact that he was not pleased with the decision. He believed that he had a strong case, which did not depend only on the evidence of the state witnesses. There were, for instance, the babies. Those babies did not make themselves. The doctor from Bloemfontein had conducted his tests, which proved conclusively that the fathers were white. His evidence would have assured the prosecution a sweet victory. The prosecutor would have got his convictions. But, of course, there was nothing that he could do. The Attorney-General's word was final.

After the magistrate announced formally that the accused had no case to answer, there was an explosion of joy in the dock. The women couldn't wait to burst out of the confines of the courtroom, to breathe the fresh air of freedom.

The sun was hiding behind dark clouds. But it did not matter. Freedom was freedom, even under a black sky.

Adam de Vries's face was beaming with pride as he walked out of the courtroom. The newspaper reporters and television cameramen saw him, and proceeded to surround him. They expressed their surprise at the withdrawal of the charges. He retorted that he was not in the least surprised. He had known right from the beginning that his clients were innocent. The black women had been bribed to frame the poor men. But he could not—or would not—say who had bribed them. It was a good thing that the women had come to their senses, and decided they were not going to give evidence against his clients. It would have been fabricated evidence in any case, as his clients had never set eyes on these women until the trial.

"I speak here not only as the lawyer for the accused, but also as the mayor of Excelsior," he added. "The people of this town are very relieved at the outcome. They believed from the start in the innocence of the people who were charged. We are a very happy community. The case has caused tension, but not as much as the press said it did. We did not like the bad publicity brought to our town by this case. People of all races in the town get on well together and live in complete harmony. Now we can go back to being just a little town as we always have been."

Maria led the women in an impromptu dance for the benefit of the cameras. Friends and relatives joined the jig of victory. Mmampe was shouting above the din that the photographers should pay if they wanted to take photographs.

"There is nothing for mahala," she was saying.

"Yes, they must pay," agreed Maria. "We need the money. We'll be jobless for the rest of our lives."

"Jobless for the rest of your lives? Why?" asked a reporter.

"What white woman will employ us after this case?" asked Mmampe. "They will think we are after their husbands."

"Prospective employers will recognise us from the pictures in your newspapers," said another woman.

"We fear that even in your Johannesburg, people will see us as the bad women of Excelsior," added Susanna.

We jeered and cheered. The women were both heroes and villains to various sections of the crowd.

We mocked Maria: "Hello, Mrs Lombard."

We taunted Mmampe: "Hello, Mrs Smit."

We leered at Niki: "Hello, Mrs Cronje."

We called each one of the women by the name of the lover with whom she had been charged. Sometimes a section of the crowd would name the wrong man for a particular woman. Another section of the crowd would proffer a correction. Then an argument would ensue among the various members of the crowd as to who the right partner for the woman really was.

We cheered and jeered even louder when Johannes Smit and Groot-Jan Lombard emerged from the courtroom. They tried to skulk away to their cars in the parking lot. But they could not escape the vigilant reporters. The men did not stop to be interviewed. They answered the questions as they walked on, with the reporters following them like hunting dogs on a chase. Except for the fact that the quarry was not running. Groot-Jan Lombard was too old and tired to run. And Johannes walked close beside him in solidarity.

"Mr Lombard," shouted one hack, "how do you feel?"

"Very good!" responded Groot-Jan Lombard, doddering on.

"And how do you feel about the Immorality Act?"

"I must speak as a party man," said Groot-Jan Lombard. "My party introduced the laws. People who commit immorality should be prosecuted."

"Yes," added Johannes Smit, "if someone is caught in the act of committing immorality, there is a good reason for prosecuting him. What sticks in the gullet is that allegations are often made against innocent people, who then have to suffer."

More people in the street joined the song and dance. Out-of-towners from the farms who had no idea what the celebration was about, and did not care. A song is a song, and a dance is a dance.

Niki—with Popi strapped in a shawl on her back—did not participate in all this jubilation. She was exhausted and just wanted to get away to the quietness of her shack. Maybe Pule would be there, waiting for her. Freedom planted daydreams in her head. Pule. He was becoming a fading memory. And Viliki. She had to see Viliki. She had missed him for almost a month. She had missed Pule, too. But that, she had convinced herself, was a hopeless longing that might never be fulfilled. Viliki was now the only man in her life. Unless Pule showed through his actions that he really meant it when he had claimed before her arrest that he forgave her because only God could judge. Viliki. She knew that he was all right. Mmampe's mother, who had never missed a day in court, reported that he was fine. He had eventually stopped asking after her. They had told him that his mother had gone to Lesotho to buy "nice things" for him.

The reporters were not prepared to let Niki escape. Cameras flashed. She hid her face behind a newspaper that she rolled in conical Basotho-hat style. But the pests were not prepared to give up. They seemed to be more interested in her than in the other women. Perhaps because her partner had committed suicide as a result of the trial. She was more newsworthy. She ran for refuge to a toilet behind the courtroom. Surely no self-respecting reporter would pursue her into the female toilet—and a racially segregated toilet at that!

RUMOURS OF WAR followed the discharge of the women. We heard of white people who were fighting amongst themselves in Cape Town. Hurling words of anger at one another in their Parliament. Scuttling around in damage control efforts at the Union Buildings in Pretoria. All because of the black women of little Excelsior, so far away. We bought newspapers every day. *Die Volksblad. The Friend.* We ravished every page that had anything to do with immorality and miscegenation. Each issue circulated from one homestead to the next. Until it was tattered. Until smokers used the pieces to roll their zols of tobacco or dagga.

The sins of our mothers had caused wonderful upheavals in the land.

The Friend, 3 February 1971:
The Minister of Justice, Mr P.C. Pelser, said in the Assembly yesterday that as long as he was Minister of Justice and as long as the Nationalist Party governed the country, the Immorality Act would not be "scrapped".

He also said that the reason why the police had acted in the Free State town of Excelsior was because Whites and non-Whites had complained that there were too many half-caste children walking the streets.

The consequences of the implementation of section 16 of the Act were actually as a result of the abhorrence which the people felt against miscegenation.

Earlier yesterday Mr M.L. Mitchell (U.P. Durban North) had

asked him during question time whether he had given any instructions in connection with the withdrawal of the case against the accused at Excelsior. His reply had been that he had definitely not done so.

Before he had formally withdrawn the case, the Attorney-General, Dr Percy Yutar, had telephoned him and had informed him that he was not going to proceed with the case. Dr Yutar had done this to prevent him (the Minister) from first reading about the decision in the newspapers or hearing about it over the radio.

The Friend, 10 February 1971:
The Coloured population of the Free State village of Excelsior has more than doubled over the past 10 years.

Excelsior received worldwide publicity because of a series of Immorality Act trials and because of the fact that the charges against 19 accused were withdrawn by the State at the last minute last month.

Preliminary 1970 census statistics show that the 273 Coloureds enumerated in the 1960 census had increased to 580—299 women and 281 men—by 1970.

The number of Whites, however, decreased from 2,800 to 2,470—a total of 1,322 men and 1,148 women—while the number of Africans increased from 19,898 to 23,594—10,908 men and 12,686 women.

The Friend, 16 February 1971:
The Minister of Justice, Mr P.C. Pelser, said in reply to a question in the Assembly yesterday by Mrs H. Suzman (P.P. Houghton) that the first indication that witnesses in the immorality case in Excelsior were unwilling to give evidence, came on 21 January.

Asked by Mrs Suzman whether any of the police witnesses were found by the Attorney-General to be unwilling to give evidence, the Minister said: "No."

Asked whether any of the other witnesses were found by the

Attorney-General to be unwilling to give evidence, the Minister replied: "Yes."

The Friend, 18 February 1971:
The Friend was criticised in the Free State Provincial Council yesterday afternoon for publishing a report last week that the Coloured population in the Free State village of Excelsior had more than doubled over the past 10 years.

"Why did *The Friend* specifically mention Excelsior only?" Mr P.W. Nel (Winburg) asked.

"The newspaper could also have noted increases in the Coloured population of towns like Boshof, Jagersfontein, Harrismith, Philippolis and Welkom."

The Friend, 28 February 1971:
The Attorney-General of the Free State, Dr Percy Yutar, said yesterday that he was aware that prosecution witnesses in the Excelsior immorality trials could have been compelled to give evidence or face imprisonment.

Dr Yutar was commenting on the widespread puzzlement at the reasons for withdrawing the charges against the 19 people, five White men and 14 African women, who were accused of contravening the Immorality Act.

It was announced that charges were withdrawn because prosecution witnesses were not willing to give evidence.

In an interview yesterday, Dr Yutar said that he was "aware of section 212 of the Criminal Procedures Act" which empowers magistrates and judges to imprison witnesses who refuse to give evidence.

"I am well aware that we were not powerless and we discussed using section 212," he said. "But we felt that in this case it would not have resolved our difficulties."

The days that followed saw Niki walking about in a daze. She was oblivious to the fact that her activities in the barn, in the yellow fields, and in Madam Cornelia's bedroom had caused such a stir nationally and internationally. She was not aware that a whole government was under threat because of her body parts. That a whole nation was shaken to its foundations by her orgiastic moans. She did not follow the national debate generated by the heat of her body. She did not read *The Friend*, which we so enthusiastically awaited every morning. Many of us who had never cared for newspapers, because they only carried news about white people, had now become avid readers of *The Friend*.

Her daze began with her first night of freedom. She had left her toilet refuge at dusk, and had slowly walked to Mahlatswetsa Location. She had opened her shack door, struck a match, lit a candle on the table and just stood there open-mouthed. Her shack had been ransacked. All her clothes were gone. Everything that Pule had bought her. Plunderers had taken the trunk that she kept under her bed. And everything in it. They had pillaged the blankets from her bed. And the duvets. They had even raided the kitchen part of her shack. They had stolen her blue and white porcelain dinner set. And her plastic table covers. And her pressure-cooker. They had left only the wobbly pan.

She had just stood there, numb for a while. Then she had walked dazedly to Mmampe's home. Mmampe's mother had welcomed her with her resonant laughter. There was a treat waiting for her, she had said. But Niki did not show any excitement. Her eyes were tiredly searching the room for Viliki.

"Viliki likes to play in the street until it is too late in the night," Mmampe had said. "Night-time is a good time for hide-and-seek. He comes home only to sleep."

Mmampe's mother had given her dumplings and chunks of meat that swam in rich brown gravy. She had gone through the motions of eating, without really tasting the food. Without feeling anything. She had vaguely heard Mmampe's mother say: "This is goose-meat, Niki. Have you ever tasted goose-meat?"

The voice had sounded as if it was coming from a distance. Mmampe's mother had been bubbling all over the place. She had announced proudly that she had cooked the goose-meat to welcome her daughters back after their resounding victory.

"Even though you are not of my womb," she had said to Niki, "here in the location a child is every woman's child."

She had explained how she got such succulent meat. A man in a brown suit and yellow miner's helmet had come selling dead geese. She had said to herself: "I must buy one of these fat birds. I must give my children a treat, especially Niki who has spent all this time in the cold jail of Winburg while my daughter enjoyed her bail outside."

The mention of her incarceration and of Mmampe's bail had made Niki fidget with uneasiness. She could not hide her discomfort around Mmampe. If it was at all true that she was the woman who had sold them out, then it would be very difficult to forgive her. Especially after Niki had lost all her valuable property.

Mmampe had laughingly accused her mother of buying stolen meat.

She had said to her mother: "The goose-man must be one of the naughty people who steal birds from the farmers' homesteads in order to sell them to the location people. They shoot geese and ducks with pellet guns, as if they are game birds, instead of shooting guinea fowls in the veld."

But Mmampe's mother had said a stolen goose tasted as well as any goose.

"When a man comes selling meat, do you ask where he got it?" Mmampe's mother had asked, not expecting an answer. "When you buy fish and chips from the Greek café, do you ask the Greek-man where he caught the fish and who dug out the potatoes?"

We continued to call Dukakis' old café the Greek café even though he had long since left Excelsior. The café was now owned by a brave Portuguese family, whose children were daughters and would therefore not be at risk of necking with Jacomina, the Reverend François Bornman's daughter, who had now grown into what *Scope* magazine would have called a blonde bombshell.

After the goose and dumplings, Niki had walked back to her

shack with an excited Viliki jumping behind her. Viliki, who had been expecting "nice things" from Lesotho, but who did not seem to care that they were nowhere to be seen. All he had cared about was that he had been reunited with his mother.

Niki had huddled up with her two children on a bare mattress on the bed.

The days that followed saw her daze being gradually replaced by self-pity. Then by anger. A silent rage. She was angry with Pule for deserting her. Angry with Mmampe for selling her out. Angry with Madam Cornelia for weighing her on the scale. Angry with Johannes Smit for raping her. Angry with Tjaart Cronje for seeing her naked. And for his horsey-horsey game. Angry with the people of Excelsior for pointing fingers at her. Angry with Stephanus Cronje for dying. Angry with everyone else but herself. Angry at the barns and the yellow fields and the distant sandstone hills and the open skies.

Her greatest anger was directed at those who had duped her. People had made promises. Messages had been sent to her cell in Winburg. Things had been whispered in her ear at Excelsior Magistrate's Court. *Do not give evidence against the white men, Niki. They will look after you and your child. They will engage the services of a good lawyer for you. They will pay for the support of your child.* Persistent whispers. Promises of lucre. Of freedom. Coming mostly through prison warders. And through policewomen, who were emphatic that they were merely the messengers. That they would deny everything if she were to reveal their messenger role to anyone. And the consequences would be very bitter for her. Messages from a faceless source. *No point in sending people to jail when you can all be free. Do not give evidence against the white men. Do not give evidence against the white men. Do not give evidence against the white men.* She had believed the promises. And had agreed with the other accused women that she would not turn state witness.

The promises were not being fulfilled. They would never be fulfilled.

She was free. And hungry.

THE BLUE MADONNA

T HE BLUE MADONNA IS different from the other madonnas. No cosmos blooms surround her. She is not sitting in a brown field of wheat. No sunflowers flourish in
her shadow. Yet she exudes tenderness like all the others. She is
drenched in a blue light. Blue and white strokes of icy innocence.
Her breasts are not hanging out. She is not naked, but wears a
blue robe. A modest madonna. A madonna with blue flowing locks
that reach her breasts. Her features are delicate. Her face is round
and her pursed lips are small. Smaller than each of the slanting
eyes. A face of brown, yellow and white impasto. She holds a
naked baby in her hands. The well-fed baby wears only white
booties. She holds the baby in front of her breasts like an offering.

That was the only madonna the trinity was going to paint that
day. Niki got up from the stool on which she had been posing, and
put Popi on the floor. Popi jumped onto a brown corduroy sofa
and sat there with her legs tightly closed. At five she was already
conscious of nakedness. A good girl never sat carelessly, her
mother had drummed into her head. During these moments of
anger, Popi's obedience to her mother's little commandments was
a reflex action. She sat motionless on the sofa and sulked.

Today's session had been different from the other modelling sessions. Niki was at ease and was not self-conscious. There was no
need to cover her pubes with her hands. She was fully clothed in a
white caftan that the trinity had given her, after telling her to take
off her brown seshweshwe Basotho dress. And her grass conical
hat and plastic sandals. She looked like a prophet of the Zionist
Church in the flowing robes.

Niki walked to the canvas and took a hard look at it. This
madonna was radiant. And serene. Though Niki had been the
model, she did not look anything like her. This was not strange.
Previous mother-and-child creations had borne no resemblance to
Popi-and-Niki of the flesh, even though Popi-and-Niki of the flesh
had been the models. What was unusual about this madonna was
that she had Popi's features. The Popi who was supposed to have
posed for the child and not for the mother. But both the madonna
and the child looked like Popi. The madonna had Popi's flowing
locks. Except for the fact that they were blue. Her face was Popi's.
Not the five-year-old Popi. The way Popi would look when she was
older.

And the gown the madonna wore was blue, even though the
caftan Niki had been wearing when she sat for the trinity was
white. The trinity, by a few strokes of wizardry, had planted Popi's
face onto Niki's body. White was blue. Niki wondered what gave
the trinity the right to change things at the dictates of his whims.
To invent his own truths. From where did he get all that power, to
re-create what had already been created?

"Popi, come and see," said Niki sweetly, hiding her disapproval
of the trinity's distortions of reality. "The Father has painted you
twice. You are now your own mother."

But Popi did not respond. She sharply turned her head the
other way, making it clear to everyone that she was not on speaking terms with her mother. She was sulking.

She had been sulking the whole day. Since early in the morning.
Since her mother had slapped her bottom very hard for farting in
bed before they woke up. Early, at dawn, when both their heads

were covered with the blankets. She had cried. And she rarely cried. She never cried, for instance, when her mother slapped her for stealing her condensed milk and sucking it from the hole in the tin. Then she knew that she had been naughty and deserved to be punished. She was never bothered by Niki's shouting at her, because that's how Niki was. Even at five she had accepted that her mother communicated with her and Viliki by shouting at them. Even when she was happy, she shouted and talked to them in stern tones. To the extent that the children were finding it increasingly difficult to tell when she was really scolding them for some wrongdoing or when she was just talking to them normally or even happily. But the slap this morning had made Popi cry so much that Viliki had woken up from his bedding on the floor, climbed onto the bed and held his sister in his arms.

Popi's deep hurt was due to the fact that she did not understand what wrong she had done. After all, Niki herself farted all the time. And said nothing about it. Not even a "sorry." And no one complained. Popi had therefore never considered farting a crime.

Popi had sulked all the way from Mahlatswetsa Location to Thaba Nchu. On the rickety bus that took them the bumpy forty-three kilometres to the trinity's mission station, fellow passengers had tried to be "nice" to her. *Coochi . . . coochi . . . coooo!* They had commented on the beauty of the blue-eyed child with flowing locks. She was a white man's child, they had said. "Her mother must be one of the Excelsior 19," one woman had observed. "Or perhaps those who came afterwards," another one had said. "It happens every day." They didn't seem to care whether Niki could hear them or not.

Niki was used to such remarks and had learnt to ignore them. They did not come from any malice on the part of the passengers, but from insensitivity. One could not crucify people for being insensitive.

An old lady had tried to give Popi a sucker. But she had sharply turned her head and looked the other way.

"Popi, how can you be rude to this grandmother who is trying to be nice?" Niki had asked.

But Popi had not responded. Instead, she had filled her mouth with air until her cheeks bulged like a balloon. She had not invited anyone to be "nice" to her. She was not used to niceness.

"This child has an ugly heart," Niki had said to herself, as she walked from the Thaba Nchu bus rank to the Roman Catholic Mission. "She is only five, yet she can hold a grudge for the whole day. What kind of an unforgiving child is this?"

Perhaps Niki had forgotten that even a child could not forgive someone who had not asked to be forgiven. Who had shown no remorse.

The trinity brayed like a donkey. Popi was determined to be strong. The trinity brayed and brayed. He was bent on coaxing her out of her anger. Popi's face began to melt a little. But just before she could break into a smile, she remembered that she was supposed to be sulking, and became stone-faced again. The trinity jumped up and down around her, braying even louder. She couldn't help but smile. Then she laughed. She laughed and laughed and laughed.

Niki joined in the laughter. She had never heard Popi laugh so much. It was good to hear Popi laugh. Just as she rarely cried, she rarely laughed. Very few things made her laugh. Yet she was the source of other people's laughter. When other children saw her in the street, they shouted, "Boesman! Boesman!" And then they ran away laughing. At first she used to cry. Then she decided that she would not go to play in the street again. She would play alone in her mother's yard. She was only good for her mother's ashy yard. She did not deserve to play with other children in the street.

She blamed her flowing locks for all her troubles. Perhaps it would be better if her mother shaved her head bald again. Then no one would know that she was different. Although her blue eyes would continue to betray her. The blue eyes and the fair hair were the main culprits. Not so much the light complexion. Many normal black people had light complexions. And no one complained about that.

The blue eyes were an aberration she could do nothing about. But the hair, she could definitely do something about that. Her mother used to shave it off with a Minora razor blade. And then she had been known as the bald-headed girl. *Cheesekop tamati lerago la misis. Head that looks like a white woman's buttock!* Until Niki was seized by a spirit of defiance. And left the locks to grow once more. No one would call her child's head a white woman's buttock again.

But Niki's defiance was not Popi's defiance. She had never been consulted on the matter. She did not want the hair. It was the curse that other children pulled when they were fighting her for being a boesman. Or that Viliki tied in knots during his wicked moments.

Popi's anger had completely melted by the time Niki carried her on her back on their way to the bus rank. Thanks to the trinity's impersonations of a donkey.

It was getting late, and Niki was worried that the bus would get to Mahlatswetsa Location after sunset. The modelling had taken longer than usual. But at least there were crisp notes hidden in her bra. Her "dairy", as she called that hiding place.

Niki wanted to be home before sunset to see to it that Viliki was home. She was very strict about that. Viliki had to be home by sunset, even though he thought he was a big boy of nine years old and should be allowed to stay out late. She had good reason to be worried about Viliki. He had started running around with older boys. Good-for-nothing boys like Sekatle, Maria's brother, who was at least six years older than him. That bothered Niki. What did Viliki have in common with fifteen-year-old boys?

As the rickety bus worked its way along the dirt road to Mahlatswetsa Location, she closed her eyes and silently prayed for the trinity's long life. For his hands that must stay strong. For his vision that must continue to find joy in cosmos, donkeys, women and sunflowers. For his passion for colour that must never fade. And for his muse that occasionally flung him into a mother-and-child mode. She pleaded with whatever spirits drove his passions to immerse him in more madonna moods before Popi grew too big to model as *the* child.

Hunger had become more of a stranger to Niki and her children because of the trinity's madonnas. They had saved her from the agony of garden parties.

The thought of garden parties flooded her with images of Tjaart Cronje. A lanky lad of twelve, chasing a rugby ball. A generous giver of cakes.

RITES OF PASSAGE:
TJAART GOES SOLDIERING

WHO IS this little girl standing against a powder-blue sky with pink flowers for stars? Big sky and pink cosmos down to her bare feet like wallpaper. Who is this little girl in a snow-white long-sleeved frock? Covering her legs down to her ankles. Delicate feet with ten toes. An unusual phenomenon. One side of her chest bare and showing a little breast that is beginning to grow. Her neck peeling down to her chest. Who is this little girl with flowing locks and big bright eyes and small lips? Hair dyed black. Roots show that it is naturally light brown. Almost blonde. Sunburnt blonde. Her hands raised as high as her head. Pleading for peace. For rain. Big hands opened flat so that we can count all ten of her long fingers. Piano fingers, the trinity called them. Who is this little girl?

The little girl was Popi, the last time she sat for the trinity. Stood for the trinity, to be exact. Bye-bye, modelling income. She was not really a little girl, although she looked like one. She was fourteen years old. And she hated the mirror. It exposed her to herself for what she really was. A boesman girl. A hotnot girl. Morwa towe!

You bushman you! Or when the good neighbours wanted to be polite, a coloured girl. She had broken quite a few mirrors in her time. A mirror was an intrusive invention. An invention that pried into the pain of her face. Yet she looked at her freckled face in the morning, at midday and at night. Every day. She prayed that her freckles would join up, so that she could look like other black children of Mahlatswetsa Location.

It was 1984: the year of passage. Popi wore a permanent frown like a badge of honour. When she posed for a photograph in front of House Number 2014—which was not really a house, but the shack in which she was born—she became blank-faced. That was the best she could do. Reduce the frown to a face on which nothing could be read.

The photographer said "Cheese!" but her face refused to break into a smile. She just stood next to the giant rose-bush that grew in front of the shack and stared at the camera. The camera captured her sombre image and the cheerful bush in full bloom with pink November roses. It also captured part of the shack, which had long since turned brown from the rusted corrugated-iron sheets. It captured the tyre on its roof whose function was to stop the lightning from sizzling the shack and its inhabitants; the hen that was roped by one leg to a small pole that formed part of the fowl run; the chicks that were feeding on the ants on pieces of a broken anthill; and the paste that Niki had made from the anthill to plaster the corners of the shack in order to stop the rain from seeping into their home.

The photographer was Sekatle, Viliki's friend. The twenty-four-year-old brother of Maria. He was not one of Niki's most favourite people because, according to her, he was "too fly", and was teaching Viliki bad things. She wanted her son to stay at Mahlatswetsa Secondary School, and matriculate, and make something of his life, instead of vagabonding with a boy who had left school even before Standard Seven. Anyway, what was Sekatle doing loitering in Mahlatswetsa Location when men of his age were already digging white man's gold in the mines of Welkom?

He and his eighteen-year-old sidekick, Viliki, of course did not consider what Sekatle was doing as loitering. Adam de Vries had given him an old box camera after Sekatle had done some gardening for him. Now he went around the township and the farm villages taking photographs of people for a small fee. After school, Viliki joined him as he clicked away at school-uniformed teenagers in the arms of village dandies. At vacationing miners who posed with their mammoth gumba-gumba radios. At babies propped up by piles of pillows and sitting on rugs in front of shacks and adobe houses. At trendsetting girls in red and black tartan skirts. Free snapshots for the pretty ones. It was a wonderful way to catch girls.

Popi's was also a free snapshot. Not because Sekatle had designs on her. He had a particular distaste for coloured girls. He knew a lot about them, too. His own sister had two such children. A girl of Popi's age, born of the Excelsior 19 days. And another girl, born years later, for miscegenation had continued unabated after the Excelsior 19 case. He had never forgiven his sister for bringing shame into his home. Very unlike Viliki, who loved his coloured sister and fought daily battles against those who rubbished her.

The free snapshot was Viliki's gift to his beautiful sister.

It took one whole month to "wash the film", as we called developing photographs. Sekatle had to mail the roll to Fripps in Johannesburg. The company was the popular place for washing films from all over southern Africa, because it sent its customers a free film for every one it developed.

By the time Sekatle brought Popi's photo, she had forgotten that he had once photographed her. She was not impressed with the result. It was too real and cold and distant. She did not feel anything when she looked at it. Unlike the trinity's depictions, it did not awaken any emotions in her. And she said so.

"It is a gift, Popi," said Sekatle angrily. "You don't count the teeth of a gift."

"Maybe it is because the photo is filled with too many things," said Viliki, trying to find a reason to excuse his sister's ungrateful-ness. "The house, the fowl run, the chickens . . . too many things."

"What do you know about taking photographs, Viliki?" asked Sekatle.

"Popi is too small in this photo," argued Viliki. "Maybe you should have stood much closer to her."

"Have you ever taken a photograph in your life, Viliki?" asked Sekatle, getting irritated by armchair critics who didn't even have an armchair.

Popi left them arguing and went into the house to wash herself. She had taken to washing herself every few hours. Not to remove the freckles. She wished they could spread and cover her whole body. Making her a whole human being.

She washed herself to remove the blood.

She was not yet used to her bleeding, as she had gone to the moon for the first time in her life only three days before. It had been a scary moment. When she saw the blood for the first time, she hid it from her mother, for she was filled with shame. She bathed secretly. It was not as if she had not known what it was all about. She had already heard at school from the biology teacher that a time would come when this would happen. And from older girls who had seen the moon before her. She had never discussed matters of womanhood with her mother. So she did not know how to tell her. Until Niki wondered at her new obsession with bathing, and found her squatting over a metal basin filled with red water.

"Why didn't you tell me?" Niki had asked quietly. It was strange when Niki talked to her in quiet tones. She always shouted. The quiet tone made Popi even more fearful.

"I am sorry, Niki," Popi said.

"This means that you are now a woman, Popi," said Niki. "You must now only play with girls your age, those who have seen what you have seen. Not the little girls you like playing with."

Popi played dibeke or rounders with little girls because they passed no judgement on her. Six-year-olds. Seven-year-olds. Eight-year-olds. They knew she was a boesman. They had heard as much from their mothers. But they were able to see past the boesman in her. Into the warm soul that was hidden by the light-complexioned and blue-eyed mask. And now, if blood meant she could no longer play with them, then blood was a punishment. Blood would consign her to the lonely life of her mother. Although Niki's aloofness was of her own choice. She had gradually withdrawn from the affairs of the location, and was in communion only with herself and her two children.

Popi's withdrawal from the world of her age-mates had been an escape from their snide remarks. Even at school, she kept to herself. And when she did, they said she was too proud to mix with them because she was a misis—a white woman. But when she tried to socialise with them, they called her a morwa—a coloured girl. Jokingly, of course. But still it stung.

"Do you have a boyfriend?" Niki asked, dreading the answer.

"No!" cried Popi. The very thought of a boyfriend disgusted her. How could Niki ask her such a stupid question?

"If you sleep with a boy, you will get pregnant," said Niki. "Don't play with boys. Don't even touch a boy. As for white men, stay away from them. Don't even talk to them unless you are buying something at the store."

THE FOLLOWING DAY, Niki and Popi went to gather cow-dung from the veld. Cattle were grazing and Popi was frolicking among them, selecting the dung that had already dried, and putting it in a sisal sack. Suddenly Niki remembered something, and sharply called Popi back.

"A girl who is in the middle of the moon is not allowed to walk among the cattle," said Niki.

"But why, Niki?"

"Because you will bleed for a long time," said Niki, shouting at her as usual. "You will bleed for days without stopping. You don't want that, do you?"

Popi laughed. There could be no connection between cattle in the veld and the workings of her body.

"You can laugh all you want, but you will cry one day," said Niki. "Don't you know that some people work their cattle with bad medicine? Precisely to make foolish girls like you sick! I warn you never walk among cattle when you are up there, especially if they are black cattle. Never go near a cattle kraal either."

"Only if they are black cattle, hey Niki? What if they are black and white like the Frieslands? Or fawn like the Jerseys?"

"I am talking of cattle that are owned by black people!" screamed Niki, losing patience with the impertinent girl. "Black people are full of witchcraft, that is why. Ba loya! It does not matter with cattle belonging to whites, because they know nothing about witchcraft medicine."

"How will I know if the cattle are owned by blacks?"

"You can always see them . . . they are emaciated. Anyway, don't walk among the cattle, full stop. Whether they are owned by blacks or whites."

Once her mother said "full stop," Popi knew that she had to shut up.

NINETEEN EIGHTY-FOUR WAS the year of passage, not only because Popi went to the moon for the first time. But also because her legs began to grow hair. The moon was part of becoming a woman. But the hairy legs were not. Even Niki said as much. Other black girls her age did not grow hair on their legs. Her peers at school discussed the changes that were happening in their bodies. The biology teacher gave lessons on how the body functioned and on proper hygiene. But no one said anything about hairy legs. About shaving or not shaving. Yet her legs grew hairier by the day. The brown hair became a source of further embarrassment. She just let it be. She dared not shave it. The belief was that those women who grew facial hair were better off leaving it like that, because if they shaved it, more would grow. Popi feared that if she ever shaved her legs, they would become even more hairy. Instead, she resorted to wearing Niki's old frocks that covered her legs down to her ankles.

It was a year of passage for Niki as well. To a world of hermitry. It had started soon after the Excelsior 19 case and gradually became the almost total solitude that we saw this year. When we came to see her, she hid herself behind the door and instructed her children to say she was not home. She was always away in Lesotho or in Thaba Nchu, even though we saw her early in the mornings gathering cow-dung in the veld. Her close friends Mmampe and Maria gave up on her. And carried on with their boisterous lives. Her only companions were her children, who had their own lives to live. At least Viliki had a life outside the confines of the home. Popi spent all her time between home and school. Between home and church on Sundays.

THOUGH NIKI SHUNNED fellowship with the men and women of her community, snatches of gossip sought her and found her. The ear is a thief, our elders have said. As it happened one afternoon when she went searching for fields that had recently been harvested in order to get gleanings. She found one such field and joined two girls whose sacks were almost full of gleaned sheaves of wheat. Niki did not greet them. They looked her over dismissively, and then continued with their business of filling up their sacks and baring their souls to one another. Niki picked up strands of wheat and put them into her sisal bag without talking to anyone.

The two girls were slightly older than Popi. The same age Niki was when she used to go on those carefree cow-dung-gathering expeditions with Maria and Mmampe. The girls were talking about the white men in their lives. Niki heard the name of Tjaart Cronje jumping about in their conversation. She gathered that one of the girls had been fired from the butchery after Madam Cornelia Cronje had accused her of being a temptress whose mission was to lure Tjaart Cronje into a deep sinful hole. They dismissed Madam Cornelia's concerns, ascribing them to the fact that she was old and manless and had no one to scratch her itch. She could not stop Tjaart Cronje if he wanted adventure. She couldn't always be looking after Tjaart Cronje. Tjaart Cronje was a big man.

"Especially now that Tjaart has gone soldiering," said one.

"And did you see how beautiful he looked in his brand-new uniform?" asked the other.

"The boeremeisies were swooning. That Jacomina Bornman . . . the dominee's daughter!"

"What does she want with him? She is much older than he is. Has already been married!"

"The boeremeisies, my dear, they see him in that uniform and they want to gobble him up!"

"They do not know . . . they do not know that I know him in ways that they will never know."

The girls laughed as they walked away, their sacks full, their pride fuller.

Tjaart Cronje . . . gone to be a soldier. The thought nagged Niki. Soldiers fought wars. Soldiers died. Tjaart Cronje was going to die. She stopped collecting the strands of wheat. And stood contemplating the meaning of it all.

Barking dogs jerked her out of her reverie. She saw Johannes Smit approach with three Alsatians on leashes. Bursting out of his khaki safari-suit as of old.

"What do you want on my farm?" asked Johannes Smit, raising his voice above the din of barking dogs. They were threatening to attack, but he held them back.

Niki had not been aware that the field was part of Johannes Smit's farm. She did not think that he would make any fuss about it. Farmers generally did not bother people who gleaned their fields after harvest. But Johannes Smit intended to do just that: make a fuss. He threatened to let the dogs loose.

"You of all people have the cheek to trespass on my farm," shouted Johannes Smit. And he released the leashes.

The dogs attacked. She tried to run. But they grabbed her brown seshweshwe dress with their teeth and ripped it off. She fell on the ground. She swallowed her screams as the dogs tore into her legs and arms. She was going to die in silence. She was not going to give Johannes Smit the satisfaction of hearing her beg for mercy.

When he thought he had given her a lesson she would never forget, he grabbed the leashes, pulled his dogs back and walked away. Niki stood up, brushed the soil from her tattered dress and limped home, leaving the bag of gleanings on the ground. She was almost naked, and her legs and arms were bleeding.

"What happened, Niki?" asked Popi.

"Who did this to you, mama?" asked Viliki.

"Tjaart is going to be a soldier," said Niki, as if to herself.

"Tjaart Cronje? Does he have anything to do with this?" demanded Viliki.

"They are going to kill Tjaart," said Niki.

"Who cares about Tjaart?" cried Popi. "What happened to you, Niki?"

"You must be nice to Tjaart," said Niki pleadingly. "Especially you, Popi. God would like you to be nice to Tjaart."

Popi did not understand why God would like her to be nice to Tjaart Cronje. She warmed water on the Primus stove and washed her mother's wounds with Sunlight soap.

RITES OF PASSAGE:

VILIKI GOES SOLDIERING

*T*HIS IS the earth-colour period. Browns and yellow ochres. Siennas: burnt and raw. Diffusing their warmth into the world. Burnt umbers. A yellow ochre man on a yellow ochre bicycle. Burnt umber face under a yellow ochre conical Basotho hat. Pedaling barefoot across the yellow ochre ground. Unusually thin outlines, almost buried by the yellow ochre. There is a dead bird on the front carrier of his bike. A red goose. Women accompany him on foot. Yellow ochre women with burnt umber faces walking on the yellow ochre earth in their yellow ochre slippers. Three women, each one with a burnt sienna goose on her head. One holding a closed burnt umber umbrella. They have left the dark-roofed yellow ochre houses a distance away, on the yellow ochre horizon. They carry their geese obligingly under a yellow ochre sky.

They came all the way from Thaba Nchu with sacrificial poultry. Relatives of Niki's. They came to celebrate Popi's passage into the ranks of the Young Women's Union of the Methodist Church. The vibrant songs of the Methodists had drawn her into their fold, away from her family's Dutch Reformed Church in Afrika, the black version of the Reverend François Bornman's Nederduits Gereformeerde Kerk or NGK—the true Dutch Reformed Church of the Afrikaner people. The Methodists held lively vigils that had captivated Popi. She had, in turn, captivated the Methodists with her voice, which reverberated against the walls of the whitewashed red-roofed church every Sunday morning. When she sang, her listeners forgot that she was the despised boesman girl, and thanked God for lending her the voice of angels.

She had learnt her scriptures well. And had passed the tests. Today she was wearing the young women's uniform for the first time. A black skirt, a white blouse, a red bib and a white hat. She stood in front of the rose-bush proudly as well-wishers congratulated her. Women of the Mothers' Union had invaded her home, to the discomfort of Niki. The front of her yard had turned colourful with their uniform of black skirts, red tops with white collars and white hats.

Her children often made it impossible for her to keep to herself. Their activities occasionally brought unwelcome guests. But she was proud of Popi for graduating into the union. And was secretly pleased that the relatives from Thaba Nchu had used the occasion as an excuse to visit her, and to find out what was happening with her. It showed that they still cared. And that they had accepted Popi. Even though at first they had kept their distance from Niki. And had said that they would have nothing to do with a woman who had brought so much shame to their family. And when she had posed naked for the trinity, and they had heard rumours to that effect, her fate had been sealed. They had said the habit of stripping for white men had been so deeply imbedded in her that she was not even ashamed to display her nakedness within God's own premises. This Catholic priest who painted women, they had wondered among themselves, why was he interested in Dutch Reformed and in Methodist women? If he was true to his calling, wouldn't he be interested only in the nakedness of Roman Catholic women?

The relatives from Thaba Nchu were extending a hand of reconciliation. The uncle with a bicycle and three aunts had walked
all the way from Thaba Nchu, with their provisions of live birds.
The uncle had walked because he could not cycle away and leave
the women to walk alone.

Now a big three-legged pot was steaming with the curried poultry they had brought to celebrate Popi's passage. Another pot was
steaming with beanless samp. Women of the Mothers' Union were
going to feast. So would Popi's fellow graduands. And then everyone would go to their homes, and leave Niki in peace.

The only sadness in Popi as that Viliki was not there to celebrate with her. He had bought her the uniform and left. He had
this tendency to disappear for days on end. And no one knew
where he was. No one but Popi, for after she had pestered him
enough, he had confided in her about his activities. He had joined
the guerrilla forces, those who were fighting to liberate South
Africa from the oppression of the Boers. He was working for the
underground political Movement.

Popi wondered what a political Movement was doing under
the ground, and how Viliki happened to get there. She imagined
him digging tunnels like a mole. The underground he was talking about, he explained, was in Lesotho. He crossed the Caledon
River every week to smuggle out young men and women who
were going to join the forces of liberation. Young men and women
who came from all over South Africa, and were directed to his
conduit by cell leaders. He took them across the river where he introduced them to his contact in Maseru—the only guerrilla leader
he met. From there, some of them would be smuggled out of the
country for military training, after which they would be infiltrated
back to cause havoc to the enemy.

"Niki will kill you if she finds out this is what you do," Popi had
warned.

"Of course she will never find out," Viliki had said confidently.
"You are too smart to tell her. You are too smart to tell anybody.
Unless you want the police to come crawling all over the place."

"What about Sekatle? Doesn't he know? Do you trust him?"

"No, I don't trust him," Viliki had said. "That is why he does not know. That is why you don't see me walking around with him any more. Sekatle has joined the system."

That meant that Sekatle was working for those Viliki was fighting against. And in Excelsior they were represented by Adam de Vries and his party machinery. Klein-Jan Lombard and his police outfit. Tjaart Cronje and his military apparatus. The Reverend François Bornman and his guardianship of the ultimate truth. Even Johannes Smit and his Brahmins and tracts of land that were as big as a small country. The more we saw Sekatle in the company of some of these people, the more his material situation seemed to change for the better. He even drove a bakkie. We never really understood how he could afford it just by taking photographs. Even Maria's house transformed before our eyes from a corrugated-iron shack to a brick house. Suddenly she lived like a princess. And the good life trickled down to Mmampe. Undoubtedly it would have trickled down to Niki as well, if she had not decided to eschew the company of good friends with whom she had been through so much!

Maria and Mmampe could not understand Niki's attitude.

"Whatever did we do to your mother?" asked Mmampe when she next saw Popi. "I hear that she had a feast and didn't even invite us."

"It was not really a feast," explained Popi. "It was just a small tea brought by the people of Thaba Nchu for the mothers of the church to celebrate my wearing the uniform of the Young Women's Union."

"So, because we are not mothers of the church, you did not even think of us," said Mmampe, laughing. And then jokingly she added, "We who looked after you when you were a baby in the cells of Winburg."

Popi did not know what she was talking about. She knew that she was a coloured girl because of some misdemeanour of her mother's. But no one had ever told her about the case of the Excelsior 19, how she had spent a month in a police cell while her skin regained its complexion after she had been a truly coloured girl. Although she had no idea what Mmampe was talking about, she didn't care to pursue the matter. Adults had a tendency to talk in riddles. It was their prerogative.

VILIKI CAME HOME some nights, but gave himself to the wandering land before dawn. He was always restless. While Niki seemed oblivious to his comings and goings, and sometimes addressed him even when he was not there, Popi worried about him. One day they might come and pick him up.

On the evenings when he was home, he sat with Popi by the brazier and roasted mielies. Popi cherished these moments. But she spoilt them by nagging him about absconding from school before completing matric in order to work for the Movement under the ground. To become a mole in the mountains of Lesotho. He responded that one day she would thank him for sacrificing his life for her and for the rest of South Africa.

Popi wondered how it had all started. What made her brother want to risk his life for the rest of South Africa, and what had brought him to the point where he cared more for the rest of South Africa than for his own safety and that of his mother and sister? How was the seed first planted in him? By whom? And where was Sekatle when this deadly seed was first planted? How did Sekatle and Viliki come to take such different directions when they had been such close friends? Why was Sekatle's choice of direction proving to be so lucrative while Viliki's was full of nothing but suffering?

Instead of answering her questions, Viliki taught Popi new songs that he had learnt in the mysterious underground. Many of these songs, he said, came from Zimbabwe. They were chimurenga songs. Songs of liberation. Zimbabwean guerrillas used to sing them when they were fighting for their liberation. They had since won it. And were ruled by a great leader who was going to take the country to great heights. Robert Mugabe. He would make Africa soar. It did not matter that the Movement had favoured another leader, Joshua Nkomo, who had been in a closer alliance with it. Robert Mugabe was the one who had been victorious in the elections. Robert Mugabe would do just as well. He too was a great African.

Then he told her about other struggles in Africa. Struggles that were inspiring the youth. Frelimo in Mozambique. Swapo in Namibia. The Polisario Front in Western Sahara. To Popi, these stories acquired the stature of folktales in her imagination. The animal tales that Niki used to tell her when she was still Niki. When they used to travel to Thaba Nchu to immerse themselves in the colourful world of the trinity. Before Niki began to hide herself inside herself.

Stories like folktales. Although folktales were better. They always had a happy ending. Viliki's stories had no ending. Just people struggling under the ground. Struggling and struggling and struggling. And singing songs.

She loved that part. She learnt all the songs and sang them in her honey-coated voice. Viliki warned her never to sing the songs in the presence of other people. But what if Popi forgot and burst out into a chimurenga song in public? That did not worry Viliki too much. The songs were in the Shona language. A language of Zimbabwe. No one would know what they were about.

While Viliki was teaching Popi chimurenga songs, Tjaart was visiting his home in a blaze of glory. He was on a few days' pass from the Tempe military base in Bloemfontein. Young boeremeisies called at the butchery and pretended to chat to Cornelia Cronje while eyeing Tjaart as he helped his mother at the meat grinder. Boeremeisies swooned and swooned. The deepest sighs were heard from the direction of Jacomina Bornman, the dominee's daughter.

The elders of the church, led by the Reverend François Bornman, his marble eye gleaming, made a point of meeting Tjaart Cronje after the service on Sunday. They commended him for doing his bit for his country. He was a good Afrikaner whose vision had been shaped by Afrikaans newspapers and the Bible. And both these publications carried gospel truths: one about the secular world that the Afrikaner was trying to shape for his children and the other about the Kingdom that the Afrikaner was striving to enter and occupy in the hereafter.

"Remember always to obey the authorities," said the Reverend François Bornman, "because their authority comes directly from God."

The Afrikaner was in the middle of a war, which he had to win at all costs. It was the duty of heroes like Tjaart Cronje and his comrades in arms to destroy all the communists and terrorists who were bent on destroying the way of life for which the forebears had fought against the native tribes and (most importantly) against the British. The Afrikaner was fighting to preserve the laws of God, which were codified in South Africa into the set of laws that comprised apartheid. Apartheid was therefore prescribed by the Bible. The future of this land to which God had led the Afrikaner of old, and the future of civilisation in Africa, were in the hands of young men like Tjaart Cronje.

Adam de Vries agreed. He spoke on behalf of the ruling National Party to which God had granted the stewardship of the country. Young men like Tjaart Cronje should never be misled by impractical solutions such as those proffered by breakaway parties like the Herstigte Nasionale Party—to which scatterbrained Afrikaners like Johannes Smit belonged. The future of the country lay in the hands of Tjaart Cronje and his peers, under the leadership of the National Party. Young men must therefore vasbyt—hang in there—and defend their country from communists and terrorists.

All the while Tjaart Cronje was standing to attention, listening intently to the town fathers. Pride swelling in his chest. His late father, Stephanus Cronje, would have shared that pride. In memory of the departed, he was going to defend this country with his life.

BLESSINGS

*H*IS SUBJECTS ARE ordinary folk doing ordinary things. Yet God radiates from them. As He radiates from the man sitting on a blue kitchen chair. Oval-eyed man wearing a red beret and a brown overall. He holds a big blue cross close to his chest. Big man in big black miners' boots sitting against a whitewashed wall with light blue smudges. Thick black outlines make him and the chair appear very robust. His head is slightly bowed in prayer.

After the prayer, Popi stood over the banana loaf cake on the "kitchen scheme" table. Tiny pink and blue candles burning on the brown cake. Four candles. They sang happy birthday to Niki. Forty years young. Yet she looked old and battered. Like a woman whose face had been exposed to many a thunderstorm. Floods had eroded it. And hydroquinone had caked it with scaly chubaba patches of black, purple and red. There was a slight suggestion of irritation in her eyes. All this unnecessary fuss!

"I told you, I don't want any of this," she said.

"Come on, Niki, don't be a spoilsport," said Popi.

"Blow the candles," commanded Viliki.

"Ja, blow the candles," agreed Pule weakly.

She blew out the candles. Everyone applauded. Popi cut the cake. She passed the plate to Niki, who was sitting on the bed. She took a slice and sniffed it before she took a bite. Popi then passed the plate to Viliki and Pule, who were sitting on the chairs at the table. Each took a slice. They all sipped green cream-soda from enamel mugs.

Popi stood in front of everyone and clapped her hands twice, calling for silence. She was radiant in her first ready-made dress. All her previous dresses had either been hand-me-downs or dresses sewn from cheap multicoloured calico by amateur dressmakers. Today she was wearing a dress that had been bought off the peg, from a real shop. A pink dress with tiny blue and yellow flowers. A knee-length dress that exposed her hairy legs. It had been brought by Pule from Welkom only the week before. He said he had looked at girls he knew to be Popi's age in order to estimate her size. His estimation had not been far off the mark, for the dress fitted her as if she had been measured for it.

Popi made a speech. She thanked God for the blessings of rain. It was a sign of good fortune. Its drops made her spinach in the backyard acquire a deep greenness and leaves that were rich and broad. Although rain muddied the unpaved streets of Mahlatswetsa Location, it was the giver of life. And of bountiful blessings. Hence our ancestors said rain heals and destroys at the same time.

She wished her mother a very long life. And thanked her for all she had done for her and for Viliki. Life had been kind to them, for rarely did they sleep with empty stomachs. All because Niki was the kind of mother who would sacrifice everything for her children. She was like a hen that protected its chicks under its short wings in the face of swooping hawks. Popi was now eighteen and Viliki was twenty-two, she reminded her mother.

"We are adults because of you," she said, "and we vow that we'll look after you, and we'll always be there for you. Don't we, Viliki?"

"Of course we do, Popi," replied Viliki.

"And we won't be leaving her alone for weeks on end," she

added. "Not so, Viliki? You vow you'll stop gallivanting all over the place?"

"You know I can't make such a vow, Popi," pleaded Viliki. "You know exactly why I can't do such a thing."

"He is always away, this boy," said Niki quietly. "He's always away. They always take my children away. They are taking Tjaart away too."

People who worked in the kitchens of white people had brought it back to Mahlatswetsa Location that Tjaart Cronje was being transferred from the military base in the neighbouring Ladybrand district, where he had been fighting the terrorists who were infiltrating the Free State farms from Lesotho. The army was sending him to Johannesburg to fight the terrorist school children who had been petrol-bombing Soweto since 1976. After hearing this, Popi had cruelly said to Niki: "Did you hear that your Tjaart Cronje is being sent away to fight real wars in Suidwes and in Soweto?"

The Suidwes part was her own invention, just to make the danger to Tjaart Cronje's life even greater. Everyone knew that the Boers were dying in Suidwes, as they called Namibia. Niki had not responded at the time. It was as though she had not heard her. But now it was obvious that Tjaart Cronje's imminent transfer to more dangerous war-zones had been eating at Niki all this time. Popi was angry with herself for having been so cruel to her mother. She could not help but hate Tjaart Cronje for having held Niki's compassion to ransom for so many years—from the time she had been his nanny.

"You know, Mother," said Viliki patiently, "it is possible that this Tjaart Cronje you seem to care so much about does not even know that you exist."

"I care about all my children, Viliki," said Niki. "Not only those of my womb."

Popi shushed them and continued with her interrupted speech. She thanked God for preserving them until their eyes could see the return of Pule. She called him "our father". *The return of our father.* Even though the mines had now eaten his lungs, she was grateful that the Lord had shown him the road back to Mahlatswetsa Location, to be sick in the bosom of his family, to be nursed back to health by those who loved him.

Viliki whispered to Popi, "Speak for yourself."

A loud whisper that everyone heard, but ignored.

Viliki was not prepared to forgive his father for deserting them for seventeen years. For deserting *him*. If Pule had a quarrel with Niki, why did he, Viliki, have to pay for Niki's sins? He was, after all, his son. A child of his blood. What had he done to be hit by stones that should have been aimed only at his mother?

Pule had returned the week before, a shadow of the man he used to be. A fleshless body that coughed blood. The doctors had diagnosed him with phthisis. As a mzalwane—a born-again Christian—he had put his faith in the Lord. He had consulted faith healers and prophets. But his mouth and nostrils continued to spew blood. Then he had resorted to traditional doctors—the sangomas and dingaka—who threw their divination bones and prescribed herbs from the mountains of Zebediela. None of which cured him. This went on until most of the pension money he had received from the mining company was gone. When the vat-en-sit woman with whom he had been cohabiting in Welkom left him for those who still had their health and wealth, he had remembered the wife he had left in Excelsior all those years ago. He had gone to town and bought Popi a ready-made dress, Viliki a navy-blue suit and Niki a red two-piece costume. Peace offerings. He had packed his few clothes into a suitcase and had boarded the maroon South African Railways bus to Excelsior.

Popi had welcomed him with open arms, Viliki with a sour face, and Niki with quiet dignity, bordering on indifference. She had thanked him for the two-piece costume, but had added that unfortunately only the cardboard boxes under her bed would wear it, as she could no longer be seen in such hedonistic clothes. Viliki had threatened to donate his suit to charity. Pule's pleading eyes had not melted his resolve not to have anything to do with this man who used to be his father.

"Now that he is dying, he comes back here," Viliki had grumbled.

This sickness of Pule's: it was like that with many men from Mahlatswetsa Location. They worked in the gold mines of Welkom, and when they came back, they were finished. Gold had eaten their lungs. Gold had drained them of all flesh and blood. They were gaunt. They were walking skeletons.

Popi continued with her speech, ignoring Viliki's snide remark. The birthday party, she reminded everyone, had been "our father's" idea. He had also paid for the cake and the cold drink. So, she was also thanking him for the wonderful gesture. For remembering Niki's fortieth birthday.

Popi suddenly stopped speaking and cast her eyes at the door. Her expression changed to one of horror when she saw a shadow looming over the threshold. The horror changed to disgust when Sekatle's head appeared at the door.

"Where is Viliki?" he asked. "Someone wants to talk to him."

"It is Sekatle," said Popi to Viliki.

"What does he want?" asked Viliki.

"Baas Klein-Jan wants you," said Sekatle.

"Come out, Viliki," said a voice that spoke Sesotho with a tinge of an Afrikaans accent. It was Klein-Jan Lombard's voice. *Captain* Klein-Jan Lombard. Viliki walked out. Without uttering another word, the captain handcuffed him and led him to the van that was parked in the street. Viliki looked at Sekatle. But his former playmate turned his head and looked the other way.

It was always a spectator sport when someone was arrested. We crowded around the police van. Children and their parents. Grandmothers and grandfathers. Stretching our necks to take a good look at the day's culprit. Squawking like mynas in a cage at feeding time. A feeding frenzy. Caged birds bearing witness to their fellow being transferred to another cage.

They got Viliki . . . What for? . . . I don't know. Maybe it's for smuggling dagga . . . It must be. They say he goes to Lesotho a lot. People who go to Lesotho a lot are dagga smugglers . . . But the quality of Lesotho dagga is not better than that of Swaziland . . . You see, there is Sekatle. He must have sold him out. They must have been doing this dagga thing together . . . Yes, where do you think Sekatle gets his money? . . . Ja, he works for the system.

Captain Klein-Jan Lombard bundled Viliki into the back of the van, banged the mesh door closed and locked it with a padlock. The captain and Sekatle climbed into the front. Niki stood at the door and watched as the police van drove away. She sighed and whispered, "They want to take away all my children."

WE SAW Pule getting finished as he walked the muddy streets of Mahlatswetsa Location, his skeletal body dragging itself from one house of a mzalwane to the next. He lived on the hymns and prayers of his fellow born-again Christians.

At night he slept on the high bed in the shack, while Niki and Popi slept on the floor. They could hear his bones rattle as he breathed with difficulty and coughed all night. One morning when everyone woke up, he did not. His soul had escaped his bones in the deep of the night. Deserting it as he had deserted his family.

As we always did when a member of the community left us, we collected a few rands together and bought him a plain pine coffin. Popi and Niki buried him with dignity.

THE METHODIST MINISTER agreed to conduct the funeral service for Popi's sake, even though Pule had not been a member of his congregation. The born-agains gave him a rousing send-off and Popi, resplendent in her Methodist uniform, sang a heartrending solo.

Viliki could not attend the funeral. He was in detention where the Special Branch policemen were torturing him, demanding a confession. He insisted he had none to make. He would rather die than betray his comrades. The more the electric current ran through his body and his genitals were clamped with a pair of pliers, the more hatred for Sekatle swelled in his body.

After six months, they released him. "We are watching you," they warned him when they dropped him in a street in town one night.

He did not shed a single tear for his father. He chided Niki for wearing a black doek, a black dress and a black cape—the year-long uniform of widowhood. Why was she mourning for a man who, according to him, had died seventeen years ago when he disappeared from their lives?

IT WAS a year of blessings. The rains fell. The harvest was good. Pule came home to die.

POSKAART/POSTCARD 1

A YELLOW STAR with six points shines on the baby.
Baby in a pink jump suit with a row of black buttons.
Pink is for girls. Baby in a blue frilled hat. Blue is for
boys. Brown baby, eyes wide open to receive the blue and white
rays of the yellow star. Baby stretching its arms to touch the
breasts of the two women kneeling on either side of it. Kneeling
on a green field of flowers. Each woman holding the baby. A black
hand. And a white hand. More accurately, a brown hand and a
pink hand. Brown hand with blue fingernails. Pink hand with pink
fingernails. Pink woman in a light blue nun's habit. Brown woman
in her Sunday best. Purple Sunday felt hat with white cosmos in
front and violet cosmos at the back. Cosmos grows from the hat-
band. Baby and women bathed in the light of the yellow star. Surrounded by hosts of sunflowers and white, violet and blue cosmos.
A wild garden floating in a turquoise universe.

Jesus tussen die Blomme. Jesus among the Flowers. By: Father Frans
Claerhout. Popi read the bottom of the postcard with deliberation.
Silently to herself. On the side that had space for a message, a ver-
tical line separated the message space from the address space. Both
spaces blank. No message. No address. No stamp on the top left

rectangle. Blank postcard that she had kept jealously ever since the last time she modelled for the trinity seven years ago. As a freckled girl of fourteen. Now she was a clear-skinned girl of twenty-one. A smooth-skinned light-complexioned woman who wore a doek all the time to hide her God-given hair. A woman who saw herself as a girl. In the guise of a child.

Jesus among the Flowers was her favourite postcard among the three she owned. Its celestial blue calmed her when she had had a particularly bad day. That is how the three postcards had survived the years without showing any signs of wear and tear: she took them out only when she needed calming. Or when nostalgia got the better of her. On normal days she hid them in an exercise book that spent its restful days in the bottom of the cardboard box where she kept her clothes.

She had taken them out today because of a bout of nostalgia. After Niki had mentioned something about the Good Father who had saved them from garden parties having moved from his old mission station to another one in Tweespruit—a reachable twenty-five kilometres west of Thaba Nchu. Her ears had snatched this information from the mouths of Catholic neighbours who attended Holy Mass and baptisms at the church in Tweespruit.

Popi passed the postcard to Niki. Niki went through the motions of looking at it, but then cast it aside, dropping it on the floor. She had seen it before.

"Niki, you will make my picture dirty putting it on the floor!" screamed Popi, taking it and placing it between the pages of her exercise book. She was now the screamer and the shouter since Niki had consigned herself to quietness.

"It is not true, anyway," said Niki as if to herself. "Jesus was not black. You have seen his photos in church."

"This is how the Father saw Him, as a black child," said Popi.

"That's a lie too," insisted Niki. "He never saw Him. And which one of these women is Mary? If it's this black woman, how come she is wearing a purple hat and a red dress like the women of today? Jesus didn't live today. And if it's this white woman, how come she is a nun, and how come she is white and her child is black?"

The import of what she had just said hit Niki. She paused and looked at Popi. But nothing had registered.

Suddenly Niki said, "Anyway, that's a stupid picture. How can a yellow star shine with such blue and white light?"

Popi laughed at Niki's venture into the world of art criticism.

"How come you remember every detail of it even when you are not looking at it?" she asked.

"You have forced it on me all these years," said Niki resignedly.

"Admit it, Niki," said Popi, "it has got into you too."

They sat silently for a while. Popi looked at the postcard intently, trying to find any traces of foolishness in it. Even in the dim light she could not detect them.

She rubbed her eyes with the back of her hand. They were red. They were crying. Not from her inability to find foolishness. Not from pain either. But from the pungent smoke of the cow-dung that was burning in the brazier. Niki and Popi had moved the "kitchen scheme" table to the side of the room, and had put the brazier at the centre, creating a cosy hearth around which they were sitting. Noisily chewing the maize on the cob that they roasted on the embers. They had closed the door and the window to keep the evil air of the night out and the warmth of the brazier in. The warmth did stay in. With it the smoke. And the tears.

"They got what they were fighting for, didn't they?" asked Niki out of the blue. "They got what they were fighting for. So now why can't he stay home?"

"Why can't who stay home?" wondered Popi.

"Viliki. Why can't he stay home?"

"They haven't got what they were fighting for yet, Niki," said Popi.

"Free Mandela. Free Mandela, they said. Now Mandela is free. And those others. The ones they released first. Mbeki and Sisulu and Gwala and others. Their names are on the radio every day. But why is Viliki never home?"

"He did explain, Niki, that now there is even more work to be done. The Boers are still the rulers. Even though his Movement has been unbanned, here in Excelsior we still only enter the hotel as cleaners. At the post office there are still two queues—one for whites and the other for blacks."

"Why would you go to the post office, anyway?" asked Niki. "We never receive letters. We never post letters to anyone."

Then she looked at Popi, and fear suddenly gripped her. "You are becoming a politician like your brother," she said admonishingly.

"These are just the truths that we see, Niki," said Popi.

"I fear for my children," said Niki resignedly.

"They have released the leaders and the exiles have come home," cried Popi. "Yet the police still harass Viliki. They just can't leave him alone."

Niki would not have admitted it, but Viliki's gallivanting had had a positive effect on the family. After one of his forages into the hinterland on Movement business one year, he had brought back a radio. A big ghetto blaster, as Viliki called it, which also played cassette tapes in two places. Hence Niki could now sing the names of Walter Sisulu and Govan Mbeki and Harry Gwala. Even though these names were popular outside the confines of her shack, for we talked about them everywhere we gathered, Niki was never part of such gatherings. If it were not for the magic of the ghetto blaster, Niki would have remained blissfully ignorant of these names. And of the radio drama series to which she had become addicted. Pale-e-Tswelang-Pele. The story that continues. The Sesotho service of Radio Bantu of the South African Broadcasting Corporation. Dramatic stories of heroes who fought against ungodly terrorists in the bush. Stories that extolled the virtues of those who chose to stay in the rural homelands, rather than go to the cities to make a nuisance of themselves there.

She would have been saved from another addiction: weekly obituary programmes. Every Friday, the announcer read in a soothing voice the names of the departed, the cause of their demise, where and when the funeral would be held, the particular people to whom the message was directed, and the names of those who had sent the message to the radio station. If she were to depart, Niki felt she would be assured permanent residence in Heaven if this particular radio announcer read her name.

Popi looked at the postcard intently. The figures seemed to assume life in the haziness of the smoke. A teardrop fell on the baby Jesus. She cleaned it off with her thumb. She sneezed as the smoke assailed her nostrils. She rubbed her neck with her forefinger. The skin was peeling off. Scales of dead skin on her neck and on part of her chest. These had been peeling off for as long as she could remember. She did not know why. It was an allergy, a doctor once said. An allergy. But Niki knew that the peeling had begun when she had roasted Popi as a baby. When she had wanted to brown her, only for her to turn into a truly coloured baby. The peeling spot on Popi's neck and chest should have stayed small as the child grew bigger. But it had grown with her. And had got bigger with her.

The peeling spot had long become a taboo subject between Niki and Popi. So were Popi's experiences in the world outside the safety of her shack. She kept her daily flagellation of taunts to herself. Taunts. Taunts. Taunts. Even though on one hand we praised her for being beautiful, and for having a wonderful voice, we continued to laugh at her for being a boesman. As we laughed at other men and women, and boys and girls, who looked like her, and were brave enough to walk the streets of Excelsior. We laughed. Until she lost hope that we would ever accept her. Until she was filled with thoughts of revenge. No one told her that vengeance had a habit of bouncing against the wall, like a ricocheting bullet, and hitting the originator. Look what had happened to Niki when she filled her loins with vengeance! It was because of that vengeance that Popi was now a prisoner of the perpetual doek on her head, of blue eyes and of hairy legs.

"One day you must send them to someone," said Niki.

"Send what to someone, Niki?" asked Popi.

"That's what they were meant for, to be posted to someone."

"Oh, the postcards? Never!"

THE SINS OF our mothers were never mentioned at dinner tables. An elaborately laid table, with a vase of red and yellow plastic roses in the middle, would have been at odds with idle talk of the misdemeanours of the flesh. Even though the Reverend François Bornman's empty eye-socket was a constant reminder that they had once been committed. They had once been written in the Big Book where all sins are recorded, although all have since been expunged. Thanks to a forgiving God.

The socket was empty because Jacomina's naughty poodle had swallowed the dominee's marble eye, which he had taken out of its socket for cleaning. After Jacomina had cleaned the eye with Dettol antiseptic in warm water, she had left it in a saucer on the side table next to her bed to dry. When she came back from another room, she had found the stupid poodle playing with it, rolling it on the carpet with its paws, and then catching it with its teeth. She had shouted at the poodle. It had been so startled that it had swallowed the eye inadvertently, as Jacomina had vouched to her father when she reported the incident.

Now the dominee's face looked like that of a naughty old man who had been caught winking at someone's wife by cruel gods— who had then decided to play a prank on him by making the eye refuse to open again. A brownish jelly oozed out of it and made Cornelia Cronje's own eyes weep.

She tried to avoid looking at the dominee. But he was sitting directly opposite her. And was chewing away at the hoenderpastei— the Cape-Dutch chicken pie—oblivious to her discomfort. It was particularly tasty, thanks to the free-range chickens that patiently awaited the occasional guillotine in the dominee's backyard. And thanks to the cooking skills of Jacomina. Everything that Jacomina touched turned into a culinary wonder that sang in one's mouth. That was why the guests had not stopped praising the crunchiness of her maize-meal spinach patties and the delicate tanginess of her tomato bredie that had been simmered in a cast-iron potjie over the coals. Or singing paeans to the colourful roasted vegetables that surrounded the brown rack of lamb. Green peppers, red peppers, green courgettes, deep red beetroot, green and white leeks, deep brown mushrooms and light yellow pattypans. And to the saffron samp cooked with sugar beans.

The cherry pudding served with custard was a sensation.

"You must give me the recipe, Mina," said Cornelia to Jacomina.

"It's very simple," said Jacomina rejoicing in her expertise. "Just make a good dough with butter, sugar, milk, eggs, flour and baking powder. Then cover the cherries with the dough and bake. Simple."

"Easier said than done," said Lizette de Vries. "My cherry pudding always turns into a mess. Even the simplest cherry crumble turns to mud in my hands."

"The secret of a good cherry crumble is: use very little sugar. Depend mostly on the sweetness of the cherries themselves."

"She takes after her mother," said the dominee proudly. "She was the greatest cook this side of the Vaal. This side of the Limpopo even. She was something else, that woman of mine."

It was obvious that the Reverend François Bornman missed his wife. He had never really gotten over her death some years ago. She had been sick for a long time, in pain from the cancer that was eating her insides. It had been a relief when she died. Her passing on to a better world had released her from the agonies of this world.

Fortunately this had happened at the time that Jacomina was having problems in her marriage to a medical doctor in Queenstown, far away in the Eastern Cape. Not that the dominee rejoiced at her marital problems. Marriage was created by God, and should last until such time that God decided to take one of the partners to His Kingdom. As He had done in the dominee's own marriage. The only fortunate thing was that Jacomina had come home when her father needed her most. And had stayed. He had never really found out the details of the breakup.

When Jacomina's husband had filed for divorce, she had refused to contest it, or to discuss the matter with her father. He never bothered her about it again. He just kept quiet and enjoyed her wonderful cooking. At least there had been no children in that marriage. Even a dominee could safely be grateful for small mercies.

The guests went for seconds. Captain Klein-Jan Lombard went for thirds and fourths, which brought a sharp rebuke from his wife, Liezl. People would think she did not feed him well at home, she said. Adam de Vries appealed to her to let the poor man eat. Policemen worked very hard. Their lot was not confined to chasing thieves. They were also burdened with the task of rooting out communists and terrorists from society.

Everyone agreed. And added that Tjaart must not be ashamed to pile his plate for the third time. After all, he was faced with a similar task. He was a soldier, a sergeant nogal, and everyone knew that military rations left much to be desired. Tjaart Cronje laughed and said that it was obvious that the speakers had not been in the army recently; otherwise they would know that military food rated with that of five-star hotel restaurants. Only Jacomina's cooking could beat it.

Jacomina Bornman smiled coyly. Cornelia Cronje looked at her uncomfortably. Then at Tjaart. She was not pleased at the interest that Tjaart had lately been taking in Jacomina. She objected to the looming relationship because Jacomina was too old for her son. Jacomina had come back from a failed marriage. Jacomina had been a wild girl who had been caught necking with Greek boys in cars. In her protective mind, Ari Dukakis had multiplied into many Greek boys. His father's Studebaker had become many cars. There was no guarantee that Jacomina had changed her ways. Perhaps that was why her marriage had failed. She must have taken her wild ways with her to Queenstown.

But it was obvious to all at the table that the two enjoyed each other's company. They made each other laugh. They laughed at small things that others considered too stupid to laugh at. They saw humour in the unfunniest of situations. They were in love.

The Reverend François Bornman opened a bottle of mampoer, the peach brandy that had been donated by Johannes Smit when he sent his apologies, claiming that he could not be present at the dinner because of another engagement in Wepener. The truth was that there was no such engagement. Johannes Smit was wary of associating with these National Party types—traitors who were busy selling the country to the communists. So he had sent a servant over with a bottle of mampoer, and a concocted excuse about some prior engagement. The dominee had welcomed the peach brandy.

Johannes Smit's pastime was to distil and brew all sorts of moonshine, and the dominee loved to sample these burning creations.

"If that's one of Johannes' concoctions, I will pass," said Adam de Vries. He was a man of refined tastes and drank only whiskey. There was a bottle of J&B Scotch on the table, and he filled his glass as if it was soda. With his fingers, he fished out two pieces of ice from the ice bucket and sank them into the whiskey. He took two big swigs and put the glass on the table.

Tjaart sniffed at the mampoer in his glass. He had never tasted it before. He had only heard stories about it, that it was a potent traditional brandy of the Afrikaners. It was his patriotic duty to have a taste. Just a little sip. Jacomina laughed and grabbed the glass from his squirming hand. She said she was going to show him how it was done, and gulped it down. Cornelia gulped the air in undisguised shock. The other two women, Lizette and Liezl, sipped their alcohol-free ginger beer nonchalantly.

"Groot-Jan would have loved this," said the dominee, pouring himself another glass of the peach brandy. "He used to enjoy Johannes Smit's little experiments—especially the cherry liqueur and the mampoer."

Groot-Jan Lombard had died about eighteen months before.

He had never really been the same since the Excelsior 19 case. His health had slowly deteriorated, until one day he had peacefully met his Maker in his sleep. The party banqueting at this table, however, did not remember him as one of the actors in the Excelsior 19 capers—victims of the sins of our mothers—but as a connoisseur of the good waters. And a great Afrikaner patriot.

"Oupa Groot-Jan was a true hero of the Afrikaner people," said Tjaart, the mampoer making him bold enough to express his views in the company of revered elders. "We read his name every Sunday outside the church as one of those who led the Great Trek commemoration of 1938. Maybe it is good that he died when he did. He was saved the humiliation of seeing the Afrikaner bite the dust."

"Bite the dust?" asked Klein-Jan Lombard.

"What are you talking about, my boy?" asked the Reverend François Bornman.

"He doesn't really mean that, Pa," said Jacomina Bornman.

"The Afrikaner will never bite the dust," asserted Adam de Vries.

"We are releasing communists from jail," said Tjaart Cronje, standing his ground. "We are allowing terrorists to come back into the country. We are now negotiating with them to be part of our government. Things are happening today that are inconceivable."

"It's all in the plan, my boy," said Adam de Vries sagely. "Nothing inconceivable."

He explained to the ignorant young man that President F.W. de Klerk was thinking only of the future of the Afrikaner people when he released the likes of Mandela from jail. It was part of de Klerk's wisdom. He would never just hand over power to the blacks without making sure that the Afrikaner had a meaningful stake. The rights of the Afrikaner would always be protected. Adam de Vries assured the doubting upstart that the Afrikaner would never lose his grip on power. The people who were being released from jail were no longer agitators. Prison had extinguished the fire in them. They were now moderates who were willing to negotiate a just settlement. That was what the referendum had been about. A just settlement. Power-sharing. The majority of the white people had spoken through the referendum, saying that they wanted power-sharing with moderate blacks. Not majority rule. There could never be majority rule. Power-sharing, the sage explained, did not mean that the Afrikaner was handing over his power. Unless Tjaart wanted to believe extreme right-wingers like Johannes Smit. The Afrikaner would always have the power.

"But how can the blacks share power with the white man in our own country?" asked Tjaart Cronje. "What does a black person know about power? All he knows is how to burn down schools. Look what is happening in their location here in Excelsior. They have forced out the Bantu councillors. The location is now ungovernable."

Tjaart Cronje was talking about the recent events in Mahlatswetsa Location. Viliki had led the community in demonstrations against the Bantu Council, a National Party government-created structure through which the Afrikaners of Excelsior governed the township by proxy through people like Sekatle. Sekatle had in fact been the chairman of the Bantu Council, and therefore the mayor of Mahlatswetsa Location. Until he was frogmarched from the council office to his house, where the people of the Movement instructed him to retire from public life. They had threatened to burn his trading store, his lorry and his new BMW 3 Series car if he refused to disband his illegitimate council. The council members, many of them schoolteachers and traders like Sekatle, did not wait to be told twice. They had resigned en masse for fear of their lives and property.

"Ungovernable?" asked Adam de Vries incredulously. "The location will never be ungovernable. I have been made the Administrator of the location and I have restored order there."

He knew black people very well, he assured his admiring listeners. Traces of doubt still showed in Tjaart Cronje's face. As a little boy, Adam de Vries said, he had played with black children on the farm. He had eaten papa and morogo in their huts. Tjaart Cronje recalled that he had done the same at Niki's home. Although he had shared papa and morogo with Viliki, he did not see this as something he could boast about in public. It was nothing to be proud of.

As a student, he had studied anthropology, Adam de Vries continued, adding more to his insights into the black man's way of thinking and doing things. Not all black people were bad. There were good black people like Sekatle. And there were bad ones like Viliki. The majority of black people were good people. When the elections came after the negotiations for a new constitution, black people would never vote for communists and terrorists. They would choose moderate people like Sekatle.

"You see, Tjaart," said Cornelia sweetly, "everything has been taken care of. Oom Adam knows what he is talking about. Leave everything to the elders."

Tjaart smiled cynically. That smile! It reminded Cornelia of her late husband. How much this boy had grown to look like his father! Poor Stephanus. She silently cursed the woman who had led him to his demise. She wondered what had happened to Niki. The traitor who had seduced her husband. She blamed her for everything. Niki had never set foot in the butchery since his death. But Cornelia had occasionally spotted Niki's coloured brat. She hated the bastard for being a smoother, delicate and more beautiful version of Tjaart.

SWEET STALACTITES

W E CALL IT a flute. It is not really a flute. It is a
penny-whistle. A metal relative of the recorder. And
it is unusual for a girl to play it. But the coloured girl
is blowing birdlike twitters on it. Boesman producing melodies
with only three fingers of her left hand. The penny-whistle has six
holes. Her three fingers commute dextrously across all the holes.
Commute between deep mellow notes and shrill piccolo-like notes.
Her other hand, the right hand, holds a brown begging bowl.
Porcelain begging bowl with a few coins rattling in it. In rhythm to
the tune. Musical bowl. Percussive porcelain.

She is sullen like the weather. Yet her tune is as bright as the
fireflies of a deep night. Boesman girl with red hair parted in the
middle. Light-coloured girl with a clown's sad face. The broadest
of strokes. Deep black strokes like the night. She wears a green
dress that is much too big for her. Her mother's dress that hangs
loosely to her ankles. Big high-heel shoes. Her mother's black
shoes. A gift from a happy madam.

The antics of the street busker would have made Popi laugh, if
she were the type that laughed in public. Everyone who watched
the busker laughed. Her deadpan expression that turned to sad-

ness when she let down her guard. Her dress that looked like it was hanging loosely on a pole. Her little feet that kept on jumping out of her shoes as she attempted what she thought was a clownish jig. All these left the spectators in stitches. But Popi's face stayed knitted in depressed lines, as if she was having a particularly difficult time releasing her bowels. She hated the penny-whistler for being gaunt and musical and funny and coloured. She hated her for calling attention to her colouredness, which in turn would call attention to Popi's own colouredness.

She had learnt ways of not calling attention to her colouredness. Her main weapon was the doek. She wore colourful doeks that hid her straight almost-blonde hair. Mammoth doeks that she rolled in many layers on her head, until they looked like Sikh turbans. Doeks that diverted the eyes of the curious from her blue eyes to the glorious top of her head. Another weapon were her slacks. Slacks that hid her hairy legs. Although in respectable places, such as the church, she had to revert to a dress. Or to the black skirt of the Methodists. White long-sleeved blouse. Red bib. White hat.

Popi sneaked away from the entertained crowd. She crossed the street and walked into Volkskas—the bank that the Afrikaners had established to pull fellow Afrikaners from the depths of poverty when the English practised their own version of apartheid against the Afrikaners. A bank that took its services deep into the harshest platteland where the English conglomerates dreaded to tread. Popi was going to cash an uncrossed cheque drawn in Viliki's favour. She couldn't make out who the drawer was.

Where do you get the money, Viliki, that comes in the form of a cheque? Is it from the underground to which you dedicate your life? No, the underground does not exist anymore. Everything is now above the ground. In the light of day. Transparency is the word that guides us. In the light of day. Everything is above ground. Almost everything. There are, of course, secret Movement matters. This is the money to do Movement work, Popi. And to pay my expenses when I travel all over the place organising workers on the farms. For the Movement. Now, stop asking foolish questions and run to the bank before it closes.

So, now you support Afrikaner banks, Viliki? Didn't you say that one day when you had money to put in the bank, you would rather keep it under your mattress than bank it at Volkskas? That was yesterday, Popi. Today it is a different world. We are reaching a settlement with the Afrikaners. Next year we have a general election. April next year. We shall be liberated and we shall be one people with the Afrikaners. That's what the Movement stands for. One South African nation. Now run to the bank and shut up with your politics. I am the politician in this house.

There was a long queue at the bank. The strange thing was that there was only one queue. Not two, as was the case not so long ago: a slow long queue for blacks and a quick short one for whites. One queue, now, for all the colours of the rainbow. Another strange thing was that the white customers did not join the one queue. They walked straight to the teller, who would immediately stop serving the black customer to attend to the white one.

It was the same when Tjaart Cronje entered. He went straight to the head of the queue.

We looked at the burly Tjaart and we looked at the tall and slim Popi. We saw what we had always whispered. They looked as if they had hatched from the same egg. Popi was just a darker version of Tjaart. We also noted that Tjaart did not see himself in Popi. And Popi did not see herself in Tjaart.

Tjaart Cronje did not see Popi at all. Just a row of faces that were not white, but were now permitted to share the same queue with white people. But Popi did see Tjaart Cronje. And was filled with hatred towards him. Popi's hatred always bubbled close to the surface, ready to erupt at the slightest provocation. She hated Tjaart Cronje for having such a tight grip on Niki's affection. The affection that should be Popi's alone. Hers and Viliki's. Yet some of it spilled over to Tjaart Cronje. Just because she had once been his nanny. And it was such a wasted love, because he was not even aware of its existence.

Anyway, what made Tjaart Cronje think he could just walk to the head of the queue and get service when she had been waiting in line for almost twenty minutes? Was it because he was Tjaart

Cronje? And she was just Popi? Well, she had news for him. She
was Popi *Pule.* She too had a surname, even though the familiarity
that bred contempt meant that all and sundry just called her Popi.
And Niki just Niki. And Viliki just Viliki. But they were born and
bred by people too. They were Niki Pule. Viliki Pule. Popi Pule.
And Tjaart Cronje had better remember that. Tjaart had better
remember that.

Popi Pule. Stealer of surnames from cuckolded men!

She was fuming inside while she displayed an indifferent outside.

Jacomina Bornman, now Jacomina Cronje, rushed in, breathing as though she had been running. She whispered something to
Tjaart Cronje. Obviously not the sweet nothings of newly-weds,
for Tjaart left her to complete the banking transaction while he
shot out of Volkskas Bank.

Jacomina took forever to finish whatever she was doing with the
teller, which included exchanging snippets of gossip. When she
turned to leave, she saw Popi. She looked at her for a long time,
until Popi feared that she might have read her evil thoughts. Jacomina slowly broke into a smile as a glimmer of recognition
dawned on her.

"Dumela," she greeted in Sesotho. Like all Afrikaners who grew
up in Excelsior, she spoke fluent Sesotho. Like almost all Afrikaner
natives of the eastern Free State.

"Dumela," responded Popi without any enthusiasm.

"I remember you," said Jacomina. "You used to sit outside our
garden parties with your mother. Why, you have grown into such a
big beautiful girl."

Popi took exception to being remembered by her. But she did
not say anything. These people had no business knowing her. Why
should this Jacomina continue to hoard memories of her back
when she used to hang around garden parties with Niki? That
must have been eighteen years ago. She had only been five then.
What twisted god had cursed this Jacomina with such a cruel

streak of memory? She, Popi, did not remember this Jacomina from the garden party days. She must have been one of the big white girls who used to pinch her cheeks before they gave her a sweet or a cookie.

"What happened to your mother? Is she still alive?" asked Jacomina innocently.

"What would make her dead?" asked Popi, taking further offence that this Jacomina should dare to associate Niki with death.

"Don't be rude, girl," said Jacomina. "I am being nice to you. It's just that I no longer see her at any of our garden parties."

As if you had invited her!

She was being nice. Like the *coochi coochi coo* women in the bus. Her memory of their niceness was as vivid as if it were yesterday. Nice. Would people ever stop this foolish notion of being nice to her? Didn't they know that she was a boesman? No one had any right to be nice to a boesman. Didn't they know that?

Popi walked home with Viliki's money hidden in her bra. At the junction where the dirt road to Mahlatswetsa Location joined the four-lane tarred road that became the only street of the town, she saw a sea of people coming her way. They were trotting and toyi-toying like prancing horses, and chanting slogans. Popi remembered that Viliki had mentioned something about Solomon Mahlangu Day. May 1993. They were celebrating Solomon Mahlangu, a young hero from Viliki's Movement who was hanged by the Boers during the Wars of Liberation. The people were using this day to demand the release of all political prisoners.

All political prisoners, Viliki? There are no political prisoners in Excelsior. How can you demand that the Boers of Excelsior release all political prisoners? Excelsior is part of South Africa, Popi. There are still political prisoners in South Africa. Even though we will have our first general elections next year. There are still political prisoners in the jails of this country. We are taking a memorandum to the police station demanding that all political prisoners in South Africa be released forthwith!

Before the demonstrating crowd could reach her—or before she could reach the demonstrating crowd—a platoon of policemen approached from the direction of the town. Policemen in police vans. Police reservists in their private bakkies. A convoy of them. They passed Niki as she walked towards the crowd. She saw that the policemen were led by Captain Klein-Jan Lombard. The police reservists were under the command of Tjaart Cronje. So that was where he was rushing! Among the reservists was Johannes Smit.

The platoon stopped in front of the crowd and Captain Klein-Jan Lombard instructed it to disperse and go back peacefully to Mahlatswetsa Location. Viliki, who was at the head of the crowd, shouted that the crowd would not disperse. The crowd was marching to the police station to hand in a memorandum. The people of Mahlatswetsa were demanding the release of political prisoners.

"That's not a local issue," Captain Klein-Jan Lombard tried to reason. "Is has nothing to do with the police of Excelsior."

"It has everything to do with the police of South Africa in every square inch of this country," yelled Viliki. "And you want a local issue, do you? We demand that Adam de Vries be removed as the Administrator of our township. Get the Conservative Party out of our affairs!"

The party that was ruling Excelsior at the time was the Conservative Party—another splinter group from the National Party. Unlike the Herstigte Nasionale Party, it was a strong group, which even had significant representation in Parliament. Hence Adam de Vries, who continued to be the leading light of the National Party, was no longer the mayor of Excelsior. The mayoral chain was now worn by the arch-right-winger, Gys Uys. Tjaart Cronje and Johannes Smit were now members of the town council, as representatives of the Conservative Party, in addition to their self-appointed task of policing Excelsior as police reservists. Although Adam de Vries was no longer mayor, and his National Party no longer had power in Excelsior, they let him run Mahlatswetsa Location as Administrator as he professed superior knowledge of "these people", knowledge gained from his anthropology courses at university.

The police reservists were getting impatient with the official police. One could not reason with these people. There was only one language they understood. Tjaart Cronje opened fire. Johannes Smit followed with his own fire. The crowd screamed and ran in different directions. The policemen and their reservists ran after them, hitting them with the butts of their guns.

Popi was not going to run. She had not been part of the crowd. She was on her way home from the bank. Home, where Niki was waiting for the money in order to buy maize-meal and candles from Sekatle's shop. Which would make Viliki angry.

Why do you spend my money at that sellout's shop? Why do you enrich the dog that has made his money from selling our people to the enemy? He is already rich, Viliki. Your buying at his store or not buying at his store will not make a dent in his wealth. Will not stop him from driving around the location, playing loud music, blowing his hooter for everyone to know Sekatle is driving by. In any case, Viliki, you do not expect us to go all the way to town just to buy a packet of candles, do you? And those shops in town, are they not owned by the enemy? Like your Volkskas Bank?

Something hit Popi on the back of her head. She fell to the ground. She saw a police boot connecting with her face. She felt another crashing into her ribcage. She went numb. She could hear as if from a distance sounds of whips lashing on her body. But she felt no pain. Her body was dead. Even the blood that was spurting out of her nose came from someone else's body. Not her dead body. She went to sleep next to her dead body.

When she woke up, she was in the back of a rattling bakkie. With many other bleeding bodies piled together. Her body was no longer dead. It ached all over.

The van stopped. Roadblock. Tjaart Cronje, Johannes Smit and a group of police reservists were manning it. Some of them waving red flags with three black sevens forming a swastika that someone had forgotten to complete.

"Where do you think you are going, ntate?" Tjaart Cronje asked in Sesotho. Calling the man "sir" or even "father". Polite, even in anger. Niki would have been proud of his upbringing.

"I am taking these people to hospital," responded the driver.

"Are you an ambulance, then?" Johannes Smit asked, also in Sesotho.

"We called the ambulance, but the town council refused to send it," said the driver.

"You are not an ambulance, ntate," said Tjaart Cronje firmly. "You'll have to turn back."

"Some of these people are terribly injured," protested the driver. "They might die."

Tjaart Cronje switched to Afrikaans. He told the man that if he did not want to join the corpses in the back of his bakkie, it would be wise for him to turn back. The man drove back to Mahlatswetsa Location.

All the vehicles that carried the injured were turned back in a similar manner.

A child died.

POPI LAY on the bed while Niki washed her wounds. The hot water with Dettol antiseptic exacerbated the pain. Niki cleaned the caked blood with a wet sponge. Soon the white water was red. Now Popi could see exactly what Viliki had been talking about. The Boers knew nothing about fair play. She was no longer going to be a bystander. Or a sidewalker who minded her own business. A sidewalker who had done no wrong and would therefore not run away.

The pain. The pain. Why wouldn't Niki mix the hot water with the cold?

Popi chuckled. Niki stood back and looked at her in amazement. Popi laughed.

"The honey," she said. "Put honey on the wounds. They say honey kills germs."

The honey. Only that morning, life had been so sweet. She had gone to gather cow-dung with Niki. She had been laughing in the veld. She reserved her laughter for Niki. She could afford to be carefree when she was with Niki. She became a child again. Replaying the childhood that she missed. She had laughed because Niki had screamed when a blade of grass had touched her calf. They had just been talking about snakes. Niki had mistaken the grass for a snake. Popi's silly guffaws had not amused Niki.

Popi had laughed until she rolled on the grass. She had rolled down a slope, gathering momentum as she left Niki far behind. She had rolled until a pile of rocks halted her progress. And it had been a good thing that she had not rolled onto the rocks, for bees had built their hive underneath them. She would have been stung to death if she had disturbed their peace.

"Niki, quick, come and see!" shouted Popi.

The rocks formed a small picturesque cave. Honeycombs were hanging from the roof of the shelter like black icicles. Sweet stalactites.

"Let's get the honey," Popi had said, when Niki arrived.

They had lit a cow-dung fire next to the hive. They had used their mouths like bellows to blow the smoke in the direction of the hive. Soon the bees were dazed. They had buzzed drunkenly around the women, perching on them without stinging them. Popi had put her hand into the grotto, drawing it out again with a dark chunk. White brood in the comb.

"Put that back, Popi," Niki had said. "It is a waste. All those young ones will die."

Popi had put the big black chunk with white grubs peeping in the hexagons aside. Her hand went in again and came back with a golden honeycomb. The inebriated bees that covered her arm did not bother her. She shook it in swift vibrations and the bees fell onto the grass. She sunk her teeth into the comb, swallowing the golden syrup and chewing the wax, and then spitting it out. Honey ran down her arms and dripped to the ground from her elbows. Some of it ran down her mouth into a number of streams on her yellow blouse. Her hands were sticky, but that did not bother her.

"Popi, you know that gluttony is a sin?" Niki had asked.

"Have some," Popi had said with a full mouth. "It is very sweet."

"Leave some for the bees, Popi," Niki had pleaded. "If you take everything, what do you think the bees will eat?"

"They can always make some more."

"If you take everything, they will move somewhere else. Leave something, they will stay and you can always come to harvest honey again next time," Niki had advised.

"What's the use, Niki? If you leave something, someone else will find the hive and take everything."

Niki had taken a small bite of a honeycomb. Honey and wax together. The women had then taken some honeycombs home. As they had no container, Popi had piled the combs into a mountain in her hands, while Niki carried the cow-dung in a sack on her head. The combs had leaked all the way, tracing a golden path that quickly turned black where the honey seeped into the soil.

The morning had begun with such sweetness.

Niki got the honey from the pot, and was rubbing some of it onto Popi's wounds when Viliki arrived. His injuries were fortunately only slight.

"These are the last wriggles of the tail of a dying lizard," said Viliki as he hobbled into the shack.

"More like the deadly kicks of a dying horse," Popi corrected him. "The tail of a dying lizard is harmless, Viliki. It wriggles and dies alone. See what happened to me?"

"Don't talk, Popi," said Niki. "You will only make the pain worse."

Viliki looked at his sister. She was lying on the bed, wearing only panties. Parts of her body covered with sticky honey. Her face was unrecognisable. Both eyes swollen. Eyelids glued together in swollen red balls. Niki spreading more honey on her body. And cleaning more caked blood from her mouth.

"I am sorry, Popi," said Viliki, eyes glassy with unshed tears. "You shouldn't have gone to that demonstration."

"I didn't go to that demonstration, Viliki," said Popi chirpily, as if her body was not racked with pain. "That demonstration came to me. But from now on, I will go to every demonstration."

"They want to take away all my children," said Niki softly.

DAYMARE

*T*HE BROWN IMPASTO WOMAN IS naked. She squats on her heels in the dark blue of the night. Her hanging stomach rests on her fat thighs. Her hanging breasts rest on her fat stomach. She has raised her thick hands to ward off the ugly spirits that haunt her dreams, turning them into nightmares.

Popi sat in a nightmare. Daymare. The light from the window shone in her eyes, almost blinding her. She shifted uncomfortably on her chair. She squinted her eyes in order to take a good look at those sitting opposite her. And on both sides of her. Imprisoning her with their heavy presence. And their strong odours. Pipe tobacco. Cologne. Sweat. There was no escape. There could be no escape. It was all of her own making. She would face the consequences without complaint.

The fan hanging from the ceiling was whirling and droning at the same time, which irritated her immensely. But the people sitting around the big brown-varnished table did not seem to mind it. Most were listening attentively to what Angela van der Walt, town clerk of Excelsior, was saying. Others had a bored look. They already knew everything she was talking about. Even more so than the town clerk herself. They had sat around this table for years. And so had their fathers before them. And their fathers' fathers.

The dirty walls were closing in on Popi. Suffocating her. Walls mapped with black streams of rain that had seeped through the ceiling to the floor. Black smudges on parts of the ceiling. Musty ceiling so high that it made the people sitting under it insignificant. The walls were moving closer, in rhythm to Angela van der Walt's brittle voice.

The town clerk was explaining the rudiments of procedure in Afrikaans, the language of the town council. The language of the black and white citizens of Excelsior. For the benefit of those who had never been in the council chamber before, she was going on at length about how to address fellow members of the council, when to raise a point of order, how the debates should be conducted, and how voting was done. She would always be at hand, she said, to assist those who needed her assistance. To guide them through the maze of rules and regulations that governed procedure in the council chamber. And through the files of the town's by-laws. It was incumbent on the members of the town council to be well versed in the by-laws, so that they might participate intelligently in the chamber.

Popi wondered why the hallowed room was called a chamber. *Chamber* in English too, when everything else was in Afrikaans. A chamber was the pot into which Niki peed at night. The thought of the chamber-pot reminded Popi that she had been suppressing her own urge to pee for the past half-hour. She did not know how to take leave of the august company around the table. Should she just stand up and rush out of the double doors, down the corridor in search of a toilet? Would she use the same toilet that the white people used? Should she raise her hand and ask, as in class, "Please, madam, may I go out"? What would happen if her urine flowed down her legs, and made a thin stream across the grey wall-to-wall carpet to the other side of the room? What would the town clerk say? What would the august members of the council say? Would they kick her out of the chamber? Pee belonged in the chamber, didn't it?

Out, Popi! You don't belong here! You are out of your league here! Out!

They would not dare. She had earned the right to belong here. Her only foolishness had been to choose a seat that faced the window. She had been the first to arrive. She had had a choice of ten seats. Ten empty chairs and she had selected the most inconvenient one. The glare of the sun was playing havoc with her eyes. The voluminous pink and violet curtains hanging on one side of the wall covered the big windows, but left a gap on just this one window opposite her. A source of light. And of irritation.

Popi did not like the idea that where she was sitting, she was directly facing Tjaart Cronje. And that she was facing a row of old Afrikaner men and women sitting on red chairs against the wall behind him. From one corner of the room to the next. Blending with the curtains behind them. Grave citizens of Excelsior who comprised the gallery. Concerned citizens who had come to witness the wonder of wonders. For the first time in the history of Excelsior, the town council had black members. And they were in the majority!

Those who came to sit as part of the gallery had come to terms with the changes that had happened in the country. With the fact that black people were in the majority and that at all levels of government, they would be in the majority. Those who stubbornly held the view that the changes were wrong, and that the Afrikaner had a God-given right to rule supreme over all, had boycotted this first session of the town council. Even though they had a councillor who stood for their aspirations—Tjaart Cronje.

Some of the members of the gallery were relatives of the newly elected councillors. But none of them came from Mahlatswetsa Location. Even though six of the ten councillors came from there. Perhaps the people of Mahlatswetsa Location did not know that members of the public were allowed in the gallery of the council chamber. Or they had not yet got used to the fact that they were now full citizens of the town. With the same rights and obligations as their white fellow citizens.

Niki was not there either, even though two of the new councillors were her children. Popi and Viliki.

That morning, Popi had dreaded entering the Stadsaal. The town hall. She had walked alone from her mother's shack to town. Viliki had left much earlier. She had stood on the pavement, and had surveyed the Stadsaal, with a combination of anxiety and satisfaction. It was as though she was seeing the beige brick building for the first time. The whitewashed concrete borders framing the door and windows. The hint of Cape Dutch architecture in the gable above the letters *Stadsaal*. Cape Dutch without the white walls and the black roofs. Only the gable-topped wall above the door.

She had slowly walked along the light brown brick paving, past the giant *Phoenix canariensis* palm trees, two on each side of the paved area. She had stood near the door to read a marble plaque on the wall. *Gelê deur Burgemeestersvrou/Laid by the Mayoress Mevr./Mrs. M.J. Coetzer 27-4-1946.*

Popi had wondered if the Mayoress who had laid this stone all those years ago would have approved if she could have seen her here. Perhaps her protective soul—which must still be hovering around the stone she had laid, as ancestors are wont to jealously guard what used to be theirs in life—thought that her presence was desecrating this building.

Popi had walked into the building. She had found herself in a corridor and had not known where to go. She had peeped into the room on the right. The room she later learnt was the council chamber. There was no one there. She had wandered into other rooms, until she came to Angela van der Walt's office.

"What do you want?" Angela van der Walt had asked abruptly, without looking at her. She had continued to scribble something on a piece of paper.

"I am looking for the meeting of the council," Popi had responded.

"It has not started yet," Angela van der Walt had said. "You can wait outside. We do not allow members of the public into the gallery until the members of the council have arrived."

"I am a member of the council," Popi had said.

Angela van der Walt had raised her head for the first time. Her face had melted into a smile, as she looked the twenty-five-year-old girl over. Girl. Not woman. The custom was that Popi was a girl. So was Niki at forty-seven. So would Niki's mother have been, if she had still been alive. Kitchen-girl. Nanny-girl. And now this girl in this hallowed hall? Council-girl? Council-girl wearing her mother's curtains fashioned into a big turban. Light-complexioned council-girl with blue eyes. Beautiful tall slender council-girl in a red dress.

Angela van der Walt had chuckled to herself and had led Popi back into the council chamber.

"The members of the council sit at this table," Angela van der Walt had explained. "You can sit anywhere you like except at the head of the table. Only the mayor, when you have elected one, sits at the head of the table."

Foolishly, Popi had chosen a place directly opposite the window. The invasive sun had not yet found its way through the opening. Angela van der Walt had returned to her office.

A few minutes later, members of the council had begun to trickle in. Three members from the National Party. Among them Lizette de Vries. One member from the Freedom Front, in the formidable figure of Tjaart Cronje. The Freedom Front, an alliance of a number of those right-wing groupings who had decided to fight for the homeland of the Afrikaner within the system, had been a late entrant in the general elections the previous year. For the local elections this year, the Freedom Front had fielded a number of candidates. Only Tjaart Cronje had been successful.

Popi had fidgeted uneasily while waiting for the five other members of the Movement she was representing to arrive. She was alone among the four Boers. They were talking among themselves, ignoring her. Discussing farm and farming matters that she knew nothing about. And weddings and christenings of people she had never heard of. This conversation was above party politics, for even Tjaart Cronje participated in it.

Soon Popi's comrades had arrived, including Viliki. The Movement was represented by six young councillors, none of them above the age of thirty. The Young Lions, as they called themselves. Popi revelled in being a Young Lion.

Her entry into the world of politics had been an unexpected one. Soon after her body had healed from its beating, she had been sucked into the Movement. The Movement had become her lover. When Niki had shown concern, Popi had told her that the Movement filled a hole in her heart. She had started by attending the rallies of the Movement. Not only those held in Excelsior. She had chased them all over the eastern Free State. Right up to Qwa Qwa, two hundred and fifty kilometres away. Niki's pleas had gone unheeded. The call of the wild had been too strong. The Movement had seduced her, and she had surrendered herself completely.

Niki had even tried to marry her off. To no one in particular.

"It's high time you found yourself a good man, Popi," Niki had said. "You will end up being a lefetwa."

Popi had laughed at the prospect of ending up an old maid. A lefetwa.

"There are no good men out there, Niki," she had responded.

"They cannot all be bad. There's bound to be a good man waiting for your love."

"Maybe when you are dead, Niki—God forbid—when you are dead, I'll think of such things."

"So it is me who is holding you ransom?"

"You are not holding me, Niki. I just want to look after you. I don't need anyone else when you are there."

"Rubbish! You are the one who needs looking after."

Niki had contemplated this exchange for a while, and then she had suddenly blurted out, "It is the Movement, isn't it? It is the Movement that is making you a lefetwa!"

"It is not the Movement," Popi had explained patiently. "Yes, I am dedicated to it. But it is not holding me from marriage. Even if I were to marry, that man would have to understand that I am dedicated to the Movement first and foremost. He would have to be a Movement man himself."

Niki had given up on her with the final mutter that they were trying to take her children away, without really elaborating on the identity of *they*. They were pillaging her heart for the last nestling that had taken refuge in its corners. Ripping it out without mercy. Leaving only emptiness.

Popi had continued with her campaigns for the Movement.

We had witnessed Popi's emergence from the battering of two years before without a dent on her willowy body. We had watched her blossom into a woman of exceptional poise, with the dimples of Niki's maidenhood. Her beauty had even erased the thoughts that used to nag us about her being a boesman. Well, not quite erased them. They had just shifted to the back of our minds. And we did not recall them every time we saw her. Perhaps our eyes were getting used to her. As they were getting used to others like her. Many others. *Walking the streets of Excelsior,* as the late and lamented Minister of Justice, the Honourable Mr P.C. Pelser, had once put it when he was explaining to his colleagues in Parliament why the police had had to act against the Excelsior 19.

Whenever we saw Popi, we praised her beauty and forgot our old gibes that she was a boesman. We lamented the fact that we never saw her smile. That a permanent frown marred her other-wise beautiful face. That her dimples were wasted without a smile. Perhaps we had forgotten that we had stolen her smiles.

It was sad that she could not see any beauty in herself.

"If only she would take off that turban she always wears like a white Winnie Mandela," some of us said.

"She will be a model one day. If only she could go to the city. Even to Bloemfontein."

"You can't be a model in Bloemfontein. She would have to go to Johannesburg or Cape Town to be a model."

"Model? Never! Haven't you seen in the magazines? They don't have light-skinned African models. You have to be pitch black to be an African model."

This, of course, was idle talk on our part. Popi had no intention of becoming a model. She had every intention of becoming a politician. Before the general elections the previous year, she had trudged the farmlands on foot, canvassing farm workers to vote for the Movement. She had told the farmers to go to hell when they fired their workers for being cheeky. She had staged fiery confrontations with those farm owners who had sent their workers packing with the message: "Go ask Mandela to give you a job," or "Go ask Mandela for a raise." Although the workers had enjoyed these confrontations, their problems were never solved. Until Viliki was called. He would negotiate with the farmers. He would tell them that it was in their interests to maintain good relations with their labour force. Sometimes he would be successful and get the workers their jobs back. But Popi would be the one they would sing songs about.

The workers loved her precisely because she was a hothead. They would exclaim in admiration, "Hey, that boesman gives the Boers hell!" They had become her ardent followers. And therefore ardent followers of the Movement.

Others had even tried their hand at propositioning her. The gift that was her body was a waste if it didn't have sinewy muscles rubbing against it. Her skills at *organising* were of no use if she could not organise the warmth of the hearth and of the blankets for the father of her future children.

But these men were crying in a void. She had no plans to become someone's wife. Or someone's anything. Her innocence was bliss. At the church gatherings, when other women of her age talked of carnal experiences, she pretended she knew what they were talking about. And proceeded to recruit them to vote for the Movement.

South Africa's first democratic general elections had come and gone. The Movement had won an overwhelming majority in Parliament and in most of the provinces. In the Free State province, some of the outstanding victories were in the districts where Popi and Viliki had campaigned.

When the local elections were held the following year, the Excelsior branch of the Movement had put both Popi and Viliki's names on the candidates' list. There had been murmurs of nepotism from some members. But the view that Popi had earned a place on the candidates' list in her own right prevailed. She had established a big following among the farm workers, who had voted for the Movement. She had worked very hard, and deserved the honour of representing a ward in Mahlatswetsa Location. Just like the Sisulu family in the National Parliament in Cape Town, one sage observed. The matriarch, Albertina, was a Member of Parliament. So was her daughter, Lindiwe, and also her son, Max. Her husband, Walter, would have been one too if he had chosen to stand. He had paid enough dues even to be President of the country. All of these family members were in Parliament in their own right as leaders who had worked for the Movement over the years, both in exile and inside the country. If there was no nepotism in the case of the Sisulus, then there was no nepotism in the case of Viliki and Popi.

This argument had won the day and Popi's name had stayed on the list.

Popi revelled in being a Young Lion who breathed fire. But in the council chambers on this first day, she sat timidly. Urine continued to build up pressure in her bladder while Angela van der Walt spoke endlessly about procedure.

The first business of the day was the election of the mayor. Angela van der Walt presided over the election. The National Party nominated Lizette de Vries. The Movement nominated Viliki Pule. The three members of the National Party voted for Lizette de Vries. The six members of the Movement voted for Viliki Pule. Tjaart Cronje abstained. Viliki Pule became the first black mayor of Excelsior.

"Now, Your Worship," said Angela van der Walt, with a tinge of sarcasm in her voice, "you have to take over the chair."

She vacated the head of the table, and left the council chamber. Popi jumped up and followed her. In the corridor, she asked the town clerk to show her the toilet.

Chairing meetings was nothing strange to Viliki. He had experience in chairing the branch meetings of the Movement. But the council, as the town clerk had explained, had its own rules and regulations. It had its own procedure, of which Viliki knew very little. Although, of course, the town clerk's little lecture had been of great help.

Viliki called the councillors to order, and thanked them for placing this great trust in him. He promised to serve them diligently and faithfully. A member of the Movement moved that the honourable members of the council should discuss the swearing-in ceremony and a big feast for all the people of Excelsior to welcome their new mayor.

"Is there a budget for a feast?" asked Lizette de Vries.

"The first thing they think about is a feast," said Tjaart Cronje. "Not the roads, not the water, not the sewerage and rubbish removal. But a feast! That's the problem with these affirmative action people."

"You can't call a fellow member an affirmative action person, Mr Cronje," said Viliki. "You will have to withdraw that remark."

"Withdraw?" asked Tjaart Cronje, with a scoffing chuckle. "Have I spoken a lie? Are you not here because of affirmative action? Aren't you people everywhere because of affirmative action? Didn't I leave the army because it was absorbing terrorists into its ranks? The very people I had been taught were the enemy of the Afrikaner race?"

"That has nothing to do with this council," said one of the National Party members.

"It has everything to do with this council!" shouted Tjaart Cronje, foaming at the mouth. "I worked hard in that army. I deserved a promotion. But did I get it? No! Instead a black terrorist was promoted. I couldn't stay in an affirmative action army and salute an affirmative action general. I resigned and came back to Excelsior to run my mother's butchery."

During these rantings, Popi had sneaked back into her seat where she sat quietly.

"Mr Cronje will have to apologise for insulting fellow members of the council," insisted the mayor.

"Well, Tjaart, you know you can't run away from these affirmative action people, as you call them," said Lizette de Vries, obviously amused. "They are everywhere in South Africa. Where are you going to go now?"

"That is why my party wants a separate homeland for the Afrikaners," screamed Tjaart Cronje.

The whole council laughed. Some members of the Movement heckled that he would not have a homeland in Excelsior.

"Questions of the homeland are discussed in Parliament," said Lizette de Vries. "Here we are only concerned with how best we can run this town."

"Don't even speak, Tant Lizette," cried Tjaart Cronje in great anguish. "It is people like you who have sold this country down the drain. You and your Broederbond. The founders of the Broederbond must be turning in their graves. When they established the organisation in 1918, its aim was to fight against the hypocrisy of the English who were discriminating against the Afrikaner in the civil service and in business. But soon the Broederbond began to discriminate against those Afrikaners who were not members. And now the Broederbond has handed this country over to the communists on a silver platter."

The members of the council applauded mockingly.

"We are not interested in your internal Afrikaner politics and your broedertwis," said a member of the Movement, laughing.

"You grew up with this man, Viliki . . . er . . . Your Worship," said another member. "You should know how to calm him down."

"He was not like this when we were growing up," said Viliki, not bothering to hide his exasperation. A chairperson who lost control of the proceedings would clearly lose the respect of the members.

WE HAD HEARD the news even before he arrived in Mahlatswetsa Location. We welcomed him into the township with ululations. We lifted him shoulder-high and toyi-toyied with him. Chanting slogans of his prowess. On the spot we composed a song: *Ruler of all. Ruler of even the mightiest and the richest of Excelsior. He who holds sway over Adam de Vries, Captain Klein-Jan Lombard, Tjaart Cronje, Johannes Smit, Gys Uys, François Bornman and the rest of the genteel people of Excelsior.* We sang until we arrived in front of his mother's shack. We called out to Niki to come and savour the victory of her loins.

But Niki did not venture out. She lay on the bed and mumbled that *they* wanted to take all her children away. That not only did they want to take these children away, they were actually doing it. Taking them away one by one. And there was nothing she could do about it.

The days that followed saw Niki's shack gaining fame countrywide. It was because of the photograph of Viliki Pule, Mayor of Excelsior, barefoot, sitting on a chair outside the shack, wearing the mayoral chain. It graced the front pages of major national newspapers.

EVERYBODY IS A HERO

AT ONE TIME AND

A VILLAIN AT ANOTHER TIME

*S*HE IS a dreamer. A raw sienna mother with splashes of crimson. And she spends her red days lying naked on the red soil between two peach trees with blue trunks. She gave birth to the trees so that they could provide her with shade. But there is hardly any shade because the trees do not bear leaves. Only pink blossoms. Born and reborn all year round. Without bearing fruit.

We were able to read Viliki's and Popi's lives in the void of their rebirth. Born again, not into some charismatic religious faith, although Popi continued to sing for the Methodists and for the dead at funerals. Born again into the suaveness of local government politics.

We called them the Pule Siblings. The people of the Movement called them the Pule Comrades. And we talked of them as though we were talking of one person. Viliki-and-Popi. A united front against retrogressive forces in the council chamber. For two years, the voice that came from their mouths was one voice. Same tone. Same timbre.

At the time, we did not know that the united front was just that—a front. That when they got home, they fought raging battles in which the brother tried to contain the tempestuousness of the sister. To the extent that a chasm was developing between them.

When Viliki visited Niki's shack, Niki would notice the tension between her children. She would mumble that *they* had finally succeeded in taking her children away. When Popi visited Viliki's house, they did nothing but argue. Her visits were becoming less frequent.

Viliki's house itself had been a source of argument. It was an RDP house, of the Reconstruction and Development Programme. Four tiny rooms. Two bedrooms, one lounge and one kitchen. A small concrete stoep at the front door. Grey walls of slightly roughcast cement blocks. Corrugated-iron roof. Big burglar-proofed windows on both sides of the varnished pine door. A small garden in front and a small garden at the back. Four strands of loose barbed wire on three sides of the yard, separating the RDP house from other RDP houses. No fence in the front.

Viliki's house had a well-tended lawn in front, and a number of the arums that are known as varkoore because of their flowers that are shaped like the ear of a pig. The arums were in bloom with white and black flowers for most of the year. Passers-by stopped to take a closer look, for they had never seen black flowers before.

The back garden had a water tap and a small patch of cabbages, tomatoes and spinach. A pit latrine in one corner.

RDP houses were the pride of Viliki's town council. A number of them had been built since it assumed power two years ago. More people had been housed than at any time in the history of Excelsior. In two years, Mahlatswetsa had become a sprawling township of grey houses and some red brick houses.

Very few shacks could be seen in the location. And those that did remain were in yards that had clear signs that construction of a more meaningful magnitude was about to begin. Or had begun. It was the objective of the council to eliminate shacks altogether. Every citizen of Excelsior deserved to live in a proper house.

Viliki had allocated himself a house quite early on. And so did the four other members of the council who came from Mahlatswetsa. Popi had refused a house, and had continued to stay in her shack with her mother. She used part of the stipend of seven hundred rands that she received from the town council to dig a foundation and buy concrete blocks. She was going to build herself and her mother a bigger and better house. A house with five big rooms and a bathroom and a toilet. No one would ever go outside again for ablutions or when responding to the call of nature. There would be no need for a chamber-pot anymore. But after two years, the house was only knee-high. Seven hundred rands a month could only go so far, especially as she also had to buy monthly groceries with it.

Viliki had allocated himself a second house, which he was renting out to some houseless family. He felt that as the mayor, he deserved a second house in order to supplement his meagre income from the council. That was the source of one of the Pule Siblings' many disagreements. Popi felt that it was immoral for Viliki to give himself a second house when there were still so many people on the list, desperately waiting for government-subsidised houses. It had been immoral, she felt, for the councillors to have allocated themselves even the first houses. She had heard that some of them had even allocated houses to girlfriends who did not qualify for government subsidies. And to their mothers and grandmothers. As leaders of the struggle, Popi felt, they should have led by example. They should have had their names on the waiting list like everyone else. Or they should have used their council stipends to build their own houses, just as she herself was doing, instead of dishing out free government houses to themselves. They should have sacrificed for the benefit of their fellow citizens.

The members of the Movement in the council laughed off

Popi's concerns and said: "We sacrificed enough when we fought for liberation. Now it is time for us to eat the fruits of our labour."

Of course, these debates did not take place in the council chamber. They happened privately when Viliki visited Niki's shack. Or when Popi visited Viliki's house, whose lounge now had two sofas, a coffee table and a big colour television. Or when the members of the Movement held their party caucus.

The first disagreement between the Pule Comrades had occurred after the very early sessions of their first year on the council. Popi had moved that the council's minutes and agenda should no longer be in Afrikaans, but in English. The three National Party members and Tjaart Cronje of the Freedom Front had objected in the strongest terms.

"We all speak Afrikaans here," Tjaart Cronje had said, standing up and glaring at Popi. "Our proceedings are in Afrikaans. Why should the minutes and the agenda be in English?"

"Maybe all our proceedings should be in English instead of Afrikaans," Popi had said, looking sneeringly at Tjaart Cronje.

"Instead of eliminating Afrikaans," Lizette de Vries had suggested, "we should rather say that our proceedings should be in Sesotho as well. We all speak Sesotho in Excelsior, don't we?"

"It is a communist plot to eliminate the Afrikaner from the face of South Africa," Tjaart Cronje had cried. "This is why the Afrikaner needs his own homeland."

"I am sure your leader will deal with the question of your homeland in Parliament," Viliki had said.

"Why don't we give him his homeland?" Popi had asked. "Why don't he and his type just disappear into their pie-in-the-sky homeland?"

"No one speaks English in Excelsior," Tjaart Cronje had observed quietly, as he resumed his seat. He had come to the conclusion that Popi, of all the councillors from the Movement, was bent on needling him. He was not going to give her any further opportunity to enjoy herself at his expense.

"We'll just have to learn English then," Popi had said with finality.

The members of the Movement had cheered and applauded.

The council had adjourned that afternoon without resolving the matter. That evening, Popi had gone to Viliki's house. She had found him watching a soap opera on his big colour television.

"You didn't express any views on Afrikaans this afternoon," Popi had said accusingly.

"Come on, Popi," Viliki had pleaded, "I am watching *Generations.* Can't we talk about this some other time?"

"No, we must talk about it now," Popi had insisted. "We are voting tomorrow and we of the Movement want to know where our Mayor stands on this crucial issue."

"You know, Popi, Tjaart was right. No one knows any English here."

"Tjaart was right? Is it you who is saying this, Viliki? You who taught me that in 1976, students died in Soweto because they did not want to be taught in Afrikaans?"

"It was being forced on them. They were right to fight against it. But this is another world and another country. It is no longer the country of 1976."

"It is another country only if you live in your own dreamland. In South Africa, Afrikaans is still the language of the oppressor."

"We have eleven official languages in this country. Afrikaans and Sesotho are two of them. And both are spoken by the people of Excelsior—black and white."

"English is an official language too. Afrikaans is the language of the oppressor!"

"Afrikaans cannot be the language of the oppressor. It is the language of many people of different colours who were themselves oppressed. Even in its origins it was not the language of the oppressor. The oppressor appropriated it and misused it. The slave masters' language was Dutch. The slaves took that Dutch and used it in their own way, adding structures and words from their own original languages . . . the languages of the Malay people . . . of the Khoikhoi people . . . of many other people. Afrikaans was a hybrid . . . a creole spoken by the slaves. The slave masters took it and made it their own. As far as I am concerned, today's coloured people have more right to the Afrikaans language than the people who call themselves Afrikaners. The true Afrikaners are the coloured people."

Popi could not counter this argument. She knew nothing of the things Viliki was jabbering about. She had often been called a coloured by those who were more polite than those who called her boesman. Yet she did not see how on earth she could have a right to the language of the oppressor. How could she be labelled a true Afrikaner? She had stomped around the small room and screamed at her brother: "Rubbish! Afrikaans is the language over which people died! And tomorrow you'd better vote with the rest of the comrades to abolish it from the council chamber."

"I am not voting," Viliki had said, not bothering to hide his relief. "I'll only have a casting vote if there is a tie."

The following day, Popi's motion had been passed. Five ayes and four nays. Viliki consoled himself that he had had no part in the foolish decision.

Another spat among the Pule Siblings blew up when Sekatle, the rich businessman who had worked for "the system" before liberation, applied to join the Movement. There were celebrations in the ranks of the Movement, rejoicings that Sekatle had at last seen the error of his ways. But Viliki objected. He said Sekatle was nothing but an opportunist. He was joining the Movement, not out of conviction, but for what he could gain from it financially.

It seemed that Viliki was taking an opposing view to that of the Movement on too many issues. Had his mayorship run to his head? Did he now think he was bigger than the Movement?

"Sekatle may be a scoundrel, Viliki," said Popi, "but he is donating a sizeable sum of money to our branch to carry out the activities of the Movement."

"That's what I am saying, Popi," said Viliki. "He thinks he can just buy his way into the Movement after doing all those filthy things against our people. He is the man who sold me out. Because of him, I was tortured by the Boers for days on end."

"Where is your spirit of reconciliation, Viliki?" Popi asked. "We forgave the Boers who oppressed and killed us for three hundred years. We are reconciling with them now. Why can't we reconcile with our own people too?"

Reconciliation won the day, and Sekatle became a member of the Movement in good standing.

Viliki gave in, and focused on his work as the mayor of Excelsior.

One of the greatest achievements of his council was the electrification of Mahlatswetsa Location. Every dwelling was wired up, even shacks like Niki's. Families threw away their paraffin lamps, and kept their candles only for the days when there were power failures.

A naked bulb hung from the roof of Niki's shack above the wobbly "kitchen scheme" table. At night it shone so brightly that it made her eyes uncomfortable. It reminded her of the naked bulb that had hung from the roof of the police cell in Winburg.

In addition to the electricity, Popi had installed a telephone. Most days it just sat there on a box in the corner without ringing. It rang only when Popi was away attending political meetings in the outlying districts. She called often to find out how Niki was keeping. And this greatly irritated Niki. She was only forty-nine, yet her daughter treated her like a senile invalid. Why couldn't she just leave her alone in her solitude, as Viliki was doing? But when a whole day passed without Popi calling, perhaps because she was too busy, or maybe because she could not find a public phonebox in the vicinity, Niki would be irritated. Why didn't the ungrateful girl call? Didn't she know that her mother worried about her?

IN THE MORNING Niki went to collect cow-dung, as she did every day, while Popi went to town to attend to matters of the council. Niki missed Popi's company during these expeditions. But Popi was too busy with the council. Or with political rallies throughout the eastern Free State.

On Saturdays, she was too busy with funerals. She was a funeral singer in one of the many choirs of Excelsior. In her red and white and black uniform of the Methodists. Singing at funerals was a pastime she had begun nine years ago, when she had sung her little heart out at Pule's funeral. Since then, every Saturday she attended funerals and sang at them. There were more funerals than ever before. In the old days, there used to be only one funeral per Saturday. Some Saturdays would even pass without a funeral. But now there were about three every Saturday. The people of Mahlatswetsa Location were dying in great numbers. Sometimes Popi would be torn between funerals. Or between a funeral and a political rally.

This did not mean that Popi had outgrown cow-dung expeditions. Once in a while, when she wanted to release the stress that inhabited her body, she joined Niki in the veld. And became carefree and happy. She became a child again. She slid down the slopes and rolled on the grass. She skipped like a kid and gambolled around like a lamb. All her bitterness seemed to dissolve.

But these moments were becoming rare, Niki thought as she gathered dry cow-dung. If only things could be as they were before *they* took her children away.

As if in answer to her prayers, Popi approached, still wearing the blue dress with tiny white dots and the blue turban that she wore for special council meetings.

"You can't collect cow-dung in your nice council clothes, Popi," said Niki.

"I haven't come to gather cow-dung, Niki. I have come to ask for your help."

Swarming bees had invaded the Stadsaal. People were scared to go in or out of the building. Popi had offered to get rid of the bees. But once she had taken a look at the place where they were swarming, she knew that she would not be able to do it alone. She needed the assistance of a greater expert. Hence her pleading with Niki to go to town with her to get rid of the bees.

Reluctantly, Niki agreed.

The bees were hanging under the eaves of the building. They had swarmed the previous day, and had clustered around their new queen. Niki piled papers and cow-dung on a corrugated-iron sheet and lit a fire. Popi stood on a 55-gallon paraffin drum and lifted the smoking corrugated-iron sheet above her head just below the swarming bees. Soon the bees were drunk with smoke. Niki climbed on a stepladder and put her naked hand among the bees. They sat all around and over her arm without stinging her.

"What are you looking for, Niki?" asked Popi.

"The one with the golden legs, Popi. That's the queen. All we need to do is to capture the one with the golden legs. The rest of her black-legged subjects will follow their queen."

Niki found the bee with the golden legs and transferred her to a wooden box that was coated with honey inside. She shook her arm and the rest of the drunken bees fell into the box.

A group of spectators had gathered around the two women.

"Some of you stink of beer," said Niki, as she shook more bees into the box. "Bees are sensitive to alcohol. They smell alcohol and they sting you."

Two or three spectators skulked away into the building. They did not want to provoke the bees with their fumes.

"We'll take these bees home, Popi," said Niki. "We'll build a hive in our backyard."

The spectators went on their way as Niki placed the box full of bees on her head. When she turned to leave, she came face-to-face with Tjaart Cronje, who had just walked out of the building. They looked at each other. Quietly for some time. Softness crept into her eyes. His remained blank. But there was a little twitch of a smile on his lips. Popi glared at Tjaart Cronje angrily, and then walked away. Niki followed with the box on her head. Tjaart Cronje walked to his bakkie parked on the pavement in front of the Stad-saal.

"I hear you and Tjaart fight like starving dogs over a dry bone," said Niki, as they walked to Mahlatswetsa Location. "It is not a good thing for you to fight Tjaart."

"I don't fight Tjaart, Niki," said Popi. "Tjaart fights me."

THE WAR OF THE UNSHAVEN LEGS

*Y*ELLOW-COLOURED YOUNG MAN in a fiery red conical hat. Fiery red overalls. Fiery red shoes. Round-nosed combat boots. Gleaming. His coal-black fingers are strumming on the invisible strings of a golden-yellow guitar. He dances in a fluid of red and yellow flames.

The Baipehi danced around one big fire. A jig of victory. The big silver moon and the tiny silver stars reflected the red and yellow flames against the clear night sky. The Baipehi: those who had placed themselves. During the day, they had marched with pieces of rusty corrugated-iron, cardboard boxes and plastic sheets, and had allocated themselves a vacant piece of land on the outskirts of Mahlatswetsa Location. They had constructed a number of shacks, about fifty or so, establishing instant homes. Tonight more than a hundred men, women and children were celebrating with songs and dances around the winter fire. Singing and dancing to a lone guitar.

The establishment of this squatter camp had caused bitter divisions among members of the Movement. Viliki, His Worship the Mayor of Excelsior, was greatly exercised by the Baipehi. They had no right to divide among themselves chunks of council land

and to build shacks on it. His council was housing the citizens of Excelsior in an orderly manner. New houses were being built every day—Reconstruction and Development Programme houses to which every family was entitled. Yes, there was a long waiting list. A backlog of a hundred names. But no one had the right to take the law into their own hands and set up shacks, which marred the landscape of Mahlatswetsa Location. For a long time, the township had prided itself as one of the very few in South Africa that did not have an eyesore of a shanty town attached to it. And if Viliki had anything to do with it, it would stay that way.

The activities of the impatient Baipehi had generated heated debates in the council chamber. At first, Popi had argued that people should be given the power to do things for themselves rather than have the government build houses for them. The Baipehi had taken the initiative in the correct self-help direction. She never forgot to remind the honourable members that she had refused an RDP house, and was slowly building herself and Niki a big house of their own. A mansion with many rooms. It had not progressed much in the last three years. It was only waist-high. But she was confident that one day she and Niki would live in it. The rusty shack that needed to be patched with anthill mud every other week would not be their home forever.

Sekatle—the rich businessman who had now purchased a big house in town only two houses from Adam de Vries's English bungalow—adopted the Baipehi and made himself their spokesman. He drove around the new settlement in his new Mercedes-Benz, making fiery speeches through a hand-held megaphone. He assured those who gathered around his car that the Movement would stand with them. The Movement had fought for liberation so that people could have roofs over their heads and bread and butter on their tables. The Movement would see to it that they were given title to the land they had already allocated themselves. The Movement would give them water and electricity and paved streets. The Movement. The Movement.

The destitute were given hope. Here was a man who stood with the people, even though he himself was so wealthy. A man who never forgot his humble origins. A man who had transformed Maria's RDP house into a gleaming palace. If he looked after his sister so well, surely he would look after the interests of his destitute brethren and sistren just as effectively.

But the members of the Movement in the council did not see things with the same eye. Whereas Viliki wanted to take a hard line against the Baipehi, others felt that they should be allowed to stay. Or that, at the very least, the council should offer them alternative land on which to build their shacks. Popi agreed with this latter position.

"I do not think we have an obligation to give them alternative land," said Viliki. "Where did they come from? Surely they must have lived somewhere before. They must go back there. We are not going to have a shanty town in Excelsior!"

"That is very callous, Comrade Mayor," Popi argued. "These people are homeless. We cannot wish them away. It is our duty as the council to see to it that they are housed."

"The land those people are occupying is earmarked for more RDP houses," Viliki insisted. "The Baipehi must vacate it."

This, of course, was a new development. The Pule Siblings/ Pule Comrades no longer spoke with one voice in the council chamber. Their voices had separated into two. Distinct. Often shrill. They no longer confined their bitter disagreements to Niki's shack or Viliki's RDP house. They started by disagreeing publicly in the caucus of the Movement, then at its branch meetings and finally in the council chamber. These little tiffs embarrassed other council members of the Movement.

Lizette de Vries and her National Party members agreed with Viliki's hard line. Tjaart Cronje, on the other hand, rejoiced at what he saw as the failure of the "affirmative action people" to govern the town in a civilised manner. He repeated that he had known things would come to this. They were definitely going to mess up a town that had been run efficiently for so many generations. The founding fathers must be weeping in their graves.

"This degeneration started three years ago when Popi Pule imposed English as the language of this chamber," said Tjaart Cronje. "From then onwards I knew that things would go downhill."

The members of the council had heard this line of argument before. Tjaart Cronje always found a way of linking any issue that arose in the council to the marginalisation of the Afrikaans language.

"Mr Cronje is out of order," Viliki declared. "We are discussing the problem of the squatters here, which has nothing to do with his Anglo-Boer War."

"It is true that the Afrikaner is still fighting the Anglo-Boer War," Popi said, laughing. "His problem with English is a problem with the English. He would have no problem if we said the proceedings in this chamber should be in Sesotho. Indeed, Tjaart Cronje has even said that the only two languages that people speak here are Afrikaans and Sesotho. He is prepared to accept Sesotho even though it is a black language and he hates black people!"

Her three years in the council had taught her to analyse things in a manner that we had never thought possible.

"I do not hate black people," said Tjaart Cronje in a pained voice. "The chair must protect me from this woman's vicious tongue."

"Ms Pule will have to withdraw those words," said Viliki.

"I withdraw them, Your Worship," said Popi, with a silly smirk in her voice. "But the point has been made."

The council members of the Movement laughed and cheered.

"You have to withdraw unconditionally, Ms Pule," insisted Viliki.

"I withdraw them unconditionally," said Popi. "All I was trying to say is that when we say the proceedings must be in English, the Afrikaner feels that English is being promoted at the expense of his own language. He sees it as another victory of the English over his people in the ongoing Anglo-Boer War saga that has lasted for a hundred years. You cannot destroy the Anglo-Boer War mentality in the Afrikaner."

"I object!" yelled Lizette de Vries. "You cannot generalise about Afrikaners."

"Since when did she become an expert on the Afrikaners?" asked another council member of the National Party.

"You are all out of order," screamed a frustrated Viliki. "We resolved that matter three years ago. Today all our minutes are in English—broken as it is. A person is free to speak the language of his or her choice in the chamber. That is why Mr Cronje always speaks in Afrikaans and Ms Pule always addresses this chamber in Sesotho. Our constitution allows that. Why should we go back to that issue now? We are talking about the squatters."

"It is because Mr Cronje is still smarting over the fact that we write our minutes in English instead of Afrikaans," said Popi, hoping that hers would be the last word on the matter.

"In rotten English!" said Tjaart Cronje. His had to be the real last word.

While the council was quibbling over irrelevancies, Sekatle had become the hero of the squatters. Not only did they sing his name, they danced it as well. In their chants he acquired the stature of the heroes of old: Moshoeshoe and Shaka. And of the stalwarts of the liberation struggle: the men and women who had languished in the prisons of South Africa and who had wandered in exile in foreign lands. Fighting for the very freedom now being denied to the Baipehi.

Sekatle is our new Mandela! Sekatle is the Father of the Orphans! Sekatle is our new Oliver Tambo! Sekatle shall free us from the pangs of hunger!

Viliki's hard line began to soften. He told his comrades that he was prepared to compromise. He would find alternative land for the squatters if they vacated the land that had already been earmarked for RDP houses.

Popi was happy at this change of attitude. She took it upon herself to go to the squatter camp to negotiate with the Baipehi to accept an alternative piece of ground.

"We cannot leave this land," a woman said. "We have paid for it."

"Paid for it?" wondered Popi. "But you just gave yourselves this land. It belongs to the government for the new houses. How can you claim to have paid for it?"

"Oh, yes, we paid for it all right. Sekatle's people collected the money from every one of us. They say it will make it possible for Sekatle to protect us from the likes of you."

"From the likes of me? I have been on your side all along."

"You are on the council, aren't you? Sekatle says we can't trust the town councillors any more. They are only looking after their own stomachs."

It dawned on Popi that Sekatle's interest in the squatters had not been fired solely by his community spirit. His keen business eye had spotted yet another moneymaking scheme. She walked to Sekatle's shop and confronted him. He denied ever sending people to collect money from the squatters and challenged her to dare remove the Baipehi even if alternative land was provided. They wanted the land they had taken occupation of, or nothing.

"Do not alienate your allies, Abuti Sekatle," pleaded Popi. "You know that in the council chamber I have supported the Baipehi. I have fought for them to be given land of their own which must have all the infrastructure."

"An ally who accuses me of stealing money from poor people is no ally at all. And please, there is the door. I am a very busy man."

Popi left the store fuming.

Viliki was alarmed when she arrived at his house at night.

"Is there something wrong with the old lady?" he asked. Although Niki was only fifty, he called her "the old lady". And she indeed looked much older than her years. It was because her face had been eroded by the skin-lighteners of her youth.

"There is nothing wrong with Niki," said Popi. "Can't I visit my brother without him getting suspicious?"

THE NEXT DAY the council was taken aback when Popi moved that the Baipehi should be removed immediately. By force, if necessary. Lizette de Vries seconded the motion. There was a division in the chamber. Popi, the three members of the National Party and Tjaart Cronje voted for the motion. The four members of the Movement opposed it. And lost. Viliki gleefully announced that the services of a private company would be engaged to remove the squatters and their camp.

The Baipehi were given one week to vacate the land. Under the revolutionary leadership of Sekatle, they stood their ground. The deadline was extended twice—by one week each time. Still they refused to move. Instead they cultivated their gardens to demonstrate that they were there permanently. Viliki seemed to be wavering.

"You cannot show signs of weakening now, Viliki," Popi egged him on. "No one will ever respect you again if you don't take action against those arrogant Baipehi. Sekatle needs to know that you are the mayor, not him."

The following month, bulldozers came thundering down the dusty roads of Mahlatswetsa Location. Men in orange overalls descended upon the squatter camp and systematically uprooted the makeshift houses. They loaded the corrugated-iron and plastic sheets, the poles and cardboard, onto a truck. Those structures that were stubborn were flattened by the bulldozers. Men, women and children ran helter-skelter in the mushrooms of dust to salvage their precious belongings. Others pleaded with the men in orange overalls to be merciful.

"How can you do this to us?" they asked. "We are black people like you."

"It is not for us to be merciful," said their foreman. "We are paid by your town council to remove this squatter camp. Go ask them for mercy. We are just doing our job."

Sekatle called an urgent branch meeting of the Movement. The Pule Comrades had gone too far. They had to be sanctioned. They had to be disciplined. Everyone was accusing the Movement-controlled council of resorting to the tactics of the past.

"We had thought that bulldozers were history," said Sekatle at the branch meeting. "Today we have seen what we used to see during the worst excesses of apartheid. We never thought we would see the day when a town council that was controlled by the Movement would vote with the Boers to drive away our people from their own land in their own country!"

"We have no blood on our hands," said the other four council members of the Movement. "We voted against the motion."

"Obviously Viliki and his sister think that they are bigger than the Movement," said Sekatle. "They forget that in the same way that we made them what they are, we can unmake them."

WE LOOKED at these events with foreboding. We all accepted that a war had been declared against the Pule Comrades.

THE MEMBERS of the Movement wanted to table the issue of the forced removals once more in the council chamber. But Viliki ruled that there was no point in discussing it. It would be a waste of time. There were other important matters on the agenda, such as the construction of the new library in Mahlatswetsa Location.

"Does the mayor think that a library is more important than the lives of our people who have been treated worse than they used to be in the days of apartheid?" asked a councillor from the Movement.

"We voted on the matter, Comrade," said Viliki, "and this council passed a motion that the squatters should be removed. We gave them ample warning. The question of the library is very important."

"Indeed a library is important," said Lizette de Vries. "The plans to build one in Mahlatswetsa have been there for a long time . . . from the time when my husband was the Administrator of the township. It is now time for action."

"The library we are talking about has nothing to do with your husband, Mrs de Vries," said Popi sneeringly. "We are talking of the library that this Movement-led council plans to build for the people of Mahlatswetsa."

"I think even before you can talk of a library, you must get your people to pay for services," said Tjaart Cronje. "The white citizens of Excelsior cannot afford to subsidise your people. Like everyone else, you must pay rates, you must pay for water, you must pay for sewerage."

Tjaart Cronje had raised a sore point. Almost every household in Mahlatswetsa Location was in arrears. Even the town councillors themselves. Except for the Pule Siblings who wanted to lead by example, and paid on time every month.

"This culture of non-payment was cultivated by the Movement," said Lizette de Vries. "Now that the Movement is in power, it must bear the consequences."

"It is true that when we were fighting for freedom, we encouraged people not to pay for services," admitted Viliki. "It was part of the war for freedom. But unfortunately the culture of non-payment set in. People got used to not paying. Now even though we are free, they refuse to pay."

"As a result, the town council has no money," said a member of the National Party.

"In the same way that they taught people not to pay, they must now teach them to pay," said another.

"Are we still talking about the library, Mr Chairperson?" asked Popi.

"Of course we are," screeched Tjaart Cronje. "People who don't pay for services do not deserve a library. In any event, black people have other priorities. A library will be a white elephant. It's like casting pearls before swine."

"You call my people swine?" said Popi.

"Black people can't read," heckled Tjaart. "A library is a waste of resources."

"If there are no resources it is because you and your people stole them," said Popi. "So now we are taking them back. If black people don't read, then we are going to cultivate a new culture of reading."

"What do you know of culture when you can't even shave your legs?" asked Tjaart Cronje, looking at Popi's legs with disgust.

"Tjaart!" admonished Lizette de Vries. "You can't talk to a lady like that."

"She is no lady," insisted Tjaart Cronje. "Ladies shave their legs. She doesn't. She is therefore no lady."

There was utter silence. Tears swelled in Popi's eyes.

For the first time, the honourable members of the council could hear crowds of Baipehi dancing the toyi-toyi dance outside the Stadsaal. Viliki could distinctly hear Sekatle's voice leading the chants.

The Mayor is a sellout! Hayi! Hayi! Hayi! Down with Viliki! Hayi! Hayi! Hayi!

26

THE SELLER OF SONGS

*T*HE PENNY-WHISTLE. We still call it a flute. But the coloured girl has graduated from birdlike twitters to the gurgling sounds of river spirits. And her face has been tanned brown by the busker's sun. Patchy brown. Her true yellow-coloured complexion peeps through in places. A tattered brown felt hat sits on her head, covering her forehead to the eyebrows. Hiding her golden-red locks. Her round eyes are wide and her brown pupils threaten to pop out and start bouncing on the brown ground to the rhythm of her melody. Her body is covered in a brown blanket. She kneels on the ground as the deep mellow notes and the shrill piccolo-like notes send shivers of prayer to those who are sleeping under it. Her fingers have learnt to close and open the six holes of the rusty metal instrument in the most dextrous manner, producing sounds that wriggle like water snakes in a warm current.

Brownness envelops her. Thin-nibbed outlines of Indian ink give an ephemeral presence to the ghost that watches over her shoulder.

We noticed that the Seller of Songs no longer spent her days busking outside the bank in town. She had decided that if customers did not come to her, she would take her music to their houses. She went from door to door playing her penny-whistle. Rich white people gave her a few coins, if only to get rid of her. When they got tired of her repeated visits, they shooed her away. Then she came to our houses in Mahlatswetsa Location. When she played outside your door, you opened and gave her some coins. She played a song or two, depending on how much you had paid her, and then moved on to the next house. Those of us who did not have money to waste on songs just clapped our hands and bade her goodbye. As she turned away from us, we would comment on how she was the spitting image of the Reverend François Bornman. And on how her eyes and ears looked exactly like those of Jacomina, the dominee's daughter and wife of Tjaart Cronje. We were able to see these resemblances quite expertly because we knew that the Seller of Songs was Maria's daughter. The Maria of the Excelsior 19. But of course the Seller of Songs was much younger. She was born several years post-Excelsior 19. Obviously Maria had continued with her escapades with white men. Could she—the temptress that she was—have continued spreading her body parts before the path of the dominee?

SUNDAY MORNING. Viliki stayed in bed and enjoyed his fingers. He loved his fingers more than he could any woman. They took him to heaven, without his first having to die. And most importantly, without his sweat mingling with anyone else's. His fingers could become any full-bodied figure he had fancied in the street during the day. Or in the gallery of the council chamber. In an instant they could turn into one of those half-naked sirens who graced the pages of *Drum* magazine.

He heard the penny-whistle. He ignored it. He had not yet reached his heavenly destination. The melody persisted. He cursed. He put on his pants and quickly went to open the door. The Seller of Songs was standing on the red polished stoop, displaying a smile that would not be out of place in a toothpaste advertisement. She could pass for a waif in her brown felt hat, whose brim almost covered her eyes, and a brown threadbare blanket hanging from her shoulders and covering her whole body down to the ankles. He smiled back.

He had seen her busking in town. On the pavement in front of the bank. But he had never really paid her any particular attention. She was just one of the light-skinned girls walking the streets of Excelsior, as the former Minister of Justice, P.C. Pelser, once so aptly put it. Later Viliki had heard from Popi that she was the daughter of Maria, Niki's erstwhile friend. Still he did not take any notice of her.

But here she was, at the door of his RDP house, smiling his knees into jelly and his palms into a sweat.

"Are you just going to stand there or are you going to play?" he asked.

"I have already played," she said impishly. "Three songs while you refused to open the door. You owe me."

"Come in," he found himself saying.

She went in. And never walked out again. At least not that day. Not that week.

In the chamber of the council, it was announced that His Worship the Mayor of Excelsior was indisposed. But in the chamber of his RDP house, he was bathing in the sweat of the Seller of Songs. And in her blood. He had gently reprimanded her when she had said she would not let him swim in her filth, as it was her bad time of the month.

"God cannot create filth," he had said. "Babies come from this blood. Babies cannot come from filth."

And to prove that he meant what he said, he had touched it and let it slide between his fingers, even though she herself was disgusted by it.

As soon as Popi entered the shack, Niki let her feel the chill of her wrath.

"How can you not tell me when my child is sick?" Niki asked.

"I didn't know it was serious," Popi defended herself.

"He has been ill for one whole week and you didn't know it was serious? I had to hear it from people in the street."

"I am sorry, Niki. My mind is full of too many things lately."

Niki mumbled that not only had *they* succeeded in taking her children away, they had built an uncaring wall between them, despite the fact that the children had come from the same womb.

Once more Popi apologised. It was her war with Tjaart Cronje that was destabilising her life, she confessed to Niki. She should have remembered to tell her mother about Viliki the very day it was announced that he was indisposed. But she had been angry and flustered by Tjaart Cronje's taunts about her hairy legs.

This was not just an excuse on her part. Indeed, since Tjaart Cronje had mentioned her hairy legs for the first time during the library debate, she had become even more conscious of her hairiness. And this had made her less vocal in the chamber lest Tjaart Cronje refer to her legs again. Tjaart Cronje, on the other hand, had every intention of exploiting this newly discovered weak spot.

Observing all this, and missing Popi's characteristic outbursts in the chamber, Lizette de Vries had taken it upon herself to hold a private tea-break conversation with her about hair and hairiness.

"I am aware that most black women don't have hair on their legs," said Lizette de Vries. "But it is quite normal with white women."

"But I am not a white woman!" screamed Popi.

All Lizette de Vries could say to this was, "Well . . . ja . . . nee . . ."

Well. Yes. No.

"I am not white," insisted Popi. "I am a Mosotho girl."

"All I am saying is that hair that grows on the legs is not abnormal. It is a normal thing for some people, and is nothing to be ashamed of."

Then she explained how white women dealt with hairy legs. Mothers who wanted their daughters to have a Barbie-doll look taught their daughters to wax and shave their legs as early as the age of fifteen. But progressive mothers taught their daughters never to shave their legs or even their armpits. Shaving legs was really a city thing. But of course some rural girls in places like Excelsior did it as well, as they aspired to be like the "with it" city girls.

"As you are so ashamed of your hair, buy a razor and shave once a week," advised Lizette de Vries. "But you must know that your hair will grow thicker and darker. If I were you, I would just let it be. Popi, you have been blessed with such beautiful legs. Be proud of them! Don't listen to country bumpkins like Tjaart."

After this talk, Popi had felt slightly better about herself. However, she continued to be angry with a God who had burdened her with the hairy problems of white people.

"This war between you and Tjaart is very silly," Niki said finally after Popi had told her of her woes.

"He is the one who starts it," said Popi. "I don't know why he hates me so."

"He is not a bad boy . . . Tjaart . . . he's really not a bad boy."

"Maybe when you looked after him . . . when he was a little boy . . . he was not a bad boy. But he has changed since then, Niki. You don't know him now. He is a right-winger."

Niki did not know what a right-winger was. She just looked at Popi sheepishly and said, "One day Tjaart will understand that he has to love you."

She took a tartan shawl from her bed and draped it around her shoulders. She commanded Popi to accompany her to see her sick child. She had cooked him her special bean and tomato soup, which she put in a blue enamel bowl that had a lid.

"Let me hold it for you, Niki," said Popi as they walked on the dirt street that was lined with RDP houses on both sides.

"So that he will think it comes from you? No thank you, I'll hold it."

Popi had this bad habit of opening Viliki's door without knocking. In this instance, she did the same. As mother and daughter entered, they were greeted by a scene that left them open-mouthed.

Viliki was sitting on his new red sofa bought from Ellerine's in Thaba Nchu on a twelve-month hire-purchase instalment plan. He was wearing khaki short pants and was both shoeless and top-less. The Seller of Songs was sitting on his lap, wearing only her navy blue knickers. The couple were watching the antics of the stope-workers in the television soap opera, *Isidingo*.

The Seller of Songs jumped up and ran into the bedroom to hide her nakedness.

"I tell you every day, Popi, that you must knock," said Viliki, going on the attack to hide his embarrassment.

"So this is how you get sick, Viliki?" asked Niki.

"And with this girl who makes a fool of herself playing a flute," said Popi.

"What is Maria's daughter doing here, Viliki?" asked Niki.

"She stays here with me, Mama. I love her."

"You stay here with someone's daughter without even asking for her hand from her parents? How many cattle did you pay for her?" asked Niki.

"He can't marry a girl like this, Niki. She is a disgrace, this girl," squealed Popi.

"Why is she a disgrace, if I may ask?" demanded Viliki.

For a moment, Popi was at a loss for words. Then she asked: "Don't you see her?"

"I see her all right," said Viliki firmly. "And I love her."

"Oh, this child will be the death of me," lamented Niki. "I come here because I heard he was sick for the whole week, only to find that he is doing a vat-en-sit with Maria's child. I spent this whole day slaving over a three-legged pot, cooking him bean and tomato soup. What are the parents of this child saying about this?"

"Nothing," said Viliki. "They don't care. No one came looking for her."

This showed how cruel Sekatle was, said Viliki. He was such a wealthy man, yet his niece had to survive by busking. Although he had built Maria a glittering mansion, he was rumoured to have said, "I am not going to toil for Maria's mixed-breed children."

Viliki vouched for the truth of this rumour. Those words looked just like Sekatle.

Viliki's harangue about the bane of his life was interrupted by the shattering of a window in the bedroom. All three rushed in, fearing that the Seller of Songs had done harm to herself. There she was, cowering in the corner. She had covered herself with her brown blanket. The smell of petrol filled the room. On the floor next to the bed was a bottle full of the liquid. There were pieces of glass all over the floor. Someone had thrown a petrol bomb through the window. It had failed to explode.

Viliki called the police on his cellphone.

"Who do you suspect?" asked the burly Afrikaner sergeant.

Viliki did not hesitate to put the blame on Sekatle. This was the second failed petrol bomb. The first one had been thrown into his house a few weeks ago. He had been at a braai that had been organised by the private company engaged by the council to remove the Baipehi. When he got back home, he had found a broken window and the beginnings of a fire in the living room. With the help of neighbours he had managed to extinguish it, but not before his sofa was burnt to ashes. Hence his having to buy a new one from Ellerine's. On that day too an ineptly constructed petrol bomb had been thrown into his RDP house.

It had to be Sekatle. Earlier that week, he had led a group of boys and girls in school uniforms. They had performed the toyi-toyi dance outside his house, hurling insults at his pedigree, at Niki's escapades with white men, and at Popi's "colouredness".

Viliki had chosen not to say anything about this because he did not want to upset his mother and sister. But this time Sekatle had gone too far.

27

SERENITY RESTS ON HER LIKE A HEAVY LOG

HE LOOKS quite different from the fruity accordion player of the glorious years of garden parties. He is of the new world. Nothing Flemish expressionist about him. The black outlines are thicker than ever. And rougher. Yet they fail to give him a robust look. He squeezes his purple and white accordion, and its folds breathe out the nostalgic wails of the mountain people of neighbouring Lesotho. The weight of the song has softened his face. He looks frail. The weight of the accordion has given his body a delicate demeanour. It is as if he will break into two. The weight of his purple boots has given him a painful gait. His purple overalls fly far above the ankle, almost mid-shin. His purple conical Basotho hat is tattered and has lost its crown at the pinnacle. His sharp knees pierce the white and yellow and purple light.

The Seller of Songs infected Viliki with music. He bought an old accordion at a second-hand music shop in Bloemfontein, and she taught him how to play it. She herself had never played the accordion before. She just pressed a few keys, listened to the notes each one produced, and created her own music. It took him a while to master the keys, but she was a patient teacher. Within three months Viliki could accompany the difela poetry and famo music of the mountain people of Lesotho. She accompanied his accordion with her flute, which in itself was an innovation, as that combination of instruments was unknown in the kind of Sesotho music that they played.

Every day when Viliki returned from the council meetings and wanted to relax, they played music together. And every day they sounded better than the day before. His RDP house was filled with songs, which the Seller of Songs felt were wasted, as he forbade her to go busking ever again.

"Your songs are mine alone," said Viliki. "I do not want you to share them with other people. The music we create cannot be wasted on people who cannot appreciate its creators . . . who call them such names as boesman."

"Have they ever called you that?" asked the Seller of Songs.

"Of course not," said Viliki. "I am not a coloured person. But they have called you that. And they have called my sister that."

"It doesn't bother me," said the Seller of Songs. "I can handle it. I don't need you to defend me."

But he continued to defend her. He defended her against Popi, who had developed a new habit of bursting into his RDP house and sniffing around as if something terrible was stinking. She would sniff close to the Seller of Songs and then, without uttering a word, she would walk out. Back to Niki's shack.

"Why does Popi hate me so?" the Seller of Songs once asked.

"Don't worry, she will get used to the idea that we are together now," Viliki assured her. "She will accept you just as my mother has finally accepted you."

"Popi . . . I think she hates me because I remind her of who she really is," observed the Seller of Songs.

Viliki gave an embarrassed chuckle.

"You should teach her that I didn't make myself to be like this," added the Seller of Songs. "In the same way she didn't make herself to be a boesman either."

Suddenly Viliki saw himself as a little boy. Knocking at Stephanus Cronje's window. He saw Stephanus Cronje reading his mother's note, putting money in an envelope and giving it to him. He saw himself running like the wind to Mahlatswetsa Location and giving the envelope to Niki. He saw himself that evening eating assorted biscuits with Fanta Orange. And then playing with the brand-new top and brand-new marbles that Niki could now afford to buy.

"Popi could never talk about such issues," observed Viliki. "You are wise. Your songs have made you such a beautiful soul."

"Enjoy my beautiful soul while it lasts," said the Seller of Songs with a naughty twinkle in her big round eyes. "Soon Maria will come and fetch me. Or perhaps Uncle Sekatle."

Viliki laughed. He knew that Sekatle had more important things to worry about than delinquent mixed-breed relatives. One of the issues that occupied his mind was the plight of two schoolboys and one schoolgirl who had each been sentenced to a one-year term of imprisonment for petrol-bombing Viliki's house. Sekatle had managed to keep his hands clean. Nothing could be found to link him to the bombers. He claimed that he had never even set his eyes on them before. But for some strange reason, he was concerned that the bombers should get legal representation, to appeal against their sentences. After all, he argued, they were minors. And they were first offenders. It would have been more just to give them a suspended sentence. Or community service. The poor children were not criminals. Theirs was a political offence. A jail term would turn them into hardened criminals.

The Pule Siblings also occupied Sekatle's mind. Especially Viliki. He wanted to see Viliki expelled or, at the very least, suspended from the Movement for bringing it into disrepute. Firstly by removing the squatters by force. And secondly, and more seriously, by falsely accusing the branch chairperson of the Movement, a disciplined and loyal member of the Movement in good standing, namely Sekatle himself, of being party to nefarious activities such as throwing petrol bombs into other people's houses.

Sekatle's word carried weight. Viliki was indeed suspended from the Movement while his case was being investigated. Popi decided to suspend herself by no longer playing any active role in the affairs of the Movement. Once more the Pule Siblings spoke with one voice. Same tone. Same timbre. Niki was happy that the wall that had been built between her children seemed to be crumbling.

The Pule Siblings remained on the council. They had been elected by the people and would remain town councillors until the next elections in eighteen months' time. But Viliki had to resign from the mayoral office as he had been elected to that position by the town councillors, the majority of whom were members of the Movement.

There was tension in the chamber when the elections for Viliki's replacement were held. The Movement would have nominated Sekatle as a candidate if he had been a member of the council, as he was now the branch chairperson. But they had to nominate one of their own council members instead. The National Party nominated Lizette de Vries. The three National Party council members voted for her. Tjaart Cronje of the Freedom Front did not abstain this time. He voted for her as well. Viliki and Popi voted for Lizette de Vries. The Movement's candidate got only four votes from its council members. Lizette de Vries, with her six votes, became the new mayor of Excelsior.

The unthinkable had happened. A Movement-run town council had elected a National Party member as mayor. In Excelsior, erstwhile rulers and creators of the apartheid system were back in power, courtesy of the former oppressed who had overthrown them in the first place.

We had thought that the Pule Siblings would not be able to walk the streets of Mahlatswetsa Location without the people spitting at them. Or even throwing stones at them. But we were wrong. No one bothered them. Perhaps the people were tired of the squabbles of the town council. They were nonchalant about the whole matter. Some of us even commented, privately lest we be called sellouts, that maybe now that the Boers were back in power, we were going to see a better delivery of services in Excelsior. We had, of course, forgotten that when they were in power during the days of apartheid, there was no electricity in our houses. No street lights in Mahlatswetsa Location. No library.

Popi continued to debate vigorously in the council chamber—since Lizette de Vries had helped her regain some of her confidence after the incident of the hairy legs—and to needle and be needled by Tjaart Cronje. But Viliki seemed to have lost all interest in the affairs of the council. He attended its sittings fairly regularly, for he was paid a stipend to do so. He cast his vote without really participating in the debates. It was as though he was in a daze. He just watched how Popi voted and then voted the same. When the new mayor reshuffled her "cabinet"—as the councillors called the management committee that comprised all ten councillors—he was given the least taxing portfolio. He was put in charge of the parks. There was really nothing to do concerning the two parks of Excelsior. They were just there. Big tracts of land with grass and bluegum trees and nothing else. No one bothered to use the parks for anything. So Viliki's work was really cut out for him.

His daze disappeared as soon as he got to his RDP house, where he made love and music with the Seller of Songs.

Popi, on the other hand, attacked the duties of her new portfolio with great enthusiasm. They included the new library of Mahlatswetsa Location. It had finally been built, furnished and equipped. It was an imposing brick structure with a green corrugated-iron roof. Its neat grounds were paved with bricks and concrete. Inside, the floors were of shining tiles, made slippery by the polish that the cleaner applied every morning. There were many shelves lined with books bought with council funds and donated by the provincial government and by overseas countries. Popi took her work as the town councillor in charge of the library very seriously. She spent all her days paging through the books, smelling them and just fondling them. We even thought she was the librarian, for sometimes she stood behind the counter and assisted students who were looking for books. The real librarian took advantage of her enthusiasm, and often sneaked out to do her washing at home. Or to go shopping for groceries. She knew that Popi would take care of the patrons. And they were many, these patrons. Mostly students from the various primary and high schools in Mahlatswetsa Location. Some adults had library cards as well. Others used the library for reading newspapers and magazines.

Popi's favourite corner was the one that had oversized glossy books on art. She paged through the colourful paintings, and read more about the European artists called Flemish expressionists who had influenced the trinity's early work. She gained a clearer understanding of what the trinity was trying to do with his distorted figures, and was no longer bothered by the fact that they were distorted. In fact, when she came across books with figures that were not distorted, that captured life as people saw it with their eyes, she was not moved. Such works, she felt, were lacking in emotion.

The library became the new thief that stole Popi from cow-dung collecting expeditions. Niki missed her. She saw her only in the evenings when she came home to sleep. Sometimes she returned only after Niki was already asleep and left early before Niki woke up. They saw very little of each other. Yet Niki continued to loom large in Popi's life. She felt Niki's presence all the time. Whether she was debating in the council chamber, fondling books in the library, or singing for the dead at funerals, Niki's aura was always with her. She could smell it. Sometimes she even felt that she was seeing everything through Niki's eyes.

Serenity had now descended upon Niki. She spent her mornings collecting cow-dung. And her afternoons sitting on a grass mat, watching worker bees fly in and out of the two hives that she had constructed in her backyard. Her face was scarred and cracked like a dried-up swamp experiencing a prolonged drought.

Her cheeks had become very hard and discoloured even as serenity set upon her. Black and blue chubaba patches blotched the rough terrain. The hair that peeked from under her doek was grey and spiky. The whites of her eyes had lost their whiteness and turned yellowish-brown.

Serenity rested on her shoulders like a heavy log.

IMMERSIONS

*T*HESE BROWN PEOPLE ARE less distorted than the trinity's usual people. Perhaps it is because they carry a load of sorrow contained in a blue coffin. A small coffin that two brown men hold in their arms close to their chests. Dark brown jackets. Light brown pants. Their eyes are closed and their brown-haired heads touch as they bow above the coffin. They have to walk sideways stepping carefully on the brown ground with their bare feet. A small crowd of brown women and children follow them. Eyes closed. A barefoot girl in a brown blanket. An older girl in a blue dress. A young woman in a white dress. Two women in brown blankets. One wearing a blue doek. A grandmother in a brown blanket and blue dress. Age has cut her height to that of the barefoot girl. The brown and blue roofs of township houses stretch to the light brown sky behind the funeral crowd.

Popi's voice rose above all voices. Its undulations carried from the cemetery to the houses of Mahlatswetsa Location a kilometre away, sending tremors of comfort even to those who had not bothered to attend the funeral. Those who had become nonchalant about funerals. They needed to be comforted, too. It was their death as much as it was that of the little boy who lay in the coffin, and of the bereaved mother who sat on a mat next to the mound that would cover her son, listening to the pastor of the Methodist Church reading the last rites.

Death lived among the people of Mahlatswetsa every day. In days gone by, a funeral was a rare occasion that everyone talked about. That everyone attended. Death was something that happened to the men who worked in the mines of Welkom, who were brought home in pine coffins after their lungs had been eaten by phthisis. Or after "the table" had collapsed on them in the dark holes where they ferreted for the gold that made white women beautiful and glittery. Death was something that happened to the aged who had lived their time on earth.

But these days death was, as the Basotho people put it in their adage, the daughter-in-law of all homesteads. Young men came home to die after being eaten by AIDS. Young women infected their unborn babies, who died soon after reaching toddlerhood. The little boy for whom Popi was singing had been more fortunate. He had reached the age of six before the disease had reduced him to a living skeleton that could not move from the bed. It was a relief for his mother when he finally gave up and breathed his last. She knew too that soon it would be her turn. Like him, she would be reduced to bones. She would be laid to rest in this very cemetery. And hopefully Popi would sing for her as well.

Popi was indeed kept busy singing at funerals. Sometimes in a single Saturday there would be three funerals, one after another. And she would sing at them all. She did not sing only at the funerals of the Methodists. She sang at Roman Catholic funerals. And mastered their hymns, which she thought lacked the liveliness and the danciness of Methodist hymns. She sang at Dutch Reformed Church funerals. And at the funerals of the Zionist Independent Christian Churches. Once she even sang at a funeral for white people. A whole family had been wiped out. Father, mother, a son and two daughters. It was one of the tragedies that had become part of the Afrikaner tradition, in which the father—faced with financial ruin and unpaid Land Bank loans—killed his whole family and then himself. Lizette de Vries, who since becoming mayor had been working closely with Popi, took her to this funeral. All eyes were on the coloured "girl" who sang Afrikaans hymns with such a heavenly voice. The Reverend François Bornman, who conducted the funeral service, stared at her and remembered Stephanus Cronje. What would he have made of this sweet-voiced creature?

Popi sang at funerals only on Saturdays. Or on Sundays, when they spilled over to the next day. During the week she immersed herself in the work of the council. Especially the library. When there were no council meetings, she spent all her days in the library, paging through books and caressing them. She took it as a blessing that she was no longer a member of the Movement since Sekatle had finally succeeded in getting her and Viliki expelled for bringing the Movement into disrepute. The Movement's patience with the Pule Comrades had finally run out when they had voted Lizette de Vries into the mayorship. After an investigation had been conducted by the big guns of the provincial executive council, Popi and Viliki were both kicked out of the Movement, without any hearing where they could defend themselves. The Pule Comrades became plain Pule Siblings, for comradeship was reserved only for those who belonged to the Movement.

The Pule Siblings would, however, remain town councillors until the next local elections. Not that Sekatle had not tried to get them kicked off the council as well. Unfortunately, the constitution of the land did not allow him to do so. Only the people who had elected them to the council could remove them through the ballot box. Popi thought it was pathetic the way Viliki insisted that he was still a member of the Movement, whether Sekatle and his allies liked it or not. He had worked for this Movement to make it what it was in the rural areas of the Free State. He was going to die a member of the Movement.

"Why would you want to remain a member of an organisation that does not want you?" she asked.

Popi felt free now that she did not have to attend branch meetings and caucuses. On the council, she and her brother were able to vote with their consciences rather than having to toe some political line. Without the demands of the Movement, she could even indulge in the occasional cow-dung gathering expedition with Niki.

While Popi was immersed in books, cow-dung and funerals, Viliki was immersed in the Seller of Songs. His body sang deep inside hers. And hers to his. Until they broke into sharp arias that sounded close to pain. Although the sharpness disturbed the neighbours and passers-by, it was celebratory in its exhilaration.

Everybody in Excelsior was immersed in something. Even Tjaart Cronje. He was immersed in anger. This was an immersion he shared with Popi. She, of course, denied that there was any anger in her. Tjaart Cronje was more honest. He did not make a secret of his anger. His people had been sold out by their leaders, he lamented. The ageing matriarch, Cornelia Cronje, joined him in his laments. She was immersed in an anger of her own. And in loneliness. The affirmative action people, as mother and son called them, were entrenching themselves in power and becoming more confident. Some would say more arrogant. Even though the mayor was a true-blooded Afrikaner woman, she was a quisling who trod lightly and didn't want to offend "these people". She was obviously being misled by Popi Pule, with whom she was seen on many occasions. This Popi must be the one who was advising her to defer to the interests of the people of Mahlatswetsa Location. Only when he got home in the evenings did Tjaart Cronje receive relief from this burning anger. In his castle, the Afrikaner was still the boss. And Jacomina was the soothing balm.

It was true that Her Worship the Mayor of Excelsior seemed to rely very much on Popi's counsel. It was Popi who had suggested that it would do Excelsior a lot of good if the town had a festival of its own. Small towns were thriving on festivals that promoted a local product. Even the dusty towns of the faraway Eastern Cape. Barkly East, for instance, had a Trout Festival. Some of these festivals gained fame nationally, and even internationally, like Fickburg's cherry festival. Although the organisers of this festival liked to claim that it belonged to the rest of the eastern Free State, it really benefited Ficksburg more than any other town. It put Ficksburg on the map. Not Fouriesburg. Not Clocolan. Not Ladybrand. And certainly not Excelsior.

Excelsior needed a festival of its own, Popi argued. Why, even neighbouring Clocolan had an event that drew farmers from all over southern Africa: the Clocolan Tractor and Farm Implement Show. Excelsior must have its own festival.

"Of what?" asked Lizette de Vries. "What are we going to promote?"

"I don't know," said Popi. "We need to think of something."

"Perhaps we should visit some of these festivals," said Lizette de Vries. "We might get some ideas."

When the time came, Popi Pule and Lizette de Vries took a casual drive in Lizette's Isuzu bakkie to Clocolan, fifty-five kilometres on a shimmering bitumen road lined on both sides with cosmos of different colours. Among these grew yellow sunflowers that had adapted to a life of wildness. They had developed small heads as a result, in order not to appear bigger than the cosmos that were hosting them. Every year, the heads of these roadside sunflowers became smaller.

The Clocolan Tractor and Farm Implement Show was one of the highlights of the year for the eastern Free State farming community. The Show Grounds turned green, yellow and red with old and new tractors, ploughs and trailers on display. There were yellow Caterpillar Challenger tractors, red Massey Ferguson tractors and green John Deere tractors. There were also the newfangled Fiat and Volvo tractors that were smaller, and which were catching on fast with trendy farmers. Although there was also giant equipment on display, such as harvesters and irrigation equipment, the crowds were drawn more to the tractors. On this occasion, the showpiece was a 1930 John Deere Model D tractor. Popi and Lizette de Vries joined the crowd that surrounded the veteran John Deere.

"Since when have you become a farmer, Lizette?" asked a voice.

She turned quickly to find herself staring into the smiling eyes of Johannes Smit. She had not seen him for quite some time. He had not been socialising much with the likes of Adam de Vries and his wife, given that he believed that they belonged to the group of Afrikaners who had sold the Boere out to the communists. A group that had been misled by one F.W. de Klerk, who had capitulated to one Nelson Mandela as soon as the Afrikaners had elected the said de Klerk President of South Africa. Johannes Smit kept his distance from such Afrikaners. And immersed himself in his farming. Occasionally he visited Tjaart Cronje at his house or at the butchery to complain about how the affirmative action people were messing up Excelsior. Soon the town would be bankrupt, the two agreed. Sewerage would run in the streets. Everything would collapse. Things would be so bad that the Afrikaner would seize power again to put things in order. He was eagerly waiting for that moment. Perhaps the election of Lizette de Vries to the mayoral position, after the affirmative action people had failed to run the town efficiently, was a step in that direction.

"Johannes!" cried Lizette de Vries. "It is wonderful to see you."

Johannes Smit looked at Popi for a long time. Until she began to fidget.

"This is Popi Pule," said Lizette Vries. "She is the town councillor in charge of libraries."

"Of course," chuckled Johannes Smit. "But she won't find any books here. Except for tractor manuals."

"I am not looking for books here," said Popi.

"Of course you wouldn't be looking for books here," said Johannes Smit coldly. "You look for them in the white library in town to take to your white elephant library in the township. You slash the budget of the library in town in order to stock the township library."

"There is no white library in town," said Popi, smiling condescendingly. "The library in town and the one in Mahlatswetsa Location both belong to all the people of Excelsior."

Lizette de Vries laughed and commented that she would never

have imagined the day when Johannes Smit would be interested in libraries and their budgets. Popi walked away to take a closer look at the showpiece.

"She is as feisty as her mother," said Johannes Smit.

"You remember her mother, then?" asked Lizette de Vries.

"I would not have known she was Niki's daughter. But you see, she looks like Stephanus Cronje. A beautiful version of Stephanus Cronje."

Then he added as an afterthought, "When he died, he was more or less the age she is now."

Popi made her way back to join them, and Lizette de Vries felt uncomfortable with the subject. She asked if Johannes Smit had anything on display. He led them to his brand-new John Deere six-cylinder turbo-charged green and yellow tractor. He insisted that Popi climb up onto the seat and showed her how to start the engine. She turned on the ignition and pressed the accelerator. The engine roared. She laughed the laughter of the peals of little bells. The second chin of the bald-headed round-bellied man with a sagging face shook with laughter. Lizette de Vries smiled and shook her head in wonder.

The next time Lizette de Vries and Popi met Johannes Smit was at the cherry festival in Ficksburg two months later. The two women were still exploring various festivals, hoping that a bright idea for the great Excelsior Festival would strike them. Although they were only at this festival for one day, they were able to sample some of the entertainment and to join tour groups to cherry and asparagus farms. Johannes Smit invited them to his stall and treated them to his cherry liqueur. An old black couple at a table nearby stared at them. The name of Stephanus Cronje and something about the Excelsior 19 escaped their lips. They thought they were whispering between themselves. But their whispers had the quality of stage whispers. They found their way to Johannes Smit's stall, and to Popi's ears.

Old people had a tendency to remember things that happened thirty years ago whenever they saw Popi. And to think of people she knew nothing about. For no one had ever given her any history lessons on the events that had shaped the town of Excelsior. She knew vaguely that there had been a scandal. Snippets of gossip about her origins had drifted her way throughout her twenty-nine years of existence. She never asked Niki anything about it and Niki never volunteered anything. Popi did not want to know. She was Pule's child.

THEY SAY our mothers no longer want to talk about these things. Our mothers have learnt to live with themselves. Niki lives with the bees. She is immersed in them. She is immersed in serenity.

AN OLD LOVE AFFAIR

S OMEONE'S PORTRAIT. A much more naturalistic head
in a battered black hat. Perhaps the trinity wants to show
that his range extends beyond distorted figures. That he
can paint real people. People who look like those we see in our
daily lives. This face, however, is not likely to be seen in our daily
lives. It belongs to the days of ox-wagons and trekkers. Although
the man does not look at you directly, his eyes are deep and penetrating. The face is as weather-beaten as the hat, with deep furrows
of wisdom roaming fervently across it. A black pipe hangs loosely
over the white beard. A blue neckerchief appears above the collar
of a heavy brown coat.

When Viliki was not immersed in the Seller of Songs, he visited
Adam de Vries at his office to engage in what de Vries quaintly
called "chewing the fat".

Viliki walked into the reception room and looked at the portrait
of the lawyer's bearded ancestor that hung on the wall next to a
flag of the old South Africa. He was a regular visitor to this office,
yet he always wondered why de Vries displayed this painful flag
when he professed to be of the new South Africa. In fact, he actu-

ally claimed that he had brought about the new South Africa. He often told Viliki about a congress he had once attended in 1982 in Marquard, another eastern Free State town thirty-four kilometers north of Clocolan. He had been one of the 260 delegates of the National Party. He could see the waves of the right-wing, he said. He had bravely stood up and told the congress that the government had no option but to negotiate with the Movement and unban it.

"They nearly crucified me," said de Vries, obviously enjoying the memory. "It was long before people like F.W. de Klerk came onto the scene and released Mandela. In fact, in those days de Klerk was one of the right-wingers. I referred the delegates to the Bible and they could have eaten me alive. I told them that in the Bible the Lord often punished His people . . . He often used heathens to punish His people. 'The Lord may punish us too,' I said. 'The Lord may use the Movement to punish us.' "

Viliki sat on a bench under a bold sign with the dictum: *A customer is always right. Sometimes confused, misinformed, rude, stubborn, changeable and even downright stupid. But never wrong!!!* And then a picture of a donkey sitting human-style on a stool.

Adam de Vries's white-haired prim and proper secretary was typing something on a rickety typewriter at a small desk behind the long reception counter. After a while, she noticed him.

"You know that Mr de Vries is busy," she said in her schoolmarmish voice. "You like to visit him during office hours. He is not idle like you town councillors, you know. He has clients to attend to."

"I'll wait until he's free," said Viliki, raising his voice so that it would sneak into Adam de Vries's office.

"Is that Viliki?" shouted Adam de Vries from his office. "Tell him I'll be with him just now."

Viliki contemplated the portrait on the wall. The old codger was stern-faced. And pensive. Yet Viliki imagined him bursting into laughter. A long self-fulfilled laughter. Until tears ran down

the furrows of his salty face. A laughter of sorrow. But the ancestor remained unmoved. And stared as he had been staring over the
years.

A young Afrikaner woman in blue denim jeans and her son of
about four, walked out of Adam de Vries's office. She greeted Viliki in the polite singsong voice of Basotho women, "Dumelang."
Viliki responded, "Dumela le wena, mme." Greetings to you too,
mother.

In Sesotho, every woman is "mother". Even when she is
younger than your younger sister.

"You can come in now, Viliki," shouted Adam de Vries.

Viliki looked at the schoolmarm and gave her a triumphant
smirk. She frowned and went back to pounding the keys of the old
Remington typewriter. He walked into the office. Adam de Vries
pointed him to a chair.

"Divorce," he said. "I don't know what is happening with young
people these days. They marry today, and the next day they part. I
hate handling divorce cases, especially when the custody of children is involved."

"I thought lawyers didn't get their personal feelings mixed up
with business," said Viliki.

"Lawyers are human beings too."

"Lawyers have no scruples, Meneer. They defend anyone who
can pay."

"A person is innocent until proven guilty by a court of law, Viliki," explained Adam de Vries. "When a lawyer takes your case, at
that stage you are innocent. Only a court of law can determine
otherwise. And it does so only after the case."

Viliki had no answer for this. Somehow it did not sound right.
But Adam de Vries had a way of twisting things so that he did not
know how to respond. He decided to be wicked. To provoke him
about his professed role in the anti-apartheid struggle.

"Hey Meneer, at your congress in Marquard so many years ago,
what made you suggest that your people should negotiate with the
heathens?"

"I was merely quoting the Bible when I talked of heathens," said Adam de Vries defensively. "You are not going to take me to the Human Rights Commission for racism, are you?"

"Well," said Viliki light-heartedly, "I can call them heathens too as they kicked me out of my own Movement. But what I want to know is, what created your doubts about apartheid?"

"I think they had their genesis in the Immorality Act case of 1971," said Adam de Vries. "I began to question some of our laws."

Adam de Vries had boasted about his old cases to Viliki before. Including the case of the Excelsior 19. And Viliki did not mind when this case was discussed, even though his mother had been one of the accused. He even joked that had it not been for the capers of those days, he would not have had a sister as beautiful as Popi.

It was obvious to Viliki that Adam de Vries was a bored man. He looked back with nostalgia to the days when he handled some of the most exciting cases of Excelsior. Today most of his business involved what he called chamber work, drawing up wills and transfer deeds. A little bit of conveyancing here; a little bit of notarial work there. Once in a while, the odd divorce case, for which he normally briefed advocates in Bloemfontein. The days of courtroom drama were gone. He could only relive them in his stories to Viliki.

"Yes, that was the greatest case of all time," said Adam de Vries. "But I tell you, Viliki, those women were bribed to frame the white men."

"And I suppose their children made themselves," said Viliki, without any enthusiasm. He had heard this version of the Excelsior 19 case so many times that he was prepared to let it pass.

"But I tell you, we were ready for them," continued Adam de Vries, ignoring Viliki's comment. "We were going to win that case. It was going to be very bad for the country. That was why John Vorster instructed Percy Yutar to withdraw the case."

"You say as a result of this case, you began to question your laws," said Viliki, "but you remained in the party for the next thirty years. Why?"

"To change it from within. People like de Klerk and I changed the National Party from within. That is why today the National Party is the party that brought about the new dispensation in South Africa."

Viliki laughed for a long time. Until Adam de Vries got irritated.

"So it's really you who brought us this freedom we are enjoying today?" asked Viliki, still laughing. "All this time we thought it was the Movement and the other organisations. What were we doing fighting for freedom in the underground when you and de Klerk were here all along to free us?"

"Listen," said Adam de Vries, not bothering to hide his annoyance, "I am busy. I cannot sit here all day listening to your idle talk. Don't you have any work to do at the council?"

"You know, Meneer," said Viliki as he made to go, "these days it is very difficult to find a white person who ever supported apartheid."

We watched Viliki walk out of Adam de Vries's office. We knew that whenever he was bored, whenever he had had his fill of the Seller of Songs' music that tingled in his veins, making his body hot to the point of explosion, he sauntered off to Adam de Vries's office in town. We wondered what it was that had drawn these two together. At least Popi and Lizette de Vries were drawn together by their work. But Viliki and Adam de Vries?

When the inquisitive quizzed him about it, Viliki would only say, "He is a nice guy, although a white man will always be a white man."

The likes of Tjaart Cronje and Johannes Smit said that Adam de Vries was Viliki's puppet. It was not enough that his party had sold out the Afrikaner; Adam de Vries was now dancing to the tune of the blacks who were taking the country down the sewer. Otherwise what would an Afrikaner lawyer have in common with an unschooled township boy?

The people of the Movement said de Vries was the puppeteer

and Viliki the puppet. The Pule Siblings no longer represented the interests of the people of Mahlatswetsa Location in the council chamber, but those of the rich Afrikaners of Excelsior.

We, on the other hand, were not bothered by these friendships. We put them down to the old love affair between black people and Afrikaners that the English found so irritating. Even at the height of apartheid, blacks preferred dealing with Afrikaners to the English-speaking South Africans. The English, common wisdom stated, were hypocrites. They laughed with you, but immediately you turned, they stabbed you in the back. The Afrikaner, on the other hand, was honest. When he hated you, he showed you at once. He did not pretend to like you. If he hated blacks, he said so publicly. So, when you dealt with him, you knew who you were dealing with. When he smiled, you knew he was genuine. One could never trust the smile of an Englishman.

We never questioned what informed these generalisations.

VILIKI WALKED aimlessly down the main street of Excelsior, which was really the only street of note in the town. The rest of the streets were lined with residential houses. The street was bustling with excited people. There was a carnival atmosphere as men, women and children walked from one shop to the next with plastic bags full of groceries. Other people gathered at the Greek café, which was really a Portuguese café, to treat themselves to Russian sausages and chips.

It was payday in Excelsior. The aged who were on old-age pensions had received their monthly grants. And their children and grandchildren were out to spend the money on both necessities and luxuries. Payday always caused such excitement. Even children knew when it was payday, because most families depended on the money that the government gave to the aged for being old. The most fortunate families were those that had one or two mentally or physically disabled members. Their disability grants, paid on the same day as the old-age pensions, fed entire families.

Viliki became part of the buzz of excitement, joining some friends from Mahlatswetsa Location who wanted to have a few beers at the off-sales liquor outlet, or bottle store, adjacent to the only hotel in town. They bought the beers and sat on the window ledge outside the bottle store, as was the custom. The owner allowed them to sit on the inside window sill in front of the counter when the weather was not conducive to imbibing outdoors.

They watched as Afrikaner men and women walked in and out of the pub at the hotel. Viliki and his friends had never been inside that pub. The thought never even entered their heads to drink there. It was the domain of the Afrikaners of Excelsior. And everyone left it at that.

Viliki saw Tjaart Cronje and Johannes Smit climb out of a four-wheel-drive vehicle, singing boisterously. Jacomina followed, reprimanding them for making too much noise. They only laughed at her and sang even louder, dancing clownishly around her as they walked into the pub.

Viliki had not seen Johannes Smit for quite some time. Since the time he had burst into the council chamber to complain about the increase in rates a year ago. To cheers of derision from the Movement council members and of admiration from Tjaart Cronje, and to the bemusement of the National Party members, he had stood up in the gallery, and had shouted out of turn, "I am a farmer! I feed South Africa! The very Mandelas and Mbekis cannot survive without me!"

Viliki sipped his beer from the one-litre bottle and wondered why people like Tjaart Cronje and Johannes Smit were so angry. Were people like Viliki, Popi and Niki not the ones who should be angry? Were they not entitled even to a shred of anger? Why should the Afrikaner hoard all the anger?

POSKAART/POSTCARD 2

*S*TREET SIGNS INDICATE that this is a crossroad. He pulls the two-wheeled unhooded cart across the crimson soil like a rickshaw man. His red hair has been tied into a big bun that hangs like a cap over his face. It is a small delicate face connected by a thick neck to a small delicate body clad in golden-yellow overalls. His grey boots have patches of red from the soil. His body is bent slightly forward from the weight of the cart. He pulls it among golden-yellow sunflowers. On the cart sits a brown Mother Mary with a brown Baby Jesus in her arms. She looks like a nun in a blue veil. Three giant candles burn in the cart: one in front, two at the back. A white giant star of Bethlehem spreads its white light between the puller of the cart and its riders. Sunflowers flourish on the crimson soil. Three giant sunflowers grow out of the blue and white sky.

Kersfees in die Karretjie. Xmas in the Small Cart. By: Father Frans Claerhouut. Popi read the bottom of the postcard and laughed. She had never noticed before that they had misspelt the trinity's name. They had added an extra *u*, which served him right, as he had mastered the art of distorting everything. Houses. People. Donkeys. Rickshaws. Sunflowers and cosmos. Even holy personages like Jesus and Mary. It was poetic justice that the printer had distorted his name too. A man who could be possessed by such beautiful madness that he placed road signs in the middle of a sunflower field deserved to have his name distorted.

It was Christmas in Excelsior, too. Popi had taken out her exercise book to look at the postcards. She wondered if the trinity would be painting on Christmas Day. Maybe the picture on the postcard was created on Christmas Day. She remembered her last visit to the trinity's studio many years ago. As a fourteen-year-old freckled girl. Before she became a woman of thirty whose tall slender frame was burdened with anger. She felt an urge to go to the mission house in Tweespruit to see him again. To bathe her troubled soul in the colourful canvases that surrounded him.

Christmas had lost the festive aura it used to have when she was a little girl. Those days, girls wore their new taffeta dresses and went to show off at church in the morning. Boys also dressed up in colourful new shirts, even when the pants of those whose parents could not afford new outfits were the old Sunday pants. Christmases were feasting days. Families used to cook special meals. After a big lunch of rice, chicken, cabbage, beetroot, tomato and onion gravy, jelly and custard, and home-baked hard cakes with ginger beer, the children would take a songful stroll to the houses of white people in town. There they would stand at the gate of each house and ask for a "Christmas Box." The white folk would send their children or maids to the gate with sweets and cookies. Late in the afternoon the children would sing their way back to Mahlatswetsa Location, where they would divide the spoils amongst themselves.

But these days, Christmas had lost its lustre. Children did not seem to care any more. They spent the whole day in their old clothes. Parents still maintained the tradition of buying new clothes. But the children refused to wear them on Christmas Day. They kept them in their boxes to wear during the year when no one would know they had been bought for Christmas.

Christmas had now become like an ordinary Sunday, except for the fact that the service was a Christmas service; the reading from the Bible was about the birth of Christ, and the preaching was about what that birth meant to the world. After the service, people went home to eat their ordinary Sunday lunches, which looked like the Christmas lunches of old except for the absence of jelly and custard, and cakes and ginger beer. Adults went to get drunk, as they did every weekend, while children just loitered around street corners in small groups.

This Christmas, unlike others, Popi had not cooked any special lunch. Neither had Niki. Popi sat on the bed and stared at the Christmas cart. She wondered why a man instead of the customary donkey was pulling it. She could never figure out the trinity. How his mind worked. Still, she enjoyed his madness, and found it moving.

Niki sat under one of the bluegum trees that lined the road leading into Excelsior. The evergreen melliodora and the black ironbark well beloved by honeybees. She sat on a white plastic garden chair, and watched the worker bees as they flew from the trees laden with pollen and nectar to the hives that she had placed on the ground. Her eyes followed the bees from the hives back to the flowers on the trees and into the hives again. The wooden hives could be seen among the long blades of grass, sometimes peeping above them, along the three-kilometre stretch of road. She had placed them randomly, facing in different directions to make it easier for the bees to find their particular hives. If the hives had been placed in a straight line facing the same direction, this would have confused the bees, as they would not have known to which hive they belonged. She had learnt, at the one-day bee-keeping course on a farm at Ficksburg Viliki had sent her to, that unlike American bees, South African bees did not know how to count.

Some of Niki's hives were placed in clusters. Four hives to each cluster. Back to back and facing in different directions. Four different colours in each cluster. Red, blue, yellow and green. In the three-kilometre stretch, there were thirty hives.

At the farm, without the knowledge of the farmer, Niki had

learnt from the labourers how to construct beehives. Each hive
had a honey chamber and a brood chamber. Each chamber had
ten frames on which honeycombs hung. In the brood chamber of
each hive were the queen and the drones and the eggs and the
brood.

Every morning Niki took her white garden chair and a piece of
bread wrapped in plastic, and walked the six kilometres from
Mahlatswetsa Location through the town to the bluegum trees.
There she sat among the hives for the whole day. Listening to the
buzzing of the bees. Watching the worker bees doing their work.
Sitting still even as some of the bees danced around her, commu-
nicating calming messages to her through their airborne hor-
mones. It was as if she shared the same pheromones with the bees.

Whenever she harvested some of the hives, Niki gave the honey
away.

The message would be relayed from one mouth to the next: *The
Bee Woman has honey.* We would then walk along the road as if we
were on a particular journey. We would see her sitting on the chair
among the hives, and would greet her in the sweetest of voices.
She would call us to come and get some honey. She would give us
honeycombs from the pile in a white plastic bucket in front of her.
She did not wonder why we happened to have containers—empty
billycans and pots—on our journey. Or why our journey suddenly
came to an end and we turned back to the township as soon as she
had given us the honey.

Her misguided generosity did not sit well with Viliki, who had
helped her with the material to construct the hives in the first
place. He had also assisted her with the construction of the catch-
boxes that were used to trap swarming bees. Right from the beginning, as the councillor in charge of the parks, he had allowed her
to place the hives in the veld near the trees that lined the road. He
had even sent her to the farm at Ficksburg to learn more scientific
ways of bee-keeping, while Popi was insisting that her mother be
left alone to keep bees in her own way, using the wisdom that her

ancestors had given her. Clearly her ancestors were talking to her through the bees, and it would be interfering with this communication if she were taught European ways of keeping bees, Popi had reasoned. Viliki had gone to all this trouble because he hoped that Niki would be able to make a living from the bees. Not just give honey away to passers-by.

Viliki once discussed his concerns with Adam de Vries, who went to offer his assistance to Niki.

"I can help you to expand your bee-keeping enterprise and make it financially viable," he had said.

Niki had thanked him for the offer, but had made it clear that she did not need anyone's assistance.

Even on Christmas Day Niki sat among the bees. And Popi sat on the bed in her mother's shack. She was getting bored with the postcards. She could not go to the library on Christmas Day. It was closed. Nor could she go to collect cow-dung. In any event, cow-dung gathering expeditions were only enjoyable when Niki was there. Popi decided to get into the Christmas rickshaw, to sit behind Baby Jesus and Mother Mary, and ride along the dusty road of Mahlatswetsa Location, until it joined the broad tarred road that led to the town, past the closed shops and banks, right up to the stretch of road that was lined with bluegum trees. There she found Niki sitting on her garden chair among the hives.

Niki was pleased to see her daughter. She was always happy when Popi came to visit her. To pay homage to her, as Popi put it. We observed that the motlopotlo that existed between them was very strong. The motlopotlo was the invisible cord that tied the child to the mother. It was the umbilical cord that remained strong even after it had been cut and buried in the ash-heap after the birth of the child. Some mothers were fortunate in that the motlopotlo between them and their children remained strong throughout their lives. The less fortunate mothers had a weak motlopotlo. Their children forgot all about them and disappeared from their lives.

Popi sat on the grass at Niki's feet. There was silence between them for some time. Then suddenly Niki said, "I did many wrong things in my life."

"I don't care what you did in your life, Niki," said Popi quietly. "I don't want to know."

"Yet some of them have had a sweet harvest," continued Niki, as if she had not heard her. "If I had not done what I did, you would not be here."

Popi did not try to make sense of what Niki was saying.

"Are you still angry with Tjaart?" Niki asked.

"I do not want to be angry with Tjaart. I do not want to be angry with anyone."

"At least now you do admit that you have some anger in you."

"I told you, I react to his anger. I become angry at his anger. Perhaps I have gone overboard with my anger. Perhaps when the people of Mahlatswetsa made me angry by calling me names, I took it out on him."

"Remember, my child, anger eats the owner."

This sounded very much like the message that Jacomina and her father were trying to transmit to Tjaart Cronje. If Popi had ridden her Christmas rickshaw to the Cronje household, she would have found Cornelia Cronje, Tjaart Cronje, Jacomina Cronje and the Reverend François Bornman sitting on the veranda, enjoying their coffee and brandy after a lunch of roast quail with berry sauce, and trying to talk Tjaart Cronje out of his anger.

As usual Cornelia was fussing over Tjaart, to the annoyance of Jacomina. Cornelia always fussed over Tjaart as if he was a child. *Did you have enough, Tjaart? Don't you want another piece of this . . . or that?* It irritated Jacomina even more that Tjaart allowed himself to become a baby whenever Cornelia was around. *Is Tjaart warm enough? . . . Don't allow him to go out in the cold like that, Jacomina . . . Did Tjaart eat before he left . . . Oh, my child this . . . my child that!*

Jacomina had once complained: "You won't be there to pick up the pieces when Tjaart gets thoroughly spoilt, Cornelia."

She called her mother-in-law Cornelia, as she had always done before she married her son.

Cornelia Cronje had mumbled something to the effect that Jacomina did not know how to look after a man properly. That was why her first husband had left.

"I heard that," Jacomina had screamed.

Cornelia kept silent as Jacomina and the dominee discussed her son's anger. It was not doing him any good, they said. He had turned thin and twisted because his anger was eating him up, they observed. Cornelia observed in her mind, without voicing her thoughts out of respect for the dominee, that her son had become thin and twisted because Jacomina was not feeding him properly.

"Every time he returns from the town council meetings he can't even eat because of anger," said Jacomina.

"It is that Popi who needles him all the time in the council," Cornelia burst out in defence of her son, unable to contain herself any longer. "Everyone in this town knows that that girl would like to see my child dead."

Tjaart Cronje admitted that his little tiffs with Popi were indeed affecting his health.

"I am fighting a lonely war on many fronts," explained Tjaart Cronje. "It is Popi on one front, who always wants to take the first opportunity to annoy me. But there is a broader and bigger front, where I fight for the rights of the Afrikaner—rights which are being trampled upon every day."

"We agreed, Tjaart, that you would not talk politics at home," said Jacomina.

"You started the subject, not me," said Tjaart Cronje.

"So now he can't even express an opinion in his own house?" asked Cornelia.

"Politics only makes him unhappy," explained Jacomina.

"Perhaps in the next local elections in November he shouldn't stand," advised the dominee.

"I certainly won't stand," said Tjaart resolutely. "Let the black people take this town and ruin it. I'll focus on my butchery, and on planning for the return of the Afrikaner to his rightful place."

"We do not need to be sombre," said the dominee, getting up from his garden chair and going to the table, which was laden with drinks and fruit. "It is Christmas! Let us have some more of your wonderful brandy, my boy."

The Christmas rickshaw left them to their Christmas cheer and returned to Niki and Popi.

They were sitting silently, listening to the bees. Niki unwrapped the turban from Popi's head and exposed the locks that flowed to her waist. She caressed her daughter's hair.

"While you are at it, why don't you scratch my scalp," said Popi. "It is always itching."

"It is because of dandruff. It is all over your head like flakes of snow. You don't wash your hair often enough."

"This hair is a curse," said Popi. "I never know what to do with it."

After thirty years, she had still not learnt how to deal with her hair. Even as a young girl she had always regretted the fact that she could not do the things that other girls her age did with their hair. She could not use the trendy hair straighteners like Dark-and-Lovely and Sta-sof-fro—all the way from America—because her hair was already straight. She had watched with envy as other girls relaxed their hair by frying it with chemicals or with red-hot copper combs. She herself was deprived participation in that ritual as her hair did not need relaxing. She could not be part of the camaraderie of braiding either. Once she had tried braiding her hair, but had had to undo it immediately when she saw her split ends sticking out all over the braids like a badly made raffia rope. She could not use extensions because her hair was already naturally extended. She had watched with envy as grease dripped down her friends' ears after a perm. She had drooled at their cornrows. At their dreadlocks. And most recently at their closely cropped kinks that had been dyed blonde. Her hair remained flowing locks. She alone, among her friends, could flip her head like a white woman.

This became necessary whenever activity or the wind blew some of her locks across the front of her face. The turban, therefore, continued to be her saviour.

"Your hair cannot be a curse, Popi," said Niki quietly. "God cannot create a curse on your head."

"The pain of my whole life is locked in my hair," said Popi bitterly.

"Hair is just hair, Popi. Hair or no hair, you are a beautiful person, Popi. A very beautiful person."

VILIKI WAS grateful. So was Niki. From the outrage of rape (that's what we called it in our post-apartheid euphoria), our mothers gave birth to beautiful human beings. As beautiful as the Seller of Songs, who could create beautiful things. As beautiful as Popi, who could not create, but who knew how to love beautiful creations like the trinity's Christmas cart that took her and her mother back to Mahlatswetsa Location that evening, after spending a comely Christmas Day with the bees.

SOMETIMES THERE IS A VOID

S HE IS NOT a madonna. Although she sits like one. There is no baby in sight. Her golden-brown body is illuminated by red streaks of light. She is naked, except for the veil of lace that flows from her head to the blue floor on which she sits. Black outlines reinforce her fullness. She looks away from the window on which the shadow of a voyeur is cast. Between her open legs is a red bowl. In front of her, two white doves are foolishly pecking at the flowers on the lace. Soon they will discover the lifelessness of the flowers and will hop to peck at the blackness of her pubes, where life throbs.

Colour goes haywire. Once more a beautiful madness. Life throbs in the green field where two black reapers cut green wheat with their invisible scythes. They put it over their shoulders, where it immediately assumes a yellow ochre colour with tinges of red. One bends to cut the wheat. He wears blue overalls and black gumboots. A wide-brimmed red hat protects him from the absent sun. Another one stands to stretch his tired back. He wears a red Basotho blanket. A black conical Basotho hat protects him from the absent sun. A black donkey pulls a red cart in the field, trampling the crops. A black man and a black child sit in the cart. Not black as in black, but black as in Payne's grey. A black hat protects the black man from the absent sun. The field is not only green. It has broad strokes of titanium white. Strokes of yellow ochre. Strokes of naphthol crimson. Green, white, yellow and crimson strokes extend to the cobalt blue sky.

A wide-eyed girl stands against a deep blue wall. The whites of her eyes are white and the pupils are black. She hides a subtle smile in her blue and green face. She stands between two reliquary figures. One is dressed in white and the other is bare-breasted. Nothing else. No other detail. Just the questions that remain in her eyes.

The same questions were in Popi's eyes as she moved from one canvas to another. *What did it all mean? Did it matter that she did not understand what it all meant? Was it not enough just to enjoy the haunting quality of the work and to rejoice in the emotions that it awakened without quibbling about what it all meant? Why should it mean anything at all? Is it not enough that it* evokes? *Should it now also* mean?

She tried very hard to identify the Flemish expressionist influence that she had read about in the oversized books in the library. The trinity had clearly strayed away from that early influence. All for the better. His work had a robustness that had escaped the Flemish expressionists. Perhaps it was the broad strokes, some of which were created with palette knives instead of the usual broad brushes. And the multiple glazes that seemed to suck her into the canvases, making her walk the same soil that the trinity's subjects walked.

She had finally come to Tweespruit. To the mission station where the trinity had been based since leaving Thaba Nchu many years ago. She had found the trinity hard at work. Not painting. At eighty-three, he was too old to mess around with pigments. Perhaps his eyes could no longer distinguish the different colours. Or he was too frail to survive the excitement of mixing different colours of oil paints, and of acrylics, to create feasts of new colours. He was hard at work spraying fixative onto a charcoal drawing of a girl reading a book in the candlelight. He was covering his nose with a dirty rag to protect himself from the fumes that assailed the crisp air.

Charcoal drawings. That was all he was capable of creating now. A world in black and white.

The trinity had led her into the living room. The walls were filled with many of his old paintings. They re-created the ambience of his studio in Thaba Nchu. It was as if she had been here before. As soon as she had entered and cast her eyes on the walls, memories of previous visits to Thaba Nchu had flooded her. She had recalled with nostalgia the visits that had made her see everybody's life through the eyes of the trinity's works.

At first, the trinity had thought she was one of the women who had come to model for his nudes. She had stood there for a while, feeling very uncomfortable. The trinity had smiled, and looked her over. Then he had told her that he no longer painted nudes. He no longer painted anything. Jokingly, he had added that even if he were still in his painting prime, she would not qualify as a model. She did not have enough flesh on her body. She was tall and slender like the models of the city. Not like the trinity's buxom models. She had felt naked as he inspected her. It was as though her yellow and blue floral dress, her fawn petticoat and matching knickers, and her red turban had disintegrated. But with the naked feeling, she was no longer uncomfortable. She had been naked here before. Many times. She had fixed her blue eyes on the trinity's. Both she and the trinity had smiled. And then he had shaped a donkey from the pages of a magazine and had emitted two brays as he gave it to her. She had known at once that he had remembered who she was.

Popi had caught a minibus taxi to Tweespruit, twenty-nine kilometres from Excelsior, on the pretext that she was going to ask the trinity to donate a painting for the library in Mahlatswetsa Location. But as she bathed herself in the light of the canvases, she knew that that was not the reason she had come. She did not even mention the donation. She just walked from one canvas to the next. Over and over again. The trinity watched her silently for a while, and then went back to his charcoal drawings.

The works exuded an energy that enveloped her, draining her of all negative feelings. She felt weak at the knees. Tears ran down her cheeks. She did not know why she was crying. She had to go. She walked out of the living room, and out of the mission station, without even saying goodbye. She had not uttered a word to the trinity throughout her visit. Yet she felt she had been healed of a deadly ailment she could not really describe.

In the taxi back home, weakness was replaced by a great feeling of exhilaration. There was no room for anger and bitterness in her any more. Yet an emptiness remained in what she imagined to be her heart. Anger had dissipated and left a void.

How was she to fill the void?

PROFOUND NOSTALGIA

*A*LL THINGS ARE bright and beautiful. Even the smile on the man straddling the light brown donkey. In the summer heat he wears a blue and white woollen cap, blue overalls and brown boots. He holds a giant white candle to illuminate his path in the bright daylight. The donkey is burdened not only by the man, but also by its huge head and tall ears. And the white brush strokes on its behind. It walks tiredly on the blue and yellow ground. A giant sunflower follows it. Strokes of white clouds rise in the cobalt blue sky. Like smoke signals to a world beyond.

Even bright beautiful days come to an end. The yellow sandstone hills of the Free State changed into dark mounds that loomed on the horizon. Fires began to burn outside some homesteads. Children sang songs of the evening. Boys and girls played hide-and-seek. Finding hiding places where they could tickle one another without being discovered. Smoke from coal stoves and braziers hovered above Mahlatswetsa Location. Over the years, some of us had gradually moved from cow-dung to coal.

The Pule Siblings sat at a brazier in front of their mother's shack. Viliki sat on an empty beer box and Popi sat on a pile of bricks. They were waiting for the coal to change from black to red-hot before taking the brazier into the shack. By which time the smoke that was billowing to the sky would be gone. Only the fumes would remain. None of them liked to breathe in the fumes from burning coal. They were used to the gentle smoke of dry cow-dung. But Niki's homestead no longer had sufficient supplies of cow-dung, now that she spent most of her time with the bees instead of gathering cow-dung. And, of course, Popi was busy with her library and council meetings. She had no choice but to buy coal from Sekatle's coal-yard and carry it home in a battered washing basin.

The Pule Siblings sat as they used to sit when they were a little boy and a little girl. They roasted dry maize on the cob on the side of the brazier where a big hole displayed the coal that was beginning to turn red. Once one side of the cob was roasted, Viliki took it from the brazier and with his thumb plucked out a row of corn, which he crunched with relish. He passed the cob to Popi, who did the same. Then she put it back on the brazier to roast another side.

They sang songs that they used to sing during the struggle. The chimurenga songs of the Zimbabwean war of liberation that Viliki had taught Popi whenever he came back home from the underground. The songs of the Frelimo cadres of Mozambique. They did not understand the languages of these songs. It was possible that they were not even pronouncing the words correctly. But it did not matter. The haunting harmonies were good enough to evoke a feeling of deep nostalgia. As did the songs whose languages they understood very well. The songs that the cadres of the Movement sang, that Viliki had also brought home for Popi's pleasure. They sang these with a new passion. The passion of those who had fought battles and won, but had not survived the victory.

A profound nostalgia for the romantic days of the struggle attacked them. Days of sacrifice and death. Days of selfless service and hope.

"At least those days we were together fighting the same war as comrades in arms," reminisced Viliki. "Sharing our suffering and moments of respite. Now others are up there and have forgotten about the rest. Survival of the fittest is the new ethos. Each one for himself or herself in the scramble for the accumulation of wealth."

It had started like that in Zimbabwe too—a liberation struggle that had inspired Viliki and his comrades during the worst moments of their own oppression. As soon as the revolutionaries had got into power, Popi wailed, they had focused on accumulating farms and hotels for themselves. Ardent revolutionaries continued to use the rhetoric of socialism, while in behaviour and outlook they were born-again capitalists.

"Of course we live in a capitalist world. What do you expect them to do?" asked Viliki, who had sharp differences with his sister on the question of capitalism versus socialism, thanks to the library books she was no longer just caressing but reading as well. The same books that had exposed her to the world of the Flemish expressionists had also taken her to Cold War era debates on political and economic systems of the world. With the basic knowledge she had gleaned from these pages, she decided that socialism made more sense to her, while Viliki, ever the loyal and disciplined cadre of the Movement that had kicked him out, followed the national leaders to capitalism.

"I expect them to be honest," said Popi. "They must not pretend that they are socialists. And they must not accumulate capital by looting the coffers of the state and by taking kickbacks from contractors."

Viliki agreed that the Zimbabwean leaders had failed their people, and that to entrench themselves in power, they were now rendering their own country bankrupt and ungovernable. They were trampling on the human rights of their own people.

The Pule Siblings consoled themselves that at least in South Africa, democracy remained intact. The human rights culture was being entrenched every day. But Viliki expressed fear for the future. For how long would the Mandela legacy of tolerance last? Already he could see signs of the arrogance of power gradually turning into racial arrogance—even within the Movement, which had prided itself on being a non-racial party. This could be seen every day in Mahlatswetsa among the leadership of the Movement, who strutted around pretending that their blackness elevated them to the ranks of angels, while the fact that they were once oppressed made them into very special people who could never be criticised. Critics, however constructive they might be, were being labelled racists or lackeys of racists. It had become treacherous for a black person to point out the corruption of a fellow black.

People like Sekatle were turning into black Tjaart Cronjes. In Sekatle's campaign for the local elections that were coming in a few months' time, he never forgot to mention that the Pule Siblings had sold out to the whites. That Excelsior was cursed with a white mayor almost six years after liberation because of their vote. The perceived friendship between the Pule Siblings and the de Vries family was frowned upon, not because of the de Vries' history and political pedigree, but because they were white. After all, Sekatle himself had a dubious history.

Niki sat on the bed in her shack and listened to her children moan about how things had turned out for them. She was happy that *they* had failed to take her children away. The nestlings—for they would remain nestlings for as long as she lived—had returned to the nest. She was happy that even though Viliki had his two RDP houses, and had the Seller of Songs, he still found time to visit the old shack, to sit around the fire with his sister, and to sing songs and tell stories.

Profound nostalgia was not the preserve of the Pule Siblings. Tjaart Cronje wallowed in it. So did Johannes Smit. They sat in the bar of Excelsior Hotel, drowning their troubles in Castle Lager, and looking back with sad fondness to the glorious days when the Afrikaner had ruled supreme, and the "kaffir" had known his place. They felt that their people were alienated from what was fashionably called "the Rainbow Nation". The Afrikaner was an Afrikaner, and could never be part of a rainbow anything. Deep feelings of resentment and anger swelled in them with each gulp of the beer. They blamed the generation of Adam de Vries for deceiving the Afrikaner.

"Adam de Vries and his wife have melted quite comfortably into the new dispensation," Johannes Smit lamented.

"We fought wars on their behalf," agreed Tjaart Cronje. "After they had taught us that the very people they are now fraternising with were the enemy. Today we are suffering the consequences of the past that their generation shaped. My career in the army was destroyed by affirmative action. I would have been a major-general by now."

"Now de Vries even has the gall to say that apartheid laws should never have been the laws of this country," said Johannes Smit.

"Hypocrite!"

"Traitor!"

"Soon they will mess this country up," Tjaart Cronje consoled his mate. "The country will be in a shambles and the Afrikaner will be called back to rescue it. The Afrikaner will regain his power."

Johannes Smit nodded his agreement. Although he was self-employed as a farmer, affirmative action had taken its toll on him as well. He was no longer getting easy loans from the Land Bank, for which he had previously qualified solely by virtue of being an Afrikaner farmer. Land Bank loans were now open to everyone, even to peasants in the villages, and like everyone else, he had to wait his turn for his applications to be approved. He now had to motivate before he could get a loan, and account for it after get-ting it. And the people he was motivating and accounting to were the very affirmative action people who had taken over everything. Even such sacred institutions as the Land Bank.

These were tough times for the Afrikaner. Especially for the boer—the farmer. Johannes Smit had had to change to a tougher breed of cattle that could withstand the rigours and hardships to which the Afrikaner was being subjected. He had sold all his Brahmins and had bought Gelbviehs, a breed of cattle that could thrive under tough conditions with minimum attention and expenditure.

Tough times called for tough measures.

BETRAYAL BY THE ELDERS

*I*N THE STARK CLARITY of the Free State, a sleepy-eyed woman follows a sleepy-eyed man. Their purple faces are delicate, shaped by the music that is ringing in their heads. Their yellow ochre hats cover their ears so that the song of the wind cannot interfere with the song in their heads. He is in a purple jump suit and purple boots. She is in a purple coat, black shirt and red shoes. Over their shoulders they each carry a heavy bag. They choose their path carefully among giant yellow sunflowers. The wide-open skies are bright with purpleness.

Viliki took to the world with the Seller of Songs. They traversed the Free State, from one farm village to another, selling their songs at people's feasts and parties. Word had spread that these two itinerant musicians, a delicately carved man and his delicately carved woman, were endowed with the power to turn the dullest of parties into torrid revelries of dance and laughter. Without the backing of the usual drums, his accordion breathed notes that set the carousers ablaze. Her flute wailed wantonly, weaving its way among the notes of the accordion. It was a combination we had never heard before, which meant that Viliki and the Seller of

Songs were in greater demand than any other itinerant musicians. We invited them to play at our weddings and at the feasts honouring the ancestors. They travelled through all the districts of the eastern Free State. They spent their days walking in the fields among sunflowers, trekking to the next village, and their nights in sweaty hovels making people dance. They even crossed the Mohokare River into Lesotho, where they played at the all-night famo dance parties.

The best moments for Viliki were among the sunflower fields, where he and the Seller of Songs had the freedom to immerse themselves in each other to their hearts' content. The two of them alone under the big sky. Away from the petty world of Excelsior, and particularly of Mahlatswetsa Location. Away from the politics and the power struggles. He was free at last and didn't have any obligations to anyone. He had never thought it would be possible to enjoy so much freedom, without any cares in the world.

The local elections had come and gone. Against Popi's advice, Viliki had stood as an independent candidate. He had lost. The Movement had regained its majority in the council in a landslide victory. Sekatle, as the branch chairperson, had become the new mayor of Excelsior. Viliki had taken to the road with the Seller of Songs. Losing the election was a blessing for which he thanked his ancestors.

While Viliki and the Seller of Songs sold songs, Popi sold her sweat. She had not stood for election, and was therefore no longer the councillor in charge of libraries. She no longer had any income from the council, and had to go out and look for something to do. Not only to put food on the table, but to resume the building of her house.

Whenever we passed Niki's shack and saw the concrete-block house that had stopped at waist height, we remarked that Popi had been foolish. She should have taken the opportunity to allocate herself an RDP house while she was a councillor. As all the other councillors had done. Viliki had allocated himself two houses, one of which he was renting out. Other councillors had allocated houses to their mistresses, girlfriends and grandmothers. But she had become a goody-goody and had decided to build her own house from her earnings. Look where that had taken her. She and her mother were shack-dwellers when everyone else in Mahlatswetsa Location lived in a proper house.

Popi had to earn a living somehow. She could not rely on the bees, as Niki gave away most of the honey without expecting any payment for it.

When the cherry harvest season came in October and November, she went to Clocolan to join the thousands of workers who scurried around the orchards picking cherries. The air was filled with their fruity aroma. She embraced the trees, some of which she was told were more than a hundred years old. She immersed herself deeply in them, as if they were her lovers. Thanks to ample rains, the crop was large and bountiful. The winter had also been a very cold one, which was good for the cherries. Warm winters resulted in late budding, which presented a problem for farmers.

Popi took to harvesting with a passion. She hoped that hard labour would fill the hole in her heart. Since her anger had dissipated, she had been left with an emptiness that she needed to fill.

She did not like to harvest yellow cherries because picking them was easier, as they were picked without stems. She preferred red cherries, as they were picked with stems, and harvesting them was therefore more time-consuming. After each day's harvest, the workers spread plastic covers over the hail netting in the orchards to protect the crop in case it rained. Rain at harvest time caused the cherries to burst open, reducing their shelf life.

At dawn, the workers woke up and removed the plastic covers. Once more the harvest resumed in earnest. Popi buried herself in the work and forgot about the world of Excelsior. Until one afternoon, the world of Excelsior came to her in the form of Johannes Smit. He was visiting the farmer who owned the orchard. Popi was picking her way between yellow cherries that were planted together with red cherries. She was wondering why they were always mixed like that.

"Wouldn't it make more sense to plant red and yellow cherries separately?" she asked the worker next to her.

"It would not make sense at all. It is for the purpose of cross-pollination. Red cherries need yellow cherries because yellow cherries are the best pollinators."

The voice that gave the explanation did not come from the worker next to her. It came from Johannes Smit, and he was standing right behind her. Popi turned to look at him.

"I know you," said Johannes Smit. "You are from Excelsior."

"We met at the tractor show," replied Popi, turning back to the tree and resuming picking.

"You are Niki's girl. How is she?"

"She is well."

"I want to see her. Please tell her that I need to see her."

"It is easy to find her. She sits with the bees near the road that leads to town."

"The Bee Woman? Is that Niki? I see the Bee Woman every time I drive past. I didn't imagine she was Niki."

The Bee Woman. We all called Niki the Bee Woman. It was her new name. She was more like the queen bee, as bees surrounded her throughout the day. Buzzing all around her. Sometimes sitting on her cracked face without stinging her.

Every dawn she put the white plastic chair on her head and walked to the bees. At dusk when they had all gone to sleep, she put her plastic chair on her head once more and walked back to her shack. Usually she found Popi waiting for her at home with an enamel bowl of hot bean soup. But during cherry harvest season the shack would be empty, as Popi was spending all her days in Clocolan working in the orchards or in the packing rooms, where red cherries were packed into plastic containers and then into boxes for export to Europe and the Middle East. Or working in the warehouses, where they preserved yellow cherries in plastic drums in a solution that turned them white for future glazing. Niki would then cook herself hard maize porridge that she ate with honey.

Sometimes her old friends Mmampe and Maria would visit her. They would boast about their jobs at the town council. Once Sekatle had become the mayor, he had employed his sister as a clerk at the registry. It did not really matter that she was barely literate and that the old Afrikaner lady who had been working at the registry for decades, and was now just waiting for retirement, did all the work for her. As soon as Maria had become a clerk, she had "organised" a job for Mmampe as a tea-lady.

Niki would just listen to them prattling on about their wonderful experiences at the Stadsaal and the important people they brushed shoulders with. These included some leading lights who had been participants in the great events of the Excelsior 19, either as magistrates, accused, police officers or prosecutors. Niki never said much during these visits. She just sat there and listened to them talk to each other. Before they left, Niki would give them each a billycan of honey.

"Please do return my containers," she would say.

Sometimes these would be the only words she uttered all evening. Except, of course, for the greetings.

"You know, Niki, Maria can also organise you a job at the Stadsaal if you want one," Mmampe once offered on behalf of her friend. "She is a very powerful person there now her brother is the mayor."

"I don't think she wants a job," Maria said. "Otherwise her son would have organised one for her when he was the mayor. And talking of Viliki, when does he think he will pay cattle for my daughter he is now eating free of charge?"

Mmampe and Maria laughed and left Niki sitting there, her face hard and blank.

Those of us who did not have charitable hearts observed that the only reason Mmampe and Maria visited Niki was for the free honey.

Niki had another visitor in the form of Adam de Vries. He occasionally called at her apiary to try to persuade her to convert her bee-keeping activities into a viable business by joining the newly formed Excelsior Development Trust. Adam de Vries was on the board of this trust, established by black and white citizens of Excelsior to spearhead developmental projects in the town. His Worship the Mayor of Excelsior, Mr Sekatle Sekatle, was the chair of the organisation. But Niki showed no interest in bee-keeping for profit. The bees themselves, for their own sake, were fulfilment enough for her.

"If you don't use these bees profitably," Adam de Vries had once said, "thieves will come in the night and steal all your honey and sell it."

But Niki did not respond. She did not seem to be worried. Perhaps she knew that none of us would ever be brave enough to go near her bees. Even those of us who had gained great expertise in harvesting wild honey in the veld and in the sunflower fields wouldn't have dared steal from her apiary. We believed that she had a way of talking with the bees, and that she had the power to make them sting unwelcome intruders to death. Even though we knew that bees normally became dazed and foolish in the darkness of the night, the Bee Woman's bees had powers that were beyond the understanding of any human, save the Bee Woman herself.

"You don't have to sit here looking after bees all day long," Adam de Vries said. "Bees can look after themselves. That's the beauty of bee-keeping. You let them be and they create honey for you."

"I do not look after the bees," Niki replied. "They look after me."

Adam de Vries did not know what she meant by this. But he did not give up. Every other week he went to the lone figure sitting on a white chair to talk about the Excelsior Development Trust. Sometimes he talked about Viliki. He was sad that Viliki was not part of the great movement for the development of the town. That he had chosen to walk the road with a coloured woman,

idling at beer parties and leading a life of wantonness. It was very
unlike Viliki, Adam de Vries said to Niki. And it was a very disap-
pointing thing. Viliki used to be a dedicated community builder.
But Niki did not respond to all this. She just smiled vaguely, as if
she knew something that the rest of the world did not know.

Sometimes the itinerant musicians' feet led them to Excelsior,
where they would play in the street in front of Viliki's RDP house.
Word would be passed around and in no time the street would be
dancing. Even the varkoore lilies and the weeds that had grown
among them would sway to the sounds that filled the air. A hat
would be passed around and soon it would be full of coins that
would be offered to the creators of such merriment.

In the evening the Seller of Songs and Viliki would sweep out
the dust that had piled up in their house during their weeks of absence. Although Viliki asked the neighbours to "put an eye" on his
house, no one cleaned it.

The following day Viliki would visit Adam de Vries, who would
express his regret that Niki and her children had taken a wayward
path instead of working for the development of their town and
their fellow Africans.

"Now all of a sudden you are a spokesman for the Africans,
Meneer," Viliki remarked mockingly. "It is good that now you people finally see yourselves as Africans."

"I have always been an African," said Adam de Vries passion-
ately. "Long before anyone else called themselves Africans, my
people called themselves Afrikaners. Africans. Unlike the English-
speaking South African, the Afrikaner does not look to England or
any European country as the mother country. His only point of
reference is South Africa. He does not see South Africa as a colo-
nial outpost. He is deeply rooted in the soil of South Africa. How
dare you question my Africanness?"

Viliki laughed and remarked that Adam de Vries was the kind
of African who viewed himself as superior to other Africans. Otherwise why had he perpetuated discrimination based on race?

"It was for the good of everyone," screamed Adam de Vries. "Things just went wrong. But there was never any intention to hurt anyone. All we wanted to do was to guide the black man to civilisation."

"Which is what you continue to do today, hey?" said Viliki sarcastically. "With your Excelsior Development Trust. Guide the natives to civilisation."

"One can never win with you, Viliki," said an exasperated Adam de Vries. "If we fold our arms and do nothing, you still blame us. You must admit it, Viliki. You need us. A black man's way of thinking is that he cannot create a job for himself. He wants the white man to guide him. Or even create a job for him."

Such debates always ended in deadlock. Viliki would walk away from Adam de Vries's office fuming and vowing that he would never visit the stubborn old codger again. But of course the next time he was in Excelsior, he would go to Adam de Vries's office again.

On the road with the Seller of Songs, Viliki admitted something he would never admit in the presence of Adam de Vries or any white man of Excelsior, lest it reinforce their I-told-you-so attitude. He told the Seller of Songs—who had very little recollection of the days of apartheid because she had been too young then—that those had been very bad days because people were oppressed.

"But at least Excelsior was clean," he added. "Mahlatswetsa was clean. Gardens were neat. The town council even gave a prize for the best garden."

We had heard this gripe about the lack of cleanliness before. It used to be Viliki's daily song even before he took to the road with the Seller of Songs: that we didn't care about beautiful gardens any more.

"Today people don't care," he lamented. "They are now free. Tall grass grows in front of their houses. They expect the government to come and clean their gardens for them. Why else did they fight for freedom if the government they elected will not remove the grass in front of their houses? People are free. They must enjoy their freedom. They must sit on their stoops all day long and the government must feed them. During the days of apartheid, they used to go out and look for work. Now they are free. The government must feed them. If Mahlatswetsa Location is filthy, it is the fault of the government. The government must clean Mahlatswetsa Location. Is that what freedom means to us?"

We observed that Viliki could afford to be critical now that he was no longer a town councillor. Didn't the dirt begin during his tenure as mayor? Those days, of course, his garden used to be one of the very few that were clean and beautiful, with lilies of different types. Now he no longer had the right to pontificate about gardens because his own garden was as ugly as the rest. It had fallen into neglect since he took to the road.

Adam de Vries did not give up on Viliki. He knew that next time he came to Excelsior, Viliki would visit his office, and the old lawyer would try once more to convince him to stay and join the Excelsior Development Trust. He was proud of its achievements. It had established a mentoring programme that he hoped would change the face of agriculture in the eastern Free State. Under the auspices of this organisation, Adam de Vries had recruited a number of Afrikaner farmers to support emerging black farmers. He had even been able to convince Johannes Smit to join the programme and mentor some emerging farmers.

Like Tjaart Cronje, Johannes Smit still believed that the Afrikaners had been lied to by their leaders, who had assured the volk that they would not just hand over the government to the blacks without making certain that the Afrikaners would continue to wield their rightful power. Unlike Tjaart Cronje, Johannes Smit was resigned to the fact that the Afrikaners had been deceived and therefore had to make the best of the situation. After all, there were some benefits in getting into partnership with black farmers. Some affirmative action contracts and tenders would surely come his way, in the name of his protégés.

Tjaart Cronje was in his butchery when he first heard of Johannes Smit's treachery. He was no longer a town councillor, as he had not stood in the local elections. He had decided to leave politics to the blacks, who would doubtlessly ruin the town and the rest of the country, making it possible for the Afrikaner to regain his power.

"Did you hear about Johannes?" asked Jacomina, as she rushed into the butchery from the bank.

"What about Johannes?"

"He has joined Oom Adam in the Excelsior Development Trust."

"No . . . not Johannes Smit . . . he can't do that," said Tjaart Cronje, shaking all over with anger.

"Maybe you should reconsider your stand too, Tjaart," advised Jacomina. "Maybe it is better for all of us to be part of this new South Africa."

But Tjaart Cronje was no longer listening. He was ranting about the betrayal of the elders. He was raving that he had fought wars on behalf of Adam de Vries, whose generation had never died at the border nor faced petrol bombs in the black townships. And now he had made an about-turn, taking many good Afrikaners with him. He would remain true to Afrikaner values even if everyone left to join the enemy camp. He was prepared to fight a lonely war.

It was clear that Tjaart Cronje had altogether lost control. He was screaming at the top of his voice, wielding a cleaver. His workers cowered in the corner. But he made no attempt to attack them. He was only interested in chopping the air in front of him. Jacomina stayed out of range while at the same time pleading with him to calm down.

"What do you expect from a man who ate pap and morogo in the huts of black nannies and boasts about it?" screamed Tjaart Cronje.

"You are not well, Tjaart," pleaded Jacomina. "You have been working too hard. Let me drive you home. You need a rest."

He seemed to calm down, and placed the cleaver on the counter. Jacomina rushed to him and embraced him.

"Don't you worry, my darling," she said, "everything will be all right."

"Okay, many an Afrikaner child has played with black piccaninnies and has eaten in their homes," he said weakly. "I myself used to play with Viliki. I had a bite or two at Viliki's home. But it is not something I boast about at a dinner table. It was just part of the reality of growing up in the Free State platteland. Something better forgotten than broadcast at a dinner table!"

Then he began to jabber and foam at the mouth. He was running a temperature. Jacomina phoned Cornelia Cronje, and then drove her husband to the doctor.

A SEASON OF WHISPERS

A SPAN OF four donkeys is pulling a cart across the emerald-green ground. A green man and a green woman sit on the cart. A big round red sun burns in the red sky. Flashes of green and white cloud float around the sun. Green hills appear on the expansive horizon. The tones are hot and sombre.

The rays of the summer sun seared through the corrugated-iron roof and through the white ceiling. They filled the room with unbearable heat. The whirling fan on the ceiling was fighting a losing battle. It stirred the hot air that was descending with a vengeance over Tjaart Cronje as he lay on a white metal bed. His gaunt body was covered only in a white sheet, which was already drenched with his sweat. He was fast asleep. A group of elders in black suits stood over the bed, looking at him sadly. Among them were Klein-Jan Lombard, Gys Uys, Adam de Vries and the Reverend François Bornman. Klein-Jan Lombard was now retired from the police service and was dabbling in vegetable farming on his smallholding. The one-time mayor of Excelsior in the good old days, Gys Uys, was the oldest of the elders.

The elders were solemn. And respectable. None of them looked like men who would not acknowledge their daughters.

"It is terrible to see him like this," said Klein-Jan Lombard, sighing sorrowfully.

"Ja, ou Stephanus's boy used to be big and strong," agreed the dominee. "He could have easily become a Springbok flank forward if he had pursued his rugby career."

"It is sad to see him like this," Gys Uys echoed Klein-Jan Lombard.

"What do the doctors say?" asked Adam de Vries.

"They are not able to put their finger on his problem," said the dominee. "He's tired. We should let him sleep. Jacomina says he was hallucinating all night long . . . something about the lies of the elders."

"And you all pretend you don't know what is wrong with him?" asked Gys Uys angrily.

"Do you know what is wrong with him, Gys?" asked Adam de Vries.

"We all know. Let's not pretend," cried Gys Uys. "We all know that we used these children to fight our wars. And then we discarded them. All of a sudden they find that they live in a new world in which they do not belong. We, on the other hand, have simply blended into this new dispensation. We were already established in our careers and in our businesses. We have the wealth and the influence and are now in cahoots with the new elite. Things like affirmative action do not affect us at all. But what about these young men who had to kill and be prepared to be killed on our behalf? They suffer the consequences. They are the ones who are on the receiving end of affirmative action and the kind of transformation that decrees that there should no longer be any white faces in any senior positions in the public sector and parastatals."

"I knew that Gys would find some political reason for the young man's sickness," said Adam de Vries. "You always want to score some right-wing political point, Gys."

"Perhaps Gys is right," said the Reverend Bornman. "We all regret the past and yet are fearful of the future."

"Don't you dare count my name among those who regret the past," yelled Gys Uys. "There was never anything wrong with the past until you people and your de Klerk messed it up. People like you, Adam, go around apologising to the blacks for apartheid. Did you ever think of apologising to these young men that you used?"

"It is people like you, Gys, who take away all hope from these young people," said Adam de Vries. "You plant in their minds the false notion that Afrikaners are now the oppressed people."

The Reverend François Bornman stepped forward and said, "Let us remember that we are here to pray for this sick boy. We are not here to poison the whole atmosphere with our silly arguments."

The elders put their hands together and bowed their heads. The Reverend François Bornman led them in prayer.

SATURDAY MORNING. Popi decided to help Niki patch the holes in their shack before going to sing at the cemetery. The shack was falling apart. They spent a lot of time attending to the leaks, patching the ramshackle structure with mud at the corners and replacing corrugated-iron sheets that had been perforated by rust with plastic bags and cardboard.

Popi was telling Niki about the cherry harvest season in Clocolan that had enabled her to put a few rands into her post office savings book. But the money was not enough to buy even a row of concrete blocks. The house would have to stay waist-high until a stroke of fortune came their way.

"The house is not important, Popi," said Niki. "We should be happy that we do have a roof over our heads."

"But I vow that one day I will finish this house, Niki," said Popi. "I tell you, Niki, one day you are going to live in this house."

Niki's crusted face cracked into a smile.

"I know," she said.

"And I'll furnish it with very posh furniture," enthused Popi.

"You know that I don't care for posh furniture, Popi. I am just happy to have you back."

"Back? From Clocolan?"

"From your politics. At least now I am able to spend a lot of time with you. But sometimes I can see that you are lonely. There is no man in your life. A woman needs a man in her life."

"You know that I do not need a man in my life, Niki."

Niki shook her head pityingly.

"I need something more substantial than a man to fill the gaping hole in my heart," added Popi.

"Sometimes I think you miss being a town councillor," said Niki.

"I do not miss being a town councillor. The only thing I am sorry about is that I left the council before we could have a festival of our own in Excelsior. And I miss running the library. Of course I can still go there to borrow books like any other patron."

"Anyway, it is a useless council. All they know is how to eat our money."

Popi laughed and asked how her mother knew anything about that.

"People talk," said Niki. "Maria and Mmampe always come with strange stories of how they eat. They say now the spout of the kettle is facing their direction. It is their turn to eat. They say my children were foolish not to eat when the spout of the kettle was facing in their direction."

"At least as a coloured person I can complain that in the old apartheid days I was not white enough, and now in the new dispensation I am not black enough," said Popi jokingly. "What about you, Niki? You are black enough, but you are not one of those who eat. What is your excuse?"

Niki laughed. For the first time in many years. She laughed for a very long time. Popi just stood there in amazement. She had not thought her joke was all that funny. Niki laughed until tears ran from her eyes and disappeared into the cracks of her face. Popi was getting worried.

"Are you all right, Niki?" she asked.

"Oh, Popi!" cried Niki. "I am so happy that at last you are so free of shame about being coloured that you can even make a joke about it."

"My shame went away with my anger, Niki," said Popi quietly.

"You are free, Popi, and you have made me free too. For a long time, I felt guilty that I had failed you . . . that I had made you coloured! Every time they mocked and insulted you, it ate my heart and increased my guilt."

"God made me coloured, Niki, not you. You have no business to be guilty about anything."

Popi and Niki embraced and laughed and cried at the same time. They were not aware of the bakkie that had stopped outside their gate. The roly-poly frame of Johannes Smit rolled out of the bakkie and up to the gate.

"I am sorry to break up this Kodak moment, ladies, but I have an urgent message for Popi," said Johannes Smit, flashing a broad smile.

The message was that Tjaart Cronje wanted to see Popi. She was taken aback. She couldn't imagine why her mortal enemy would want to see her. The temerity of it all was that he expected her to go to his house.

"He wants to see me, so he must come here," said Popi. "He cannot just summon me as if he is the baas."

"He is sick, Popi," explained Johannes Smit. "Very sick. He wants to talk to you."

"He wants to make peace with you, Popi," said Niki. "I think you must go."

"How do you know he wants to make peace with me?" asked Popi.

"His ancestors are telling him to make peace with you, Popi. You can't go against the wishes of the ancestors."

Popi laughed and said, "White people don't have ancestors, Niki."

Niki offered to go with her. But Johannes Smit said Cornelia Cronje would not be pleased to see Niki in her house. Popi said that if her mother was not welcome, then she would not go either. Johannes Smit relented and allowed Niki to accompany her daughter.

Niki sat in the front of the bakkie with Johannes Smit while Popi sat in the back.

"This is a good opportunity to speak with you, Niki," said Johannes Smit as he drove out of Mahlatswetsa Location. "Why don't you join our mentoring scheme with your bee-keeping project? It could benefit you a lot."

Niki did not answer.

"I think we must declare a truce," pleaded Johannes Smit. "We can't live in the past forever. Bygones should be allowed to be bygones, Niki."

"This is a strange way of asking for forgiveness," said Niki. "I do not understand all this nonsense about a truce. I don't remember any war between us. You, Johannes Smit, wronged me. You stole my girlhood. And now you talk of a truce?"

It was Johannes Smit's turn to be silent. He held his peace until they reached the Cronje homestead.

He led the two women through the kitchen door, as was the custom. He asked them to wait on a bench while he went to look for Jacomina. Niki's eyes ran around the room. It had not changed. The varnished oak cupboards and the cast-iron pots and pans that hung on the wall were as she remembered them. So were the wooden table and the six heavy wooden chairs in the centre of the room. The antique coal stove was still there. But it was no longer in use. There was a cream-white electric stove and a matching fridge. These were the only new additions.

Jacomina came and led the women to the bedroom, without greeting them. Tjaart Cronje was lying in the antique metal bed. Niki recognised the bed at once. She shivered slightly as she remembered lying on it. It was possible that Popi had been conceived on that bed. If not in the sunflower fields. Or in the barn. The white bed still looked like a hospital bed to her. And the fact that a gaunt Tjaart was lying in it, covered with a white sheet, enhanced its hospitalness. The atmosphere in the room reeked of a hospital.

"Niki, you came too?" said Tjaart Cronje, his eyes brightening. "You are lucky my mother is at the butchery. Otherwise you would not leave this house alive."

Then he laughed weakly at his own joke. No one else laughed. Jacomina left the room. Johannes Smit gestured to Niki that they too should leave. But she did not move. Her eyes were fixed on the framed portrait on the wall. A dashing Stephanus Cronje, frozen in a perpetual state of youthfulness. Johannes Smit gently took Niki's arm and led her out. Popi's eyes remained fixed on the portrait.

"I wish you had known him, Popi," said Tjaart Cronje in a quivering voice.

"Known him?" asked Popi.

"Our father," responded Tjaart Cronje. "He was not a bad man."

"*Your* father."

"*Our* father. Surely you know that by now."

"I have heard whispers."

There was an uneasy silence for a while. Then Tjaart Cronje made some small talk about their days on the council. He did not talk about their fights. He recalled only some of the funny moments when the joke had been on him. Self-deprecating moments. Soon Popi was laughing. An uneasy kind of laughter. After a while, Tjaart Cronje said he was tired and wanted to sleep. He thanked her for coming. But as she was about to walk out of the door, he called her back.

"I have a little present for you," he said, giving her a container of Immac hair remover. "It is a cream that will make your legs smooth."

For a moment, anger flashed across Popi's face. Her hand did not move to take the insensitive gift from his shaking hand. But when she saw the earnestness of his face, she took it and said, "I don't shave my legs, Tjaart."

"You are a beautiful woman, Popi. Very beautiful. That cream is going to enhance the beauty of your long legs," he said.

Popi smiled and whispered, "I do not shave my legs, Tjaart."

"But you must," cried Tjaart Cronje. "You are a lady. A beautiful lady."

Popi was blushing all over. No one outside Niki and Viliki had ever called her beautiful before. At least, not to her face. Apparently she never knew how we used to gossip about her beauty, grudgingly praising it despite our public denunciations of her being a boesman.

"Lizette de Vries told me that progressive women don't shave their legs," she said. "Not even their armpits."

"Lizette de Vries is an old-fashioned old fart," he responded, chuckling at his own joke again.

"I'll take the cream, Tjaart, because in my culture they say it is rude to refuse a present. But I will never use it. I love my body the way it is."

Once more she bade Tjaart Cronje goodbye and left the room. Niki was waiting for her in the passage.

"I wonder what is eating him," Popi whispered to Niki.

"Anger," Niki whispered back. "It is as I told you, Popi. Anger does eat the owner."

"He didn't say much. I wonder why he wanted to see me?"

Johannes Smit and Jacomina were waiting for them in the kitchen.

As they walked back to Johannes Smit's bakkie, they heard Jacomina whispering to Johannes Smit: "She looks so much like Tjaart."

It was a season of whispers.

FROM THE SINS OF OUR MOTHERS

*T*HE REAL NEW MILLENNIUM has dawned. Four women with pointed breasts walk in single file. Their long necks carry their multicoloured heads with studied grace. Their hair is white with age, but their faces glow with youth. They do not lose their way, even though they undertake their journey with closed eyes. They walk straight and rigidly, their brown shoes hardly leaving the naphthol crimson ground. Their profiles foreground a white and yellow sky. The woman in front wears a green dress. Her face is pink and blue and green. She holds a bunch of white cosmos. The second woman wears a red dress. Her face is blue and orange. She holds a bunch of violet cosmos. The third woman wears a brown dress. Her face is blue. She carries a bunch of pink cosmos. The fourth woman wears a green dress. Her face is brown and pink. She holds a bunch of white cosmos.

It was the time of the cosmos. And of the yellowness in the fields and the sandstone hills. Niki walked among the cosmos between the sunflower fields, collecting cow-dung in a sisal sack. She walked along the path that bordered Johannes Smit's farm. She could see from a distance the barn that she used to know so well. Although it had fallen into disuse, its skeleton stood proudly as a monument to a breathless past. She could see with yesterday's eyes the barn assuming the shape of a wanton temple, with female supplicants walking into it. She could hear with yesterday's ears moans and groans escaping through its cracks and drenching the whole valley. Echoes of pain and pleasure relayed throughout the eastern Free State.

Niki was pleased that Popi had remained at home that day. Otherwise she would have had to explain the sudden change in her breathing. It had become fast and furious.

She had wanted Popi to come with her. But Popi had been very busy admiring herself in the mirror. Lately Popi spent all her mornings looking at herself in the mirror, admiring her blue eyes, and brushing her long golden-brown hair. She no longer hid it under huge turbans. She wondered why she had been ashamed of it all these years, why she had never noticed its beauty. She brushed it and combed it over and over again. It was so long that it reached behind her knees when she stood up straight.

She did not only admire her hair and her eyes. She loved her yellow-coloured face and her long neck that had the spot where the skin continued to peel off. She loved her body and everything about it. She had taken to wearing the isigqebhezana, the micro-miniskirts of the new millennium, displaying her long yellow-coloured legs that bristled with golden-yellow hair. She was no Barbie doll: she would not shave her hairy legs. Her hairy arms. Even her armpits. She rejoiced in her hair and in her hairiness.

She enjoyed her own beauty and celebrated it.

When Niki returned with the cow-dung, Popi was still admiring her beauty in the full-size mirror that she had placed against the corrugated-iron wall.

"It is a beautiful thing to love yourself, Popi," said Niki. "But don't you think you are overdoing it now? Preening yourself in front of the mirror all day long?"

"I am making up for lost time, Niki," giggled Popi. "Let's go to the bees."

"We must eat first," said Niki.

She took out the wobbly pan from the cupboard and fried eggs on the Primus stove. Popi knew that it was a special day. Niki only used the wobbly pan on special days. Memory days. It was the only thing left that linked her to Pule. It and the velveteen on the headboard that had become black and shiny with dirt, and tattered with age. The pan, especially, brought Pule very much alive in the shack.

After a meal of eggs and stiff maize porridge, Popi and Niki walked through the town of Excelsior to the hives by the road. Niki carried her white plastic chair on her head. She refused when Popi wanted to help her with the load.

Popi smiled back at those of us who looked at her with strange eyes. We had not yet gotten used to her wearing the narrow strips that passed for skirts. The red one she was wearing today with a white blouse hugged very tightly and gave us a full view of her long slim thighs and legs.

Popi remarked as they passed Adam de Vries's office: "Viliki would have been in there had he not decided to give himself to the world."

"Even Adam de Vries . . . I do not see him any more," said Niki. "Is he still up and about in that organisation they wanted me to join?"

"I think he is old and tired now," said Popi.

Indeed, Adam de Vries sat all day long in his office, drawing up the last wills and testaments of his fellow citizens.

That afternoon we saw Niki sitting on her white chair among the hives of different colours. Popi was sitting on the grass, her head resting between Niki's knees. The wind was blowing very hard. In its whines, they could hear the songs of Viliki and the Seller of Songs that the wind carried from distant villages and farmsteads. They could also hear their moans of pleasure coming from distant fields of sunflowers.

And then the bees began to swarm. They buzzed away from one of the hives in a black ball around the queen. And then they formed a big black cloud. We saw Niki and Popi walking under the cloud, following the bees. Or were the bees following them? We did not know. We just saw the women and the bees all moving in the same direction. Until they disappeared into a cluster of blue-gum trees a distance away.

We knew that the bees had succeeded in filling the gaping hole in Popi's heart. Popi, who had been ruled by anger, had finally been calmed by the bees. The bees had finally completed the healing work that had been begun by the creations of the trinity.

Yet the trinity never knew all these things. His work was to paint the subjects, and not to poke his nose into their lives beyond the canvas.

FROM THE SINS of our mothers all these things flow.

ACKNOWLEDGEMENTS

The research for this novel was made possible by a generous grant from the National Arts Council of South Africa.

I would like to thank four lovely women—Debe Morris (Toronto, Canada), Sara Gonzalez (Barcelona, Spain), Berniece Friedmann (Cape Town, South Africa) and NomCebo (from my childhood world of Orlando East)—who read each chapter as soon as I finished writing it and e-mailed me flattering remarks. In the manner of true muses they nourished my imagination.

Zakes Mda